The Wizard Corps

By
Guy Antibes

STRINGS OF EMPIRE

BOOK ONE

THE WIZARD CORPS

By
GUY ANTIBES

CASIE PRESS

SALT LAKE CITY, UT

The Wizard Corps

The Wizard Corps Copyright ©2024 Guy Antibes. All Rights Reserved. No part of this book may be reproduced without the permission of the author.

~

This is a work of fiction. There are no real locations used in the book; the people, settings, and specific places are a product of the author's imagination. Any resemblances to actual persons, locations, or places are purely coincidental.

Published by CasiePress LLC in Salt Lake City, UT, July 2024
www.casiepress.com

ISBN: 979-8333682871

Cover Design: Kenneth Cassell (modified illustration utilized Adobe Photoshop AI)
Book Design: Kenneth Cassell
Reader: Bev Cassell

Author's Note

The first book in a new series is always fun to write. I get to create fresh characters with different kinds of relationships, challenges, and cultures. I often develop an ensemble of support during the first book, but perhaps you'll find The Wizard Corps a little different. Our hero lives in a very biased world, and he is born on the wrong side. There are glimmers of friendliness amidst all the naked hate that must be accommodated, however, our hero being a hero, makes an effort to survive as his wizardly talents grow.

— Guy Antibes

Map of South Fenola

- To North Fenola →
- Gussellia
  - Nornotta
- Bocarre
- Racellia
  - Fort Draco
- Vinellia
- Quint's District

South Fenola
Barellia

STRINGS OF EMPIRE
BOOK ONE

THE WIZARD CORPS

CHAPTER ONE

QUINTO TIROLO HATED SITTING INSIDE THE FAMILY COTTAGE on a warm summer's day with his hands held up, thumbs extended, letting his mother use his body as a rack while she wound the wool threads she made into a ball. Quint looked outside through the wavy glass of tiny diamond-paned windows.

He wished his life would change. He had just finished his time at school, and since Quint's parents didn't work a farm, he did other chores that wheelwright children did when his siblings were already married and out of the house. Unfortunately, helping his mother wind wool balls was one of them. Now that he had finished schooling, it was time to formally become his father's apprentice.

Quint was already caught up on chopping firewood, and his father was out selling wheels as he delivered another order in the town three villages away. The frustration was making him squirm in his seat. A hot flush overcame him, and Quint shook his head.

"What's wrong, Quinto?" his mother asked.

"I don't know. I felt hot suddenly, and I still feel odd," Quint said.

His mother carefully put down her wool ball and put her head on his forehead. "Put out your fingers."

Quint did as his mother said, with the wool skein still hanging from his hands.

"I'm not quite sure how this works," Quint's mother said, furrowing her brow. "I wish your father was here." She concentrated on Quint's fingers.

"Try pushing power out of your fingertips as if you were going to touch me from across the room."

His mother gasped, and she backed up, sitting in her chair. "Look!"

Quint had his eyes on his mother, but when he looked at his fingertips, he gasped. Little sparkly lines came out of each fingertip. Each one seemed to be a different color. "Magic?"

His mother sighed. "If I'd say anything, you are much stronger than your father."

"He only knows a couple of strings," Quint said. "I don't know how to use these," he waved his fingers through the big loop of wool.

"You can start by willing those energy tendrils to stop." Quint's mother shivered. "I don't have any magic, nor do any of your siblings. All your father can do is shock you with a string and light a candle. Neither of us can teach you very much."

Quint practiced turning the tendrils on and off while he helped his mother. He thought he didn't have much to say but had to ask. "Will having magic change my life?"

"Has it changed your father's?" she asked her son, shaking her head. "In a village like ours, magic is a curiosity. I wouldn't get your hopes up."

That seemed to seal the conversation until Quint's father returned from his merchant work.

Just after dark, Quint heard the wagon clattering into the yard. He ran out to greet his father and was glad to see the wagon was emptied. His father had a successful trip. Zeppo Tirolo always returned in a great mood when he sold out.

"Put the wagon away. My rear end is sore from all the driving today," Zeppo said as he climbed off the wagon and left Quint alone with the wagon and their horse.

Putting the wagon away was more than driving it across the yard to the big workshop. When Quint was younger, he was always excited to drive the wagon by himself and have one of his brothers brush the horse, but those days were long gone. Now, it was a chore, but his father wasn't getting any younger, and Quint needed to lighten the load around the house.

Quint faced two serious faces at the kitchen table when he entered the cottage.

"Sit. We can talk while I finish dinner," Zeppo said. Quint's father took another big spoon of the stew and didn't speak again until he swallowed and sipped his watered wine. "Tell me how you felt when you got your magic?"

Quint explained how he felt. The expanded feeling was still with him, but he was getting used to it.

"Show me," Zeppo said. His expression hadn't lightened since Quint walked in.

Quint put out his fingers, and in the darkness of the cottage, the light emitting from his fingers was even brighter. Zeppo shook his head.

"Your talent is going to complicate your life," Zeppo said. He put out the gnarled fingers of his hands and showed tendrils that were faint compared to Quint's.

"We will see the hedge wizard tomorrow," Zeppo said, sighing. "I've been putting off bringing your brother Rezzo into the business, but it's time you learned other things. People with your strength don't cut down trees for a living."

"People with my strength?"

Zeppo sighed again. "I had hoped I could give you the woodcutting warrant, but…"

Quint didn't like how his father didn't finish the sentence.

☙

Pogi, the hedge wizard of Quint's village, finished wrapping a young girl's sprained wrist. Hedge wizards generally earned more money healing than selling their magic, Zeppo said as they walked across the village to the wizard's hut.

Quint asked the girl if she was all right, and she nodded. They had often played together with other village children. Quint felt he was too old to play now that he had taken up the wheelwright trade.

They sat in Pogi's examination room. Quint didn't jump on the table like he would if he was injured.

Pogi looked at Zeppo. "What is this all about?" the hedge wizard asked.

Zeppo nodded to Quint, who lit up the room with the tendrils of magic coming from his fingers.

"Do you know how to do anything with those?" Pogi asked Quint.

"How would he learn anything?" Zeppo asked. "I know two strings, and I also know enough that I can't safely do more."

Pogi nodded. "He needs instruction, then?"

Quint sat there as if he were an object, not a person, and that was precisely how he was being treated. He took a deep breath.

"What are my options?" Quint asked. "I only know you do something with your fingers to create a string, and the string does all the work."

"It doesn't quite work that way, but the general idea is right," Pogi said. "As part of my duties in the village, I train newly discovered magicians. Those who learn more easily have options after we've done some training."

Pogi looked at Zeppo. "Can I have him for an hour if I don't get a patient running through the door?"

"He knows the way home," Zeppo said, standing up. He looked down at his son. "Learn well. I think you might be one of those who learn easily, son. The world will open to you if you do. Pogi can tell you about it."

Zeppo sighed and hugged his son before walking out the door.

"Is this training going to hurt?"

Pogi shook his head. "Not in any way that you've hurt before," the wizard said. "What do you know about wizards?"

"I know we call you a hedge wizard, but I don't know what that means. I've never seen you behind a hedge before."

Pogi laughed. "It's an ancient term. Eons ago, some local wizards were untaught, but they managed to figure out a few strings. Most of them turned into hermits because people were frightened by those who did strange things. The term stuck. I know more strings than your father and have had a little training."

"Where did you get your training?"

Pogi smiled. "From another hedge wizard. I've tried to learn more strings from books, but it's hard to do when one can't read much more than their name. I can start fires and extinguish fires if they aren't too big. I can find water in the ground, which is unusual for a hedge wizard, as it happens. I'll never do much, so I offer my services to this village and the one south. I have a certificate from the Racellian High Council to practice."

"What if another hedge wizard shows up?"

Pogi shook his finger at Quin. "That isn't going to happen since I have a certificate giving me a territory. I must pay a fee every year to keep it up. Healing is my work, and I make more money from that."

"I can learn as much as you?" Quint asked. "I've already graduated from school and can read and do numbers."

"You are already fifteen? I'm sure you are about to grow in the next year or so. Hubites are slow in their development," Pogi said.

The hedge wizard was one of the few willots in the village. Hubites were taller, with lighter skin, blond or reddish hair, and blue eyes. Willots seemed to be born with a tan, dark hair, and all the willots had brown or black eyes. Hubites and willots couldn't breed, or so his teachers had said. Besides being a little taller, Quint hadn't detected any difference between willots and hubites, especially in the summer when everyone had tanned skin unless they took off their hats.

"How do we start?"

Pogi pursed his lips. "Show me your tendrils again."

Quint was getting the hang of showing off his magic.

Pogi shook his head. "Too strong. First, we will learn how to control your magic tendrils."

Pogi showed Quint what the process looked like. "Making strings is not just intertwining tendrils to create a power pulse. The tendrils are woven into threads, and the threads are woven into strings, but not all the strings are made at the same power level. Master wizards can work a hundred strings of various types."

"They don't teach us about magic at school. Why not?" Quint asked.

"It is a touchy subject. Willots, who dominate Racellia, feel uncomfortable around magic-wielding hubites. Although there are hubite hedge wizards and some hubite masters, they are confined to cloisters. You don't have to worry about that."

Quint thought willots were touchy about everything. Quint would never tell his father that, but he was happy to live in his corner of Racellia, where there were many more hubites than willots.

"Back to work. You practice amplifying your tendrils and tamping them down the rest of the day. Tomorrow, after lunch, show up again and we will investigate changing the intensity, finger to finger."

Quint thought that impossible, but his father seemed to support the training.

※

CHAPTER TWO

Zeppo sent Quint into the forest to tag trees for cutting, something that Zeppo had taught Quint when he was twelve. He returned for lunch and sat down with his parents.

"Did you learn much from Pogi?" Zeppo asked.

"I learned to control the intensity of my tendrils as a group. Tomorrow, Pogi will show me how to do the same with each finger."

Zeppo laughed. "I only have one intensity. I don't know where you got all your talent."

"It comes and goes, dear," Quin's mother said. "Lately, it has mostly been gone in my family."

"We talked briefly about willots and hubites," Quint said.

"Not a good subject to bring up in mixed company," Zeppo said. "I don't entirely trust Pogi; I've known him for twenty years, and I still maintain that Willots are known for their deviousness."

"And hubites aren't devious?" Quin's mother said.

"You know what I mean," Zeppo said.

Quint could pick up the rising anger in his father's voice. "I could have expanded my business to more than three villages and a town, but my warrant hasn't been expanded no matter how many times I ask. Every damned person on the Racellian High Council is a willot. Don't tell me they don't give their own people every advantage."

"Quiet, dear," Quint's mother told Zeppo. "You can get into trouble speaking ill of our betters."

Zeppo growled. "I know!" He stared at Quint. "Eat!" Zeppo barked.

Quint bent his head down and concentrated on his stew. He knew his father wasn't mad at him but at his circumstances.

"What happens to me if I exceed Pogi's abilities?"

"You will, Quinto," his mother said. "That's what worries me. Even if you have a lot of promise, I'm afraid you won't be able to shine as brightly as you should. Always leave a little of your talent in reserve. Show too much, and people will get angry."

"Listen to your mother, son. Willots are an overly sensitive race."

☙

Quint spent the morning controlling his tendril intensity. He tried to energize a finger at a time, which was much easier than he had thought.

When he walked across the village to Pogi's hut, he could extend his tendrils independently, make them bright, and then recede like the waves in the wheat fields.

Pogi was shocked Quint could learn that on his own and went right to teaching Quint a simple string.

"The process is simple," the wizard said. "You extend a tendril with the proper power and roll your hands until the tendrils wrap around each other into a string and then send a pulse of power into the string. However, getting everything aligned is not easy. I have mastered six strings I can consistently weave in all my years. I'm lucky that one of them is a water-dividing string. That makes me the most money. Everyone wants to know where to dig their wells. That divining weave is almost a psychic string. I can disinfect wounds, which is my only healing string. The rest are physical."

"So, psychic strings are the most lucrative?" Quint asked. "Should I be thinking about becoming a hedge wizard?"

Pogi laughed. "I believe you can do much better than that, but you need more training than I can give."

"How can I get that?"

Pogi smiled. "You can always try to get admitted to a cloister. It is a place where wizards live to improve their magic." The wizard shivered. "I spent six months in a cloister near the border with Vinellia, and that was six months too many. However, that was where I learned the divination spell. Few in the cloister could do that."

"What can my father do?"

Pogi sighed. "Everyone with magical talent can do some kind of fire. You ball everything together and give it a pulse. You don't need to create much of a thread since the disorganization of the magic creates the heat. Zeppo, your father, is so weak in magic that it is one of only two strings he can weave. The organization of the string gives magic a purpose."

"Isn't that dangerous?" Quint asked.

"It can be, but failed strings generally fall apart before they organize because part of your will binds the tendrils and without a focused intent, a proper job of thread organization, nothing happens. Most wizards create their strings step-by-step to take much of the guesswork out of their castings. That kind of approach creates milder magic, and that is a good thing."

"So magic is safe?"

"Safer than swimming a mile in the ocean. Safer than jumping off a fifty-foot cliff. Strings have been known to snap back on the caster. Shall we start with fire?"

Quint didn't get very far. He could manage his tendrils, but he didn't have the knack for the weave. Pogi said a few times during Quin's failed attempts that it was the most challenging part of wizardry.

A patient showed up, and Quint left the wizard's hut, returning home in time to help Zeppo assemble a few wheels before dinner.

After dinner, father and son returned to the wheel workshop and assembled a few more before dark.

Zeppo sighed as they finished their last wheel for the night.

"I think we have saturated my region for a while," Quin's father said. "We must wait for our customers to break more wheels before life is good again."

"Why don't you apply for another region or work with another wheelwright whose territory needs more replacement wheels?" Quint asked.

"The government in Bocarre won't permit it. Although a bribe might do something, your father doesn't have that kind of money. We will do as we always have: tighten our belts until the wheels age. I must be satisfied with my forest to cut, and my other woodworking to sell before life will be good again. Show me what you've learned," Zeppo said, leaning against a workbench, wiping his hands with a damp towel.

Quint thrust out his fingers and initiated tendrils that lit up the space. He tried to weave a string, but just as he was going to give it a pulse of power, another thing he had yet to learn, the tendril unwound, and Quint was back to where he started.

Zeppo laughed. "Practice with a single tendril twisted into a string. Don't bother managing ten; you'll only fail, fail, and fail again. Move on from there. Use the tendril from your right middle finger. On most wizards, that will get you enough flame to light a candle."

"What if I have more power than you?" Quint asked.

"Then don't point your power at anything flammable!" Zeppo laughed.

Twisting a single tendril into a string was something he could do. His father was right. He willed a modest pulse of power, and a flame bright enough for a torch burned three inches in front of his palms, shaped as if they were holding a ball. It was much like his father had done countless times, but Quint felt he had more power.

Quint willed his power off, and the flame popped as it went out.

"I just said, don't point your string at anything flammable," Zeppo said. "Let's go outside where you won't burn anything."

Quint duplicated the first string. He barely applied power to his string and was able to make a two-inch flame. Quint hadn't expected to go to bed that night knowing a magic string, but his father was the better teacher.

"Now a big flame," Quint said. He took a deep breath, willed a strong tendril followed by as powerful a pulse as possible, and pointed his string across the bare dirt yard.

The flame was almost a foot in diameter and flamed out ten yards before him. Quint was gasping for breath after the demonstration.

"Why am I so weak?"

"There is a price for power. You save it up, and as you use magic, your strength goes into the magic."

"Do I have to eat more?"

"Food helps a little, but sunlight gives you real power. My magic capacity is so meager that my daily outside activities are enough for me. I imagine it won't be enough for you. Rated wizards will have tanned skin from exposure to the sun. Heat helps a bit, but sunlight is best," Zeppo said. "Pogi didn't tell you about this?" Zeppo asked.

Quint shook his head. "He is bringing me on slowly on purpose," he said. "Why?"

Zeppo shrugged. "We don't have many wizards discovered in our little village," Quint's father said, "but it happens occasionally. Sometimes, a newly discovered wizard will vanish." Zeppo shrugged as he locked the workshop doors. "It's better not to be curious about that, but with you, I suppose my interest has picked up a bit."

Ricco, the village headman's son, a willot, walked into the yard. He was an on-again, off-again friend of Quint's.

"I heard you came into your magic. I just saw what you can do," Ricco said.

Quint looked at his father, who gave Quint a tiny head shake.

"When I learn a little more," Quint said. "I'm taking instruction from Pogi at present. I'd rather learn a few strings and then show you something impressive."

"As if you could impress me," Ricco said in his typical self-important way.

"I'm not learning to impress you, and you asked."

Ricco smiled. "I did, didn't I? Well, I suppose you are on your way. I'll check back with you in a few days," he said, disappearing up the road past Zeppo's wheelwright shop.

"That's not good," Zeppo said. "I never did trust that boy, and now the entire village will know you can cast fire. That was an awesome flame, my boy."

Quint smiled. "It was, wasn't it? But this is only the start, and maybe just the start of the beginning, for all I know."

☙

Pogi was impressed by Quint's demonstration, although Quint could tell the wizard was trying to look calm. "Your father knows how to teach," Pogi said.

Quint nodded. "He taught me the only string he is capable of weaving. You know more than him. Now that I've proven I can create a string, it's time to learn a few more tricks."

Pogi pursed his lips and then worked them as he thought. Quint could tell Pogi was stalling. The hedge wizard's hesitant demeanor had destroyed his credibility, and Quint felt lost. Who could he trust? Not his brothers and sister. Not Ricco, and not Pogi.

A tiny stab of fear punctured him inside. Would this training end up being a disappointment? Quint feared it would, but he had no choice but to continue.

Pogi inhaled. "I suppose we can try two more simple threads. One is a levitation spell. It isn't too powerful, but you can lift and transport a few pounds of material. The other is a heat string. Heat differs from a flame, the thread your father knows."

"The levitation spell teaches you how to create the string and change the focus of the string on the object. That is lifting and carrying the floating object and setting it down."

"That is an easy string?" Quint asked.

Pogi smiled in a self-satisfying way. "All strings are difficult except for the fire string that your father uses because it is caused by the disorganization."

Quint leaned forward. "I'm ready to learn."

The wizard drew two crude hands with fingers outstretched before sketching lines from two fingers on one hand, three from two fingers, and a thumb on the other.

"There are the tendrils for the string. You must get them to twist into a left-hand weave," Pogi said drawing the direction the tendrils were to twist. "Do you really think you can do this?"

Quint shrugged. "I can give it a try." Inside, he was more determined than he let on. He vowed to succeed.

Pogi smiled again and sat back, folding his arms. "Try."

Quint first extended tendrils from each finger separately before making the pattern that Pogi had drawn. It was more complicated than he thought. The wizard was right; the fire spell was simple compared to this.

He finally got the right combination of tendrils and then put his hands closer together with the hands almost in a ball as he willed the tendrils to move toward a single point. With many tries, that was all he could do. He had difficulty keeping the threads twisted while he tried to get them to weave.

Pogi gave him no encouragement as he struggled for success. Patients came and went while Quint made his failed attempts.

Discouraged, Quint left the wizard's hut and walked home. Pogi had drawn the diagram for heat. At dusk, he attempted to make the levitation string work but set that aside and examined the heat string. It seemed easier.

There were three strings loosely woven. Not as loosely as the barely woven fire string.

Quint found it easier to manipulate the tendrils in a loose weave, and after six tries, he generated a tiny cloud of heat from his balled-up hands. The heat was warm but not hot. He put more power into the string, making the cloud wax and wane.

After trying unsuccessfully to move the cloud away from his hands, he let the string unravel and looked at the three strings. They were dimmer than when he started, but Quint applied more power, and the tendrils glowed brighter and twisted tighter, making a warmer cloud.

Quint thought that Pogi's levitation spell wasn't correct. Making this string after a few tries was easy, but the levitation string seemed impossible. He made the simple change of winding the teleportation weave in the opposite direction and the string felt right and produced a stable string. He concentrated on a small fallen branch at his feet and focused on making the string extend to touch the branch, and then he moved the branch off the ground with his will. Will seemed to be another significant component in making a string work.

He could move the branch about ten paces from him before the object fell to the ground. Quint stood over the fallen branch and reproduced the string. He concentrated on it being two feet in front of his chest as he walked around the yard.

"What are you doing?" his mother called from the front door to their cottage.

Quint turned around, and the distraction killed the string.

"Practicing what Pogi taught me," Quint said.

He had to get a book on strings since he couldn't trust Pogi to give him the correct information.

CHAPTER THREE

~

THE NEXT DAY, RICCI, QUINT'S FRIEND, SHOWED UP ON HIS DOORSTEP, offering to walk to the village with him. Quint thought it strange, but Ricci was always a harmless distraction once you got through the hubite jokes that he occasionally told.

They took a shortcut that Quint took occasionally when the weather was good. When they were about to cross a lane, Quint heard a shout.

"Stop right there, boys!"

Quint's first response was to run, but Ricci pushed him from the side, making Quint trip over his feet falling to the ground. As he rose, Quint was surrounded by men in green uniforms with an officer dressed in black.

Irons were clapped to his wrists as he struggled, but then he saw the officer in the group pull Ricci aside.

"This is for you, and this is for the wizard," the officer said.

Ricci opened the envelope and smiled. There had to be paper money inside. Pogi's envelope looked fatter. Quint stopped struggling. He had been sold to someone, and that was that.

He couldn't overcome one soldier, much less nine. Ricci gave Quint a smirk and gave him a mock salute. "Have fun for the rest of your life, hubie."

"Hubie" was a derogatory term for hubite.

"Don't give him no mind," the officer said, looking disgusted as Ricci skipped away without a backward glance. "We do the same thing for willot wizards."

"You collect wizards?" Quint asked, trying to catch his breath after his futile struggles.

"How do you think we staff our country's wizard corps? Welcome to the Racellian Army, Wizard Corps Division."

"I'm only fifteen," Quint said. "I haven't even begun to shave!"

The officer shrugged. "I've pressed thirteen-year-olds before, but most are closer to eighteen. You'll just be better sooner. Behave, and we won't have to beat you," the officer said.

Quint looked at the soldiers surrounding him. "I'm not worth it," Quint said.

"Your village hedge wizard thought you were. You'll be tested when we get to the fort."

"How far is that?"

"Three days away. Behave, and we won't put leg irons on you," the officer said.

Quint merely nodded. He would have to wait for a chance to escape, but surrounded by green-uniformed soldiers, it wasn't the proper time.

They headed north in the opposite direction from the village. They skirted two villages and arrived at Polenza, the town that was the limit of Zeppo's warrant. Any chance to see his father would be here or not at all. They walked through the town without Quint seeing a familiar face, and Quint wondered if he'd ever see his parents again.

※

They spent the night in another town. Quint had never been so far from home in his life, and that little bit of information excited him, but it wasn't enough to overcome his dread.

The food was the same, and people talked and dressed the same, but more willots were walking the streets than hubites, which was new. In the morning, the soldiers left Quint locked in his room until the officer unlocked it.

"Downstairs. We will eat lunch and then head for the fort."

Another unfortunate pressed recruit sat at one of two tables occupied by the soldiers. This willot looked eighteen or older. The newer recruit stared at Quint's wrists.

"They even press hubites," the young man said with distaste written on his face. He certainly dressed better than Quint.

"We invite all kinds into the wizard corps if they are magical. If you don't qualify, you get to serve in the Racellian army," the officer said. "I warn you, give us a hard time, and you won't make it to the training fort. Give the officers a hard time, and you won't leave the training fort."

Quint didn't know if the officer was scaring him to make sure he didn't give his captors any trouble or if he was serious. The scare tactics were working, Quint conceded.

The officer shepherded all the men outside. Two soldiers were on each driver's seat, and the other soldiers split up, jumping into the wagons. One recruit was put into each wagon. The officer rode a horse.

Quint looked at one of the soldiers. "Why didn't you bring wagons when you captured me?"

The soldier almost sneered. "It's easier to walk when we press in rural areas. Sometimes, we have a dandy chase. Your friend's shove put a stop to that."

"He's no friend of mine," Quint said.

"They never are, in the end."

The other soldiers looked bored, but this was all new to Quint. He had never seen these lands. They drove through a city that looked huge to Quint. Every person was a willot. He didn't know how people could exist in such a place. Where did they get food and water?

As they rode through the city streets, Quint answered his own question. There were fountains and wells at regular intervals, and he spotted wagons like the one he rode laden with grain sacks and vegetables. They even passed a large, barred wagon with sheep standing behind the bars on their way to be slaughtered.

Quint felt like one of those sheep.

They spent another two nights at inns, and then the wagons followed the officer down a long dirt road to Fort Draco, so said the sign. There was a coat of arms on either side. He guessed it was the symbol for the wizard corps since it had two hands connected by lines in the shield.

Quint didn't know what the fort defended. It sat in the middle of a meadow in a valley. It was like a town with a stone wall surrounding it. As they rode under the gate, Quint flinched. None of the soldiers did.

Was it a magic barrier? He would find out soon enough. Quint wondered if whatever made him flinch was his childhood being stripped away. He wouldn't be surprised if it were.

They rode past a training field where black-garbed soldiers trained in combat. He expected magic duels, but he didn't see anyone making strings. They stopped.

"Two recruits," the officer said, handing two envelopes to another officer in black standing at the top of steps to a three-story building. "One with promise and one, not so much," the man who had kidnapped Quint said to the other.

"Very well. Here is your next assignment." The officer walked down the steps and gave a thick envelope to the kidnapper. "You made it in time for lunch, and you and your squad can be away in time to make it to the next town to the north."

The soldiers helped Quint off the wagon, but they didn't get down. The drivers took the wagons away, deeper into the fort, leaving Quint and the other potential wizard standing in front of their new guards. Quint wondered which recruit he was: the one with promise or the one, not so much.

☙

"Inside. We will process you, and then you'll be tested," the new officer said. "You can call me Lieutenant Drabano. I will be your superior for the next few days until you are assessed."

They followed Drabano into the building. The two guards, flanking the lieutenant, walked behind as Drabano led the pair to the counter facing the front door.

"Sarza?" Drabano asked.

"That's me," Sarza said. "I'm the older one."

Drabano looked weary. "I think I can tell that." He asked Sarza a series of questions and at the end, asked him how many strings he had mastered.

"One," Sarza said. "Fire."

Sarza wasn't any more accomplished than his father, Zeppo.

"You are Quinto Tirolo?"

"I go by Quint."

"No, you don't. It will be Tirolo or Recruit, or if you are nice or are in trouble, it will be Recruit Tirolo," the officer said.

"Yes, sir."

"You know how to address me. Good." Drabano glared at Sarza. "Did you get that?"

Sarza nodded.

Drabano exhaled with an exasperated look on his face. "That is 'yes, sir.'" He looked at the two soldiers. "Take him to the punishment room. Five stripes should be enough to wake him up."

Sarza struggled with his captors, but there wasn't anything he could do with his hands still in irons. One of the soldiers created a string and sent what looked like a thick, bright tendril into his stomach. When it hit the recruit, it made a "zzzt" sound.

"That's one, Sarza. You get four more," Drabano said, dismissing the soldiers dragging Sarza away with a wave. '

Drabano looked at Quint with raised eyebrows. "Did you learn something?"

"Yes, sir!" Quint said, scared half to death by the quick punishment and dread of the punishment itself.

"Good. It's testing for you." He began to walk out of the room but stopped and twisted his head toward Quint. "Follow me, recruit."

Quint hurried, and the pair walked out of the foyer. They stopped at the door. It said, oddly enough, "Testing" on the door.

"In you go. Give this to the tester. He's the one in a white robe," Drabano said, walking briskly away without looking back.

Quint turned the doorknob and received a shock that numbed his hand. He tried his left hand, and then he had two numbed hands. Quint had to pull the sleeve of his tunic over his hand and was able to negotiate the door without a shock.

"You passed the first test!" the bald older man in a white cotton robe said as Quint walked in.

"That is a string?" Quint asked, looking back at the door.

"Sir. That is a string, sir?"

"I don't know the rules, sir," Quint said.

"You better learn them fast, or you'll have more than your share of stripes and shocks, young recruit." The tester held out his hand for the document.

He didn't spend much time reading it. "Fifteen years old. Which string do you know?"

"Fire. I've been learning two more, but I only learned about my magic a week ago, sir," Quint said.

"Which two?"

"Levitation and Heat, sir," Quint said.

"Show me where you are with heat."

Quint was stuck. He would do heat but use Pogi's instructions for levitation. His heat was at a feeble level.

"I'm still practicing, sir. I had only three lessons."

"Three lessons? Can you diagram this string?"

Quint did as he was asked.

"Interesting." The tester scribbled something on the form.

"Show me your fire string, but I don't want you burning the place down."

Quint started with enough power to light a candle and ended with a foot-long spear before turning the spell off.

"That was the first one I learned. My father taught me the basic string, sir,"

"He had the control that you displayed?"

Quint shook his head. "He doesn't have as much power as I do, sir," Quint said.

"Your trainer really tried to teach you a levitation string?"

Quint nodded and then said, "Yes, sir. I couldn't quite get it to work."

"Diagram it."

Quint made sure the twist to the wave was on the left side like Pogi taught him, not the right.

The tester looked it over. "Try it with the weave on the right side. Your trainer either didn't know the string or was playing games with you."

Quint was trapped. "What should I levitate?"

The tester had a polished steel sphere on his desk. "Lift this."

Quint lifted it to eye level and put it back down. "Like that, sir?"

"You know too much for a hubite. And you were the weak one." The tester snorted, shook his head, slipped the page into another envelope, and sealed it with wax. "I've seen enough. Take this across the hall."

"Yes, sir. Forgive me, for I don't know how to salute."

"Don't worry about it. You haven't been registered yet. That comes next. You are dismissed."

Quint turned around and walked across the hall and knocked on the door. It didn't have a sign.

"Come in," a voice said.

Quint stepped inside. Three clerks, two men, and a woman, were sitting behind desks doing paperwork.

"Recruit?" One of the clerks answered. He was dressed in black, but his uniform was like the guards, not the officers.

Quint raised the newly sealed envelope. "Yes, sir."

"You don't 'yes, sir' us. We are soldiers all, which you will be soon enough," the man who asked the question said. He extended his hand, and Quint handed him the envelope, which the clerk quickly unsealed.

"Quinto Tirolo?"

"Recruit Quinto Tirolo," Quint said.

The clerk's eyebrows rose. "Three string recruit? He was found in the wild?"

"Who were you asking, sir?" Quint asked.

"You trained for how long?"

"Three days, sir."

"I will take you to your next destination," the clerk said.

In the corridor, the clerk asked Quint which strings he mastered.

"I wouldn't say I've mastered them," Quint said. "Fire, heat, and levitation."

The clerk coughed. "Levitation? The tester wrote it down, but I thought he was mistaken. You'll be asked to duplicate it before your induction interview."

☙

The Wizard Corps didn't waste any time in the following interview. Quint was led to a room and sat on a hard wooden chair facing a pair of tables arranged end to end with four empty chairs behind.

"You wait here. The panel will assemble in a few minutes."

"What about the other recruit?" Quint asked.

"He lost his chance for the wizard corps," the clerk said. The man held up his hand to forestall a comment by Quint. "Don't ask me more."

Quint shook his head. "I won't, sir."

"Sir is appropriate here. I'll be leaving you."

Quint waited a long time, but three men and one woman finally paraded through a door and sat down. Each one had a folder, which they all opened.

The woman spoke. "This is your induction interview. Unless you attack us or show gross disrespect, you will be accepted into the Racellian wizard corps. State your name."

"Quinto Tirolo, sir."

The men laughed.

"You address a woman as ma'am, recruit," the woman said.

"Yes, ma'am."

"That is better. You are obviously a hubite. What activities were you engaged in before you were pressed into service?"

"I had finished my letters and numbers in school in the spring, and I've been working with my father, a wheelwright, ever since."

"When did your magic come to you?" One of the men asked.

"A week or so ago."

That raised a few eyebrows, and some notes were made.

"Are you and your father members of any hubite organizations?" another man asked.

Quint shook his head. "No, sir. Most of the people where I come from are just hubites, but I don't know anything about organizations. My father has drinking friends, but I don't think that counts."

Two of the men smiled, but the other one and the woman were impassive.

"You will demonstrate your three strings," the woman said. "Even if you aren't fully adept, we'd like to see you perform."

Quint started with fire. It was the easiest, and he didn't manipulate the flame like he could. He stood and tried to levitate the chair. It was almost too heavy, but Quint was able to lift the chair half a foot off the floor. Heat was easy after levitation, but Quint didn't go crazy with that, either. He performed better than he intended. Quint was getting more used to making magic.

He sat back down and waited for a response after all three scribbled something.

"You learned those three from scratch since you could see tendrils?"

"I did, ma'am," Quint said.

"What do you think about Racellia?" one of the men asked.

Quint shrugged. "It's where I was born and likely where I'll die unless I'm unlucky in fighting."

That answer seemed to satisfy them. They continued to ask questions about Quint's upbringing, how many siblings he had, and what they were doing. A few seemed disappointed that magic hadn't manifested itself among the rest of his family.

The woman closed her file and stood. "You are now a Recruit in the Racellian wizard corps. When you learn ten strings, you will be accepted as one of the High Council's wizard soldiers. Remain seated while we arrange an escort to the training barracks."

CHAPTER FOUR

~

After an inordinately long wait, Quint was escorted by two young soldiers to the training barracks, an attic in one of the fort's other buildings. There were eight beds on either side of the attic, which almost ran from end to end of the building. One end held a washroom and toilet facility.

Quint quickly learned that a string drew water uphill, so the attic had a water supply. He also found that the trainees were elsewhere, and he was shown to his bunk just before his escort left him alone. Quint used the water closet while he was alone. The water began to fill the tank without his intervention. Quint wondered what kind of string did that.

It was clear that there were twelve trainees. Quint made it thirteen, and Sarza, the missing recruit, would have made it fourteen.

His bed had no sheets or blankets. The chest at the foot of his bed was empty, and Quint possessed the clothes on his back and a few coins in his pocket.

Quint walked to the dormer window by his bed and saw a column of black-clad young wizards marching toward his building. He went to every window and surveyed his new home.

Fort Draco was in the middle of a forest. From his vantage point, Quint saw the haze of a large village or a town a few miles away to the north. The forest or the distance hid everything else. A range of hills lined the horizon from the southeast to the northeast.

He stood by his bed as he heard steps on the only stairs that led to the dormitory.

The column of young men filed into the room and an older man ordered them dismissed. Everyone converged on Quint, the new recruit. None of the eyes were friendly, and a few looked malevolent.

"I thought there was to be two of you," the man in charge said as he walked to Quint.

"I don't think he was acceptable," Quint said.

The man slapped Quint in the face. "Who are you talking to?"

"Am I talking to a 'sir?'" Quint asked.

"You are."

"I don't think he was acceptable, sir," Quint said, resisting the urge to rub his injured face.

"One less recruit suits me just fine," the man said. "I am Sergeant Deck."

"My name is Quinto Tirolo, sir. I'm from southeast Racellia."

"You don't have to remember where you are from. All you need to understand is the here and the now. You are a member of Wizard Corps. Any life before today is gone, washed out, invisible."

"Yes, sir," Quint said.

"You are a recruit. How many strings?"

"Three, sir."

"How long have you been a wizard?"

"A week and a bit," Quint said.

Sergeant Deck paused. "You must learn ten strings before you rise to Soldier." The sergeant looked away from Quint. "Falco!"

One of the younger recruits stepped smartly to the side of Deck and saluted, hands clasped together and thrust forward.

"Yes, sir!" the boy was probably younger than Quint.

"First floor supply room. Get this recruit some clothes so he can dress for dinner."

"Yes, sir!"

Quint followed Falco out the door and down the stairs. His stomach rumbled. He had missed lunch through all the testing and the interviews.

Falco didn't say a word while Quint walked behind the recruit until they walked through a door emblazoned with the sign "Supply."

"New recruit, sir," Falco said to the man behind the counter. "He didn't bring anything with him."

"Pressed?" the man said.

Falco shrugged. "I guess, sir."

The man came from around the corner, measured Quint, and told Quint to stick out a foot. He disappeared and returned with a filled bag and a rolled-up blanket.

"This is your first kit. Name?"

"Quinto Tirolo, recruit, sir," Quint said.

"Sign, Recruit Tirolo," the man said, flipping around a ledger on the counter and giving Quint a pencil.

"Should I see what's inside, sir?" Quint asked.

"Do you think I'm a crook!" the man said.

"No, sir. I won't bother you."

Falco pulled on Quint's sleeve, and they walked back to the stairs with Falco carrying the bedroll.

"Lisina didn't give you a list, so what are you going to compare what you have with?" Falco said.

Quint sighed. "He is doing a fiddle, isn't he?"

Falco nodded. "I don't know what a fiddle is, but if it involves a swindle, likely, yes."

"I hope there is a uniform and underwear," Quint said.

When Falco and Quint returned to the dormitory, Sergeant Deck was gone, but eleven angry stares greeted Quint. All were willots. Quint didn't know if that was going to be a problem or not.

"We heard you were responsible for what happened to the other recruit," one of the others said.

"No," Quint said. "He was asked his name, which he didn't say, and nodded instead of saying 'yes, sir.'"

"A likely story," another said.

They converged on Quint. Falco took Quint's bag and stepped away.

"It is a capital offense to fight with strings," one of the recruits warned.

Quint settled in for a beating. He looked at all the older bodies and decided to drop to the floor and curl into a defensive ball like he used to when his brothers were angry at him. The expected fists and feet pummeled him while he was down. In a few minutes, steps were heard, and the recruits ran to their beds, pulled out books, or ran into the washroom while Quint struggled to stand and hobbled to his bed before opening the bag of his new possessions.

Deck walked into the room. He had a smirk on his face.

"Did you give Recruit Tirolo a wizard corps welcome?"

"We did, sir," one of the older boys said. "He slipped walking up the stairs from Supply, sir."

Deck stood over Quint. "Is that so?"

"Actually, I slipped walking down, sir," Quint said.

"I see. Dinner in half an hour. Get your uniform on and those rags on your body stowed."

"Yes, sir," Quint said.

He sighed as he dumped the bag on his bed now that the other recruits ignored him. It appeared he was supposed to have three clothing changes, but he only had three sets of underwear and two uniforms.

The uniform fit surprisingly well, and the boots were perfect. Quint looked at his reflection in the only mirror in the dormitory. Quint looked like the others, he guessed.

He put everything else away, transferred his coins to the pants he wore, and sat down, waiting to march to dinner or whatever his captors did.

Quint thought of them as captors, and he knew he had to watch out for himself since no one else would care what happened to him. Acting the part of the subservient hubite was an easy enough role since he had practice at various willot establishments in their district.

His beatings had still raised cuts and bruises on his body. Quint noted that his face and hands weren't touched in the beating. Perhaps that was a rule that Deck created.

Quint marched in the back by himself as they made their way to the commissary, where meals were served. Quint was surprised that the food was more than acceptable in quality and quantity. Maybe they fed the wizards a proper diet to promote magic. He wasn't going to complain.

They marched back to the dormitory and stood in formation, with Quint still behind.

"For the benefit of the new recruit, we will have school in the morning and string training in the afternoon. You have the rest of the evening to practice," Deck said. "Don't do anything that will bring me upstairs. Dismissed."

Deck went downstairs, and everyone ignored Quint, even Falco. Everyone had books and practiced strings. The dormitory was large enough to permit sixteen recruits to spread out.

After reorganizing his hastily stowed possessions and making his bed, Quint decided to work on levitation. He took off a boot, laid it on the bare mattress next to him, and sat staring at the boot on his bed.

He looked at his hands and took a deep breath. The threads came easily enough. He had a little practice earlier in the day when he was tested. He lifted the boot. Since it was lighter than the steel sphere of the tester, Quint raised it slowly. He concentrated, and the boot turned around. He made it turn the other way and then had it rotate vertically before setting the boot down.

When Quint finished, the dormitory was silent. All eyes were on him.

"How long have you been doing magic?" one of the older boys said.

"Less than two weeks. I only know three strings. This, fire, and heat."

"But levitation is almost a psychic string," another recruit said.

"That's what the tester said, but I don't know what a psychic string is. I suppose I'll find out tomorrow."

"We aren't learning them yet. Our instructor said we won't learn them until we leave the fort."

Quint shrugged. "I'm new at all this. I was pressed into service four days after my magic came."

"Don't show us up," another recruit said. "You won't want another beating, will you?"

"I don't even know how I'd do that," Quint said.

"Learn too quickly," the young man said.

Quint intended to do that. His withholding of his talent hadn't been very successful, and he didn't think playing around with a boot was threatening. He had a lot to learn.

❧

Quint thought he had left his schooling behind, but he was mistaken. When he entered the classroom, the teacher told him he would have to catch up and gave him four books on Racellia: history, geography, military history, and military strategy. They wouldn't touch the other typical subjects.

The class began, and Quint saw that the subjects were tilted towards supporting the High Council of Racellia and puffing up Racellia's willot past. His village teacher taught a less glorious version of history.

Quint would learn the subjects but would be wary of swallowing every positive story. Maybe most soldiers needed to be fed one-sided versions to become good soldiers. Quint didn't feel that way, and his cynicism surprised him. Remembering Sarza's fate when he didn't toe the line in the lobby the previous day, Quint would learn the history and adequately respond to what was taught, no matter how he felt about the truth of everything.

Everyone learned together. Quint was as well-educated as any of them, he thought. Military history was fascinating but had to be taken with a grain of salt. Military strategy seemed to be the most interesting of the four.

Quint marched with the others to the refectory for lunch before magic instruction. He wondered how it would differ from what Pogi, the village hedge wizard, taught.

Lunch was no different from the other two meals. At least Quint wouldn't starve. They returned to the barracks for a break while Quint stored his books in his chest like the others. The recruits each carried a portfolio to the next session.

Magic class was conducted three times each week. Quint had arrived on an off day. The recruits walked into a large room the size of their barracks, but tables and chairs lined the wall. The instructor was a gray-haired older man with many badges sewn onto his uniform, standing behind the instructor's table and holding his left hand behind his back.

Since Quint was the only raw recruit, he didn't feel like disrupting the class by asking simple questions. He would hold them until he could get the instructor alone or if it fit into the afternoon activities.

"I see we have a new recruit," the instructor said, looking at Quint. He looked down at a paper on the table. "You are Quinto Tirolo, correct?"

"Yes, sir," Quint said, straightening up.

"My name is Geno Pozella. I have achieved the rank of Master in the service of Racellia's wizard corps and have chosen to teach magic." Pozella walked from behind the table, exhibiting a severe limp. He took his hand from behind his back and showed Quint a fingerless hand encased in a black leather glove. "As you can see, I wanted to be useful since my magic days are behind me."

Quint noticed a few smirks from the other recruits, out of sight of the master. Quint had never dreamed of even meeting a master wizard in his life. They had to know fifty strings to begin to qualify. Even without his magic, this man would be a font of information.

"You know three strings?"

"I do, sir. Fire, heat, levitation."

"When I get everyone started on exercises, come to me and demonstrate," Pozella said.

"Yes, sir."

Pozella ambled to a wall that had a curtain over a board. He drew the curtain and the recruits' progress was recorded for all to see. Magic progress was a public affair in the Wizard Corps.

Quint was astonished that only three recruits knew more strings than he did.

"You need to learn ten strings to graduate to soldier," Pozella said, still talking to Quint. "The others know what to work on." Pozella turned to the others. "What do you need to do to learn a string?"

"Practice, practice, practice, sir!" the recruits said in unison.

"Very well. Spread out and get to work. When you are ready to demonstrate, find me."

The recruits did as ordered, leaving Quint standing by himself. Pozella limped over. "Now, show me. Don't tell me which string you are demonstrating."

"Yes, sir." Quint didn't understand why Master Pozella would give him that instruction.

Quint went through his three strings, saving levitation for last. One of the tables scattered around the room was close by. He was able to raise the table a foot off the ground, but he kept the table level and lowered it slowly.

Pozella sat on the table. "That was impressive for your first year."

"I've been a wizard for nearly two weeks, sir."

"The levitation spell?"

Quint sighed. "That took me four hours of intense practice, sir," responding in as quiet a voice as he could.

Pozella sputtered. "Four hours?" He stared at Quint. "Do you have the same amount of control of the other strings?"

"I suppose I do, sir," Quint said.

"Show me flame from an inch to a pace."

Quint pursed his lips. He didn't want to show off but couldn't reject Pozella's command. The flame string was the easiest to control.

"Excellent," Pozella whispered to Quint as he told the recruits, looking at them to return to their practice. "You are a wild talent, I suppose?"

"Wild? My father can generate a small flame, sir."

"As in lighting a candle?"

Quint nodded. "Yes, sir."

"That isn't what I meant. You are a wild talent if you have no wizards in your immediate family. You are the only one in this batch of recruits, so I won't publicly press you too hard in this class. We will concentrate on getting you to Level 2 before you leave, but they won't realize that. If they find out, your life will be miserable."

"I understand, sir. I was reminded of what that entailed last night, sir."

"I'm sure being the only hubite and a talented one didn't help."

Quint didn't respond and hoped that would be acceptable.

"Do you know what string diagrams are?"

"I think I do, sir," Quint said. "The local hedge wizard drew them out for me. He gave me the wrong direction of a weave for the levitation string."

"And you figured it out."

"I was lucky that was the only change. I don't think Pogi could do the string. He knows a few healing strings."

"Let's go up front and give you a few strings to work on," Pozella said.

Quint had five diagrams to work on. Pozella told him to complete them fully, one at a time and when he controlled them, to do it during his free time, in secret, preferably.

"Practice makes the string stronger, so go through all your strings when you practice here," Pozella said. "Make diagrams for your three strings so you can document your progress. When you have completed a string, I will sign your diagram. Do you understand? Strings are harder than they look. Some people take years of practice to get the weaves right and the strings repeatable. Most wizards don't get much past Level 1. We fail half the recruits, but I think you will be an exception."

"Yes, sir."

Quint returned to the table that he had levitated and shuffled through the strings. They seemed to be ordinary things: light, wind, water, cold, dry.

As Quint thought about them, any could be destructive if a lot of power was applied.

Quint laid them out and wondered which he could start. All but the bright light needed a partner to evaluate if he was successful or not.

Pozella was crossing the room when Quint slid close to him. "How do I evaluate these, sir?"

Pozella started at Quint. "That's up to you to decide. Aren't you up to it?"

Quint thought for a moment. "Is there a block of metal that I can use for heat and cold, sir?"

Pozella smiled. "That cabinet in the corner has various objects to use. Now, let me continue with the other recruits."

Quint saw two recruits practicing by a table with an object. Most of the others seemed to be struggling with tendrils and weaves.

The cabinet held all kinds of objects. One was a metal pitcher that would work for dry, water, and cold. He would start with cold since that was probably related to flame.

Quint took the pitcher and put it on the table, spreading out the diagram, and looked at his hands. He suspected learning a spell was more complicated than looking at the diagram, duplicating the tendrils, creating the threads, and wrapping them together to form a string that would work.

He tried to complete the spell and couldn't get the tendrils to emerge from his fingers in the proper pattern. It wasn't as easy as he thought. Quint spent the rest of the class learning to control the tendrils, but hadn't succeeded when Pozella called on the recruits to stop.

Quint closed his eyes and fixed the feeling of the tendrils in his mind before opening his eyes and slipping the diagram into his portfolio.

"Bring a chair," Pozella said.

Quint did as the others did, carrying a chair from the wall and setting them in two lines facing Pozella.

Pozella looked at Quint. "Don't forget to return your object to the cabinet when we are through."

"Yes, sir," Quint said.

Pozella talked about weaves, showing them examples of how tendrils were wrapped. The village wizard had never enlightened Quint about the complexity of weaves. He wondered how a wizard could learn a hundred strings with only ten fingers, but different weaves could produce opposite results.

 The master made sure everyone understood that they had much more to learn. Quint returned to the barracks, overwhelmed with learning strings.

⁂

CHAPTER FIVE

~

Quint spent four days working on the cold string when he could generate the proper tendrils, and he hadn't gotten to weaving them. He returned to the empty practice hall on the next off-day afternoon and began working on the cold weave.

The solitude settled him down. Quint looked closely at the weave. It had a tight weave at the bottom and a looser weave at the top. There were nine tendrils instead of the ten with a flame string.

He spent an hour working on the weave and found the transition between tight and loose was the hardest part. His head began to ache when he finally succeeded in creating the string. He pulsed it, aiming at the metal pitcher.

He gave the string another pulse before he broke the string and ran to the pitcher. The metal surface was cooler than it had been before. He continued to work on intensity, using a more precise weave on the string.

After three tries to get the string wound, Quint pulsed the pitcher with a more robust effort. He didn't have to run to the pitcher since the surface sent up a few wisps of mist. He wouldn't increase that pulse for fear the pitcher might be damaged.

Someone clapped behind him. Quint turned to see Pozella grinning as he continued to clap. "If I didn't see you struggle when you came in, I wouldn't have believed you could make my cold string work."

"It's not the tendrils that are the problem; it is setting up the weave, sir,"

Quint said.

"How did you figure out the change in the twist?"

Quint took a deep breath and inhaled slowly, nervous to be talking to a master wizard about strings. "Concentration, sir. I gave myself a headache using my will to do it. It is like a regular string weave, and then I had to relax my mind to create better precision. I've never done that before."

"None of your fellow recruits can do that. It is actually the hardest string of the five I gave you. The rest is modulating your power, right?"

Quint nodded. "That and making tendrils is easy for me."

Pozella sat down. "And then you should slow up. I suggest you work on string weave exercises. Pull up any number of tendrils and work on different patterns. Tomorrow, I'll give you a sheet with different combinations. Use four tendrils; you'll find it easier than nine. If you go too fast, the other recruits will get jealous. You should complete no more than one string per month. I honestly think you could complete one or more every week."

"I can do that, sir."

"You could be a master in less than a year if your memory can stand all the information. That would not be good for you. Even so, I don't think promotions will come easy for you. Hubites are barely tolerated in the corps."

"Should you be advising me like this, sir?" Quint asked.

"No. Absolutely not, but I've seen few wizards with your command of tendrils. The weaving seems hard to you now, but that's because it is new."

"If the corps can't tolerate me, why am I here, sir?"

"One way or another, the wizard corps must have every competent wizard filter through their organization. If they don't need you, you are useless to the High Council," Pozella said. "If I couldn't reposition myself as an instructor, I wouldn't be standing before you and would either be confined to a cloister or worse."

"Then I'll have to walk the fine line of learning what I can and not using it, sir."

Pozella smiled. "You keep that in your mind, always."

༺༻

Master Pozella's advice was correct. When Quint asked probing questions about military strategy, his favorite class, his fellow recruits roughed him up again. He had to keep his string practice to himself, but he could practice weaves without the others noticing.

Four months later, the three recruits who were more advanced were promoted to Soldiers and left the fort, assigned to one of the six wizard corps battalions stationed around Racellia and on the border with Barellia, where the Racellian forces were engaged in border skirmishes. Four of the original twelve were dismissed along the way.

The High Council wanted an empire, and Barellia was deemed the first step. That fact wasn't stated in the military strategy class, but it was in the military history class. Quint could see the strategy clearly, even from what little he learned.

The geography class concentrated on learning the topography of South Fenola. Implicit was that officers in the Wizard Corps would use that knowledge in the years to come.

In those four months, as more recruits were added, Quint's seven strings led the barracks, and it was hard for Quint to hold back. He knew sixteen strings with varying degrees of proficiency since he couldn't practice with magic. That would have been enough to earn him the rank of Corporal once he was released from training, but he was content to stay in familiar surroundings as long as the beatings didn't go too far.

Two more recruits achieved Soldier and left. Four recruits joined them. None were pressed. They came from prominent willot families who lived in Bocarre, the Racellian capital. Their arrogance repulsed Quint, but all of them were man-sized and were at least a couple of years older than him. They could end up like Sarza if they didn't respond to the fort's discipline.

They were a vicious clique who disrupted the classes and demanded most of Master Pozella's time.

"How could a hubite learn five strings in five months," one of them said. "How much are you paying the master?"

Quint snorted. "Where would I get enough money for that? Anyway, I've never seen Master Pozella take money for advancement. He is already spending most of his time helping you."

"Are you accusing us of bribing him?" another said.

"No," Quint said. "He does what he does. He wants all four of you to move quickly to your next ranks."

The recruit closest to Quint pushed him to the floor. "Just what are you getting at? We don't need favoritism to succeed in this place."

Favoritism or not, Quint had to endure minutes of kicking. The other recruits looked on. Quint could see the fear in their faces.

"Why are we doing all the work? Help us humble a hubite!"

In a moment, every recruit was beating on Quint, and when they tired of their sport, Quint had lost consciousness.

He woke in a tiny room. Quint rolled over, a painful experience, and looked out the window. He was in a different room on a different floor.

His possessions were tossed in a corner. Quint tried to get up but was unable to. He thought he had a broken wrist and a broken ankle. He laid back down and added a few ribs to the list.

The door opened, and a woman wearing a white coat over her black uniform entered.

"You regained consciousness. Good!" she said. "We didn't know if you were going to make it. Sergeant Deck has been demoted and reassigned to the Barellian border. The four recruits received slight slaps on the wrists and are still in barracks."

Quint gulped a breath, but the woman stopped him from speaking. "You won't be returning to the barracks," the woman said. "The fort commander was not happy that he had to reassign the sergeant, but if the four had killed you, Sergeant Deck would have been executed for dereliction of duty. You will have this room as your own until you are promoted out of this fort."

"What about my classes, ma'am?"

"You will continue your studies. Master Pozella thinks you can qualify on your magic alone and will work with you."

"Why am I not discharged, ma'am?" Quint asked.

"One of the boys is the grandson of a High Council member, and he is unhappy with his son's son. He is ordering you to be successful to spite his grandson."

"Won't that make the four recruits treat me even worse?"

"If the High Councilman hadn't intervened, you would have been left for dead. Don't spit on good fortune," the woman said. "As you may know, magical healing isn't much better than common medical treatments, but they will help knit your broken bones. You can be released for classes in two weeks. Master Pozella might not wait that long."

She worked on Quint. The pain of wizardly healing was almost as bad as the beating, but Quint didn't know when the woman left since he had lapsed into unconsciousness again.

※

"Twenty!" Master Pozella said. "Ten more, and they must classify you as an officer. Outstanding, Quint."

"I'm a Level Two, sir?" Quint asked. He knew the answer, but he felt he had to continue to hold back. Quint knew six more strings than he had demonstrated to Pozella. Four more, and he could leave the fort as an officer. The minimum rating that Pozella thought Quint could survive with.

"When you get your next ten, it is doubtful you will get a commission," Pozella said, "but your standing will keep you out of a barracks, which is your greatest danger."

"Do I get tested again?" Quint asked.

"Most certainly, and it won't just be magic this time. That was why I wanted you to wait a year. You'll have more strings than you need; now, your education will determine what battalion you will be assigned."

Quint still worked with the wizard healer to gain physical strength. He had started to grow into a man. He was skinny, but his bones were lengthening, and with more painful treatments, the healer claimed his bones would be stronger than usual because of her magic.

Quint had no reason to doubt her, but also, he had no reason to believe her. But he did feel stronger as he grew and worked out with the soldiers, not the recruits in the training field. His appetite was healthy and sometimes the commissary servers grumbled about all his extra helpings.

"You can start sunbathing," Pozella said. "You must use good judgment. Too much sun can ruin your skin and make it dry and diseased, but not enough will not give you enough power now that you are adult-sized. Here is the pass to the tanning compound. Your skin can get as brown as a willot, but that is when you have overdone it."

"I understand," Quint said. "I'm ready to prepare myself for the outside."

"Once you are in the wizard corps, you never are truly on the outside again," Pozella said.

Quint spent all his time concentrating on his four subjects. When he felt he had learned all he could out of the four books, he had mastered thirty-three strings, including four psychic strings: lying detection, weather, portents, which was a very unpredictable form of divining the future, and confusion, which was useful when you wanted your opponent to think less clearly. He was still working on a mental shield from strings that affected the mind. The weave was very complex, and Pozella said even he couldn't rely on achieving the weave consistently.

"The fort commander insists on demonstrating all thirty of your strings," Pozella said. "I know you can do it, but it will take a full day, and you will have to do it all over again wherever you are assigned."

"There is resistance, sir?" Quint asked.

"For you, there will always be resistance, Quint. You know that."

Quint frowned. "Then I will work on the shield string. I don't trust a test that isn't normally given."

Pozella sighed. "I can't deny that would be a proper plan. I can stall them for another week."

"I'll get it done, sir," Quint said.

Quint worked on the mental shield weave four times daily for an hour and a half each session. He interspersed more work in the classroom texts.

On the fourth day of concentrated work, he found the correct technique for the weave. The string split into five compound threads midway up the string before reverting to the original pattern. Making his tendrils durable for the time it took to weave the string probably gave wizards the most difficulty.

Quint spent another whole day working on speeding up the weave and found Pozella in his office.

"I am ready."

Pozella struggled to his feed. "Shall I test you?"

Quint nodded. He had already cast the string before he walked into Pozella's office. "But you can't make strings," Quint said.

Pozella chuckled. "Even though I lost my fingers, some of my ability to generate tendrils returned. I've never told anyone. I lost my taste for fighting when I lost my mobility. I suppose it also comes with age."

"Do your worst."

"You don't mean that, but I won't hold back on the strings that could be thrown at you."

Quint stood at attention while he could see Pozella create strings and toss the magic at Quint. He could feel the buffeting of the wizardry, but his shield seemed to hold until Pozella shot a string at him that slammed him against the wall.

It took a moment for Quint to catch his breath. "What was that?"

"A levitation string," Pozella said. "One you don't know. Relying on one defense is dangerous. It is a lesson I wanted to leave with you."

"And my mental shield?"

Pozella shrugged. "It did what it should. You are as ready as any sixteen-year-old I've taught. I'll see if we can set up a panel for tomorrow."

☙

Quint recognized two of the three panelists. Pozella sat in the back of the room. He faced the woman who had interviewed him before, the wizard who had tested him, still wearing his white coat, and a uniformed officer with many badges adorning his chest.

The officer introduced himself as the fort commandant and lifted a sheet from an open file. "Recruit Quinto Tirolo. You have been recommended for promotion. You must learn ten strings to advance, but Master Pozella claims you can demonstrate thirty. Is that right? Don't lie. We demand that you demonstrate all thirty. Fail to do so, and you will suffer consequences."

"I have a question, sir," Quint said.

The officer nodded and waved his assent.

"Some threads require objects."

"No need. Our distinguished testing officer can see threads and you will be judged on your weaves.

Quint had already protected himself from mental strings, so the tester wouldn't have to see Quint create the protection he felt he needed.

Quint stood before the panel and went through each string as he had learned them. Some of his strings were offensive for use in the field of battle, and the officer flinched a few times during the demonstration. Quint felt the pressure of psychic threads cast at him, but they didn't affect him. He included all four psychic threads and sat down, eventually demonstrating thirty-two.

The testing officer stood and clapped. "I knew you'd excel!"

The commandant glared at the testing officer and requested that he sit down.

"You have learned another thread you didn't disclose," the commandant said.

The door to the conference room opened, and an older officer came in. "He didn't stutter or fall asleep, did he?" the older man asked.

"No, he didn't," a perturbed commandant said before turning to Quint. "You used a shield thread."

"I know one," Quint said, "and I invoked it before I came. I didn't want to be distracted while progressing through my strings."

The testing officer slapped his knee, grinning, earning him another glare from the commanding officer.

"We have had some precocious recruits through here demonstrating twenty or more threads, but you are the first who have gone past thirty," the commandant said. "I have no choice but to promote you to a Level Three rating. That doesn't mean you will get a command, but there are privileges to the rating. You will travel to Bocarre in two days and be presented to the Wizard Corps headquarters, where you will demonstrate your strings again and answer questions regarding your classroom training. You are dismissed."

The woman raised her eyebrows, the testing officer winked at Quint and Pozella escorted Quint from the conference room as quickly as he could.

"You dodged a string," Pozella said. "I thought the commandant was going to charge you for insubordination for having prepared yourself with the protection string."

"He tried to throw me off."

"Indeed, he did. Your instincts are better than mine, I suppose. Let's get you ready for your journey."

Quint shrugged. "What is there to get ready? I have my four books, my portfolio of string diagrams, and three uniform changes. I even have a bag to put them all."

Pozella stopped and stared at Quint. "I suppose that is all you need. When you pass the wizard board, you will get a dark green uniform if you go out into the field or a black uniform if you are assigned a non-fighting position."

"They will let me fight?" Quint asked.

"Anything can happen, but every wizard has to go out into the field occasionally," Pozella said. "Be warned that no one will take a teenaged Level 3 seriously. You had to put on a show for the fort commandant, but forget about it. You made everyone at Fort Draco proud, although few will admit it. Be wary, and good luck."

Two days later, Quint was put on a horse after being shown how to tie his bag on the horse and was given a few minutes of riding tips.

The week-long trip to Bocarre was a painful experience, physically, but Quint marveled at the changes in the countryside as he traveled through his country to its capital. For all the time spent together, Quint's traveling companions hardly acknowledged Quint's existence. On a sunny morning, Quint and the six other riders from the fort arrived at the gates to Bocarre. All the other riders had been to Bocarre before.

Bocarre impressed Quint to no end. He couldn't believe a city could be so large and so ornate. His staring stopped when they came to a black building fronting a large square.

"Welcome to the headquarters of the Racellian Wizard Corps," said one of the aides who came to take their horses.

CHAPTER SIX

THE WIZARD CORPS HEADQUARTERS BUILDING'S FOYER was primarily black, but the many windows of the facade let in abundant light, eliminating some of the gloom. Quint presented his documents to the woman in uniform at the front counter. His riding companions walked through the lobby and off to their destinations.

"A new soldier?" she asked, looking at Quint's young face.

"Maybe something more, ma'am," Quint said.

The woman laughed. "A little snip like you hinting like you were something special. That won't work on me, young man," she said.

After reading Quint's papers, she cleared her throat. "I suppose it did work on me after all," she said with a blushing face. "You will see Captain Bavora, and he will arrange everything for your testing."

Quint nodded. "Where do I go, ma'am?"

The woman gave him a printed map and put an "X" on Bavora's office.

"I wouldn't tarry, Recruit Tirolo. You won't be a recruit for long if you really are a Level 3."

As Quint walked the halls searching for Captain Bavora's office, he thought of the change in the woman's attitude once she read his papers. Quint recounted what Pozella told him about no one wanting a teenage officer.

Quint reached his destination on the second floor and was shown into the anteroom of Captain Bavora's office. The room was filled with seven black-uniformed young men as well as himself.

"You are here to be tested?" Quint asked the young man sitting next to him.

"Of course. We are tested and interviewed before getting our greens."

"Greens?" Quint asked.

"The uniform of wizards in the field."

Perhaps that would be his fate, as well, Quint thought.

He waited for three hours. The first six were gone, replaced by three more recruits, but Quint was finally called into Captain Bavora's office.

"Did you use your time waiting?" Captain Bavora asked after offering Quint a seat in front of his desk and receiving Quint's papers.

"I went over strings, sir."

"How long could that take? You learn ten to progress," Bavora said.

"I learned more than ten. They are listed in there, sir," Quint said.

"An achiever. Good. The few qualified hubites need to work a little harder to get recognition in the Council's wizard corps." The captain coughed when he got to the list. "Thirty-three! You have met the wizardry qualifications for an officer."

"I know, sir, but I lack other qualities. I'm sure age is one of them," Quint said.

"It certainly is. I doubt the testing and interviews will be sufficient for the corps to grant a commission, but you will likely get a wizard rank if you back up what is on this document," Bavora said.

Quint shrugged. "I will serve as I am able, sir," Quint said as a matter of form.

Bavora filled out a document and opened a thin pamphlet. "You will at least merit a room to yourself while you stay with us. You will spend the next few nights at headquarters like the other recruits before getting your first assignment." Bavora stood and gave Quint a casual salute. "You have a building map? Give it to me." The captain marked a circle around room 221 in the annex, the inn for visiting wizards. "Stay in your room. Someone will be at your door to give you instructions for tonight and tomorrow. Dismissed."

Quint wandered around the headquarters until he found the corridor that linked to the annex. He followed the hall signs and easily found room 221.

His temporary quarters were much better than the large closet that he had occupied for the last few months at the fort. A window looked over the street that ran behind the headquarters entrance.

Quint sat on the single chair in the room and stared out the window at the street below, watching people scurry about their business. He didn't have the time to take in the buildings of Bocarre on the ride in, but now he had a chance to absorb what the capital felt like. Most people seemed to be driven as they walked below with fast paces and expressions of anxiety.

No one strolled along the street to relax like Quint would see when he people-watched at his village. All the citizens seemed to be ordered to go somewhere and do something.

He turned at a knock on the door.

"You are Quinto Tirolo?" a woman said, standing in front of the door with a male companion. Both wore black uniforms.

"I am, ma'am," Quint said.

"Good." She proceeded to spout a set of rules that were duplicated in a packet she would give him.

Quint received a badge for meals and another badge to identify him as a recruit undergoing evaluations.

"Your identify badge will allow you to use the headquarters refectory," the woman said. "Doctor Enzia will perform a physical examination before you can begin a proper evaluation."

"Now, ma'am?"

She nodded. "Now."

Quint didn't appreciate the probing and prodding. Doctor Enzia used a metal hook to draw back his lips to reveal teeth and gums. He pressed uncomfortably hard to get a pulse reading. The woman dutifully recorded the doctor's results.

The doctor put a little hammer he used to make Quint kick his legs. The training facility never had an examination so thorough.

"You are fit enough for service. Your youth displays a healthy body. You are fifteen, sixteen?"

"Sixteen," Quint said.

"This time next year, you will be a bigger boy," the doctor said with a grin.

"I've been told that at the training camp, doctor."

"It's true." The doctor put his instruments in a black valise and left the room. "But that is generally true of sixteen-year-olds."

The woman stayed. She marked another location on the map, the refectory, drawing a line from his room to where he would eat.

"Make sure you show up when the refectory is open, or you'll miss a meal." She gave Quint a professionally curt smile and left him.

If he hurried, he could make lunch. Quint didn't see a key anywhere and used one of his newly acquired strings to freeze the lock on the door before he rushed out to the refectory on the main floor of the annex.

The refectory wasn't much different from the eating area at the fort, except there were more choices for the food. Quint filled his metal tray and ate by himself. Two of his riding companions from the fort ignored him as he stood in line a few diners away. He mentally shrugged. Quint decided he wouldn't let slights bother him at the headquarters any more than they had done at the fort.

☙

After dinner, Quint returned to his room and locked the door. He went to the window and looked at the lights of Bocarre blinking on as night fell. He decided to turn in early since tomorrow might be draining on his magic.

The city lights were blacked out by three figures entering through the window. Quint struggled to stand but was dragged off his bed. He knew what was in store and curled up into a ball. If they had blades to kill him, he was a dead man. The assailants beat him senseless, and the same woman awakened Quint the previous day as she pounded on the door. He was able to stand and unlock the latch.

"You look like you had a rough night," she said, unsurprised by Quint's appearance.

"I fell out of my bed," Quint said, glancing at the not-quite-closed window.

"I will wait down the hall while you clean yourself up, and then I will escort you to your first interview, which is generally a demonstration of your strings. Most recruits come to us with ten or a few more, which takes an hour. I suppose yours might be closer to three hours, so prepare yourself."

"Yes, ma'am," Quint said. He visited the washroom and wiped the blood off his face; most of it was from a bloody nose. Less visible was the pain from bruises that had mainly blossomed from his beating. Quint returned feeling better, but not good.

They left the annex and stayed on the main floor, entering a conference room. Unlike the last test, tables lined one wall, filled with objects.

Three officers stood chatting as the pair walked in. Two wore black uniforms, and another wore a dark green uniform with the same cut.

"Recruit Tirolo is here for testing and evaluation. His medical examination and history are in the files," the woman said before leaving the room.

"Sit down while we look at the files," said the officer sitting in the middle of a row of three tables for the interviewers.

"How long were you training at Fort Draco?"

"About nine months, sir."

"What was your magical training before entering the wizard corps?" the green-uniformed man asked.

"I had three days with the village hedge wizard, sir," Quint said. "I started my training when I came into my magic."

They scribbled something in their files.

"We might as well get started. Demonstrate the strings that you have learned."

"All thirty-two, sir?"

"I have thirty-three listed," the man in the center said.

"The shield weave. I can do that first," Quint said.

"Do that, and we will test your shield."

The inquisitors looked closely as Quint looked at his hands as he created tendrils. He put his hands into a ball and manipulated the threads into a string before pulsing the string with power. He felt the shield fall into place and stopped applying magic.

"It is done, sir."

The three of them began weaving strings and tossing them at Quint. The pressure of the magic assaulted him as if the inquisitors threw soft little pillows at him. Ultimately, the second black-uniformed man threw a string at Quint, making him freeze.

"That one got through?" the officer asked.

Quint couldn't respond. The officer created the counterspell, and Quint could feel a tingle as the freeze thread dissipated.

"Remember, you are exposed no matter how good you think your shield is. But I would rate your string as very good, and that is the hardest string to master on your list."

"In your opinion," the officer in green said.

"The relative strength of all strings is based on experience and opinion," the second officer said.

The green uniformed officer nodded.

At that point they went through every string and wanted as actual a demonstration as was possible in a room inside a building. The woman had guessed that the ordeal lasted over two hours but not three.

"Definitely a Level 3. Have you been working on any other psychic spells?" the officer in the center asked.

Quint didn't want to tell him about any, but he said he was still practicing three.

"Take your time with those," the officer in green said. "I'd rather you get some years on you before learning more strings."

"Yes, sir," Quint said, although he thought the comment wasn't an order.

"Now, it's time to see how much you've learned about the military."

Quint spent another hour answering questions about what he had learned in his nine months at Fort Draco.

"I would rate his military as competent," the man in the center said before looking at Quint. "Few recruits are given that rating with only one year of training."

Quint's history rating wasn't as good, but military history was also competent, and geography was adequate, which the officers considered better than average for recruits.

"I think we've seen enough, Recruit Tirolo. You can return to your room. You will receive your assignment tomorrow after lunch. Enjoy Bocarre." The officer tossed a purse on the table. "At the corps' expense."

He gave Quint a tight smile, and the three officers filed out. After barely reaching the refectory after missing breakfast, Quint went to his room and removed his uniform jacket to nap. The interview was grueling, and the schooling questions were more challenging than demonstrating strings.

☙

Quint exited from the front door of the annex. At the gate he was stopped by a guard.

"Tirolo?"

"I am Quinto Tirolo," Quint said.

"Good. Your escort is waiting on the other side of the gate. You can pass to meet her."

A female? Quint thought. He expected the woman who had helped him manage the interviews, but the female was a young woman, maybe not even that: someone his age.

"I have a guide?" Quint said.

The pretty girl flashed her thick eyelashes. She had large brown eyes and smooth tan skin. Her dark hair had thin ribbons mingling with her long ponytail was tied with a ribbon and a bow at the bottom. Racellian maidens wore long hair unless they were working. Most girls worked in his village, so the ribbons and the ponytail looked fetching to Quint.

"You do if you are Recruit Quinto Tirolo."

Quint smiled. "I suppose I do. Do you have a name that can be disclosed?"

She smiled. "I am Talia Occo. I'm nearly eighteen if you were wondering. If I was told correctly, you haven't been sixteen for very long."

"I haven't," Quint said. An older woman would escort him, he joked to himself. "Do you have a plan of what we will see?"

"There is a market a few blocks away. I can show you some prominent buildings on the way. The High Council Palace is in a different part of the city along with most Racellian administration buildings. One hundred years ago, the Wizard Corps was frowned upon about the time the Wizard Corps building was getting too small. I understand the headquarters was built a good distance away by mutual agreement."

She began walking, and Quint obediently followed.

"And what is your connection to the wizard corps?"

Talia smiled. "I'm a soldier in the corps. I am sometimes called upon to escort Recruits around the city. I was a young inductee, like you. I earn some extra money doing this. You do know you'll be buying me dinner?"

"I do now," Quint said. At least he wouldn't be eating alone in a few hours.

"Were you pressed into service?" Quint asked.

She giggled. "Oh, no! I volunteered. My father works at the headquarters. I work for a division that has its own building in Bocarre."

"What is interesting about Bocarre?" Quint asked. "I've never been in a city before. Where I live, I can move between four villages and a town, and that is it."

"Most of Racellia is like that. We call it the one-day rule. Everyone lives in a district."

"My father needed a warrant to sell his wheels to other towns."

Talia nodded with a smile. "It makes everything so much more orderly. The cities are exceptions since people are needed for special services, but most people stay within the city limits."

"What if you want to tour the country?"

"You get a tour warrant. They are a little dear but not impossible to get."

Quint realized he had led a sheltered life, partly because of Racellia's one-day rule.

Talia gave Quint a guided tour, which was well-rehearsed. He wondered how many recruits she had guided through the city. It certainly wasn't a punishment, but Quint felt the tour was odd.

They reached the marketplace. Quint expected to be impressed, but once they started through the market lanes, the goods had more variety, but Quint thought the market would have been something special, and it was a bit of a letdown.

Talia suggested he buy a civilian outfit. She was confident he had enough money in his purse for one. After a quarter of an hour looking at the marketgoers, Quint had a feel for the local style and bought a conservative set of clothes and regular shoes rather than boots.

He paid for a large valise to put his purchases, and Talia directed him to a pub.

"The food is good, but not too expensive. You'll have something left in your purse."

Quint was all for that, and they went inside. Quint had eaten in pubs with his father in the four villages and the town in their little district, and this one was only a bit bigger, but it smelled the same.

A menu was posted around the place on chalkboards.

"Roast chicken," Quint said. "My father always avoided stews since they often contain different kinds of meat, not all of it good."

"A wise man, your father," Talia said. "I'll have the chicken, too."

They ordered, and Talia ordered a mug of ale for both. Quint raised his finger.

"If I'm going to drink alcohol, I'd rather it be wine. My father always drank white wine with his chicken."

Talia frowned. "Are you sure about that?"

Quint nodded. "I'm not much of a drinker. My father let me nurse a small goblet from time to time."

"White wine for him and ale for me," Talia said.

Quint watched her looking at the patrons rather than the surroundings. She had been here before, it seemed. Quint wondered if this was a unique situation or one that had been played repeatedly for recruits coming through headquarters to be rated and assigned.

As he gazed about the pub, while waiting for their food, Quint realized he had no preference about his rating or assignment. He had insufficient experience to evaluate anything except for the current situation, whatever that might be at the time.

Regardless, Quint had to be careful, so he wasn't automatically disadvantaged. He didn't know how to survive in the constantly changing environment of the Wizard Corps, but he wanted to give himself the chance to survive.

"Does your father ever complain about his lot in life?" Talia asked after the pause that Quint used to think.

"He cares about his business making wheels. The demand for his work comes and goes. It is currently going, and he is worried about maintaining his business. I'm hoping his savings will grow with me out of the way. One of my brothers might come into the business, but he isn't trained yet. None of that is my business, now, is it?"

"I suppose not," Talia said. "Does he get enough to eat?"

Quint shrugged. "I never went hungry," he said. "My father is a good, earnest man who knows who he is and what to do about it. He makes the best wheels for miles around."

Talia leaned closer. "How do you know that?"

"Because I've been his apprentice since I was ten. He has trained me to evaluate wheels, and his wheels hold up better than any others. It's almost a curse. When he's replaced most of the wheels in our area, he knows his business will suffer because his wheels last longer."

Talia laughed. "A successful business can be a curse. I'll have to remember that," she said. "Does the government keep him from succeeding?"

"If he ever gets around to asking for a warrant to sell in other areas, he is always denied, but Father is happy about his lot in life."

"Are you happy with yours?" Talia asked.

"I don't know what my lot in life is at this point," Quint said.

He wasn't happy about being probed. Either Talia was exceptionally nosy, or she was performing an interrogation. He thought the interrogation was most likely.

"Are you happy with your lot in life?" Quint said, trying to get on the offensive with the girl.

Talia raised her eyebrows. "My father is high up the ladder in the wizard corps. I have a job that I like, so I suppose I am happy."

"But what about your next step up? If your father is highly ranked, don't you have a plan to reach as high as him?"

Talia smiled at the question. "Women can only go so far in the Racellian armed forces, including the wizard corps. For example, the leap from lieutenant to captain is one few women successfully make. I'm not sure I'm made of the right disposition."

"And does the same situation apply to hubites?" Quint asked. "Who is the highest ranked hubite you know of?"

"I don't know of any hubite captains. I don't know all the officers," Talia said.

"Levels are measures of magical capability, but the real acceptance in the wizard corps is military rank and directing officers below you. Am I right?"

Talia nodded.

"You and I suffer from the same problem. There is a finite ceiling that determines our lots in life. I don't know if that restricts my happiness," Quint said.

Talia sat back as their food was served with a frown on her face.

The roast chicken looked delicious, with browned skin and roasted potatoes swimming in a chicken gravy. Quint sipped his wine. It was watered down so much that it was almost flavored water.

"Eat," Talia said with a grin.

If anything, Talia enjoyed her dinner. She ate more of her chicken than Quint did.

They walked back to the annex in companionable silence.

As they came to the gate, they stopped.

"I will go home. My father doesn't live at the headquarters, but his flat is a few blocks away. I live with him when I'm not on duty at my division." She looked up at the annex behind Quint's back and then looked into Quint's eyes. "I think you've given me more to think about than the opposite. Thanks for the dinner," she said.

Quint gave her a little bow. A salute wouldn't be appropriate since she was in civilian clothes. "I think I can say the same. Thanks for the tour and your advice on getting these." Quint lifted the bag of his new civilian outfit. "Good night."

"And a good night to you."

He walked through the gate after showing his identity tag. Once in bed, Quint stared at the dark ceiling and wondered how he did with Talia. He realized he had made a mistake in pointing out they both had a hard limit in the wizard corps. At this point, Quint didn't care, but that might not always be the case.

Did his test, for he was sure the evening out was a trial of some kind, affect whatever decision would be made the following day?

☙

Quint was left to his own devices in the annex for breakfast and lunch. The woman who had escorted him to his magic test finally rapped on his door.

"Time to find out what the wizard corps has in store for you," she said.

She led Quint to the same waiting room for his first interview and left him sitting in a chair, waiting for the next meeting. No one bothered him as he sat for half an hour waiting for the door to open. It finally did, and a man exited. He was older than a recruit and didn't look exceptionally happy.

Quint watched him walk out, wondering what his reaction would be.

"Recruit Tirolo," a voice called him in from the corridor.

Quint walked in and stood at attention. Only one officer was behind the long table meant for maybe five people.

The voice belonged to the second officer, who talked little while he was evaluated and tested the previous day.

"I won't take much of your time. We have made a difficult decision regarding your rank and first posting. You will be recognized as a Level 3 wizard. That gives you certain privileges. You will be housed as an officer and eat in the officer's mess, should you choose. However, your military rank will be that of a corporal due to your age and inexperience. Your day-to-day duties will be that of a corporal and you will be given duties befitting a corporal.

"My pay grade, sir?"

"We are on firmer ground with that. There are always two components to pay in the Wizard Corps. You will be paid as a corporal with the standard bonus for achieving Level 3. The bonus is twice that of a Level One corporal's pay."

"Thank you, sir." Quint could send some money home. With a lowly rank and more money than any of his peers, he would do some saving.

"Your studies at Fort Draco presented us with an opportunity to give you a challenging posting. You will be assigned to the Strategic Operations division of the Wizard Corps. Their operations are closer to the city center, and you will merit a billet in the building for your first year of service."

"And then, sir?"

"You will be allowed to procure housing outside the headquarters. Most personnel live outside," the officer said. "There is a housing allowance for corps members serving in Bocarre."

Quint had to repress a frown. He had to find out about the allowance before sending money to his father. Quint didn't know how to do that, so he would have to learn a lot since he had no idea what strategic operations entailed.

"Yes, sir. When do I have to report?"

"Since you will be living in Bocarre, you will take a carriage to the headquarters after breakfast tomorrow. Here are your orders. Do not read the sealed envelope. Give those to the officer in charge. Any questions, Corporal Tirolo?"

"No, sir," Quint said.

He saluted and left the room. Quint was sure his expression matched the one of the soldiers who had preceded him.

CHAPTER SEVEN

THE CARRIAGE LET QUINT OFF IN FRONT OF A BUILDING that looked more like a mansion or a lord's manor in the middle of a block of similar structures. At least this one wasn't black, but black-uniformed officers were guarding the gates.

Quint showed them his identity tag and let them read the address on his orders before they would let them into a graveled courtyard.

A brass plaque beside the ornate doors proclaimed that the building housed the Strategic Operations Division of the Racellian Wizard Corps. Quint didn't know if he should feel proud or disgusted.

He walked into a foyer. The architecture was fancy, but there were no decorations on the walls. The headquarters building he had left had arms and armor displayed and depictions of magical battles on murals on some walls.

"These are my orders," Quint told the soldier behind the counter.

"I am to deliver this to the officer in charge," Quint said.

The soldier pulled a distasteful face and called out for the Officer of the Day. A man came out and took Quint's orders. He casually unsealed the envelope and looked at Quint before reading.

"Interesting, a hubite. Come with me," The officer said. He led Quint down into the basement to an office with a large window looking out into the corridor.

"A new worker," the officer said. "This one is a Level 3 and has been given the rank of corporal. I'm sure you know what that means."

The woman in the office looked at the orders. "I do. He will have to work in a full uniform and take up one of my two extra rooms."

The woman didn't sound happy.

"I'll leave him to you. He is to participate in field operations. We won't schedule any magic sessions. He needs time and experience to catch up."

The woman blinked. "Level 3, you say. A prodigy to learn how to get his hands dirty, but I doubt he will do any catching up while he's down here."

"Whatever. We have our orders from headquarters." The officer winked at the woman.

She laughed and nodded. Quint didn't know what communication was exchanged, but it wasn't favorable for him. It was clear he was assigned to be a servant.

"Come with me," the woman said.

Quint noted that after she read the papers in the sealed envelope, the officer snatched them back. Quint followed the woman to his new home.

✂

The woman was correct about the uniform. The other servants wore gray uniforms. Quint had to wear his black uniform, but his duties were the same.

He mopped floors and emptied garbage. When required, he used some simple strings in his work, like lighting candles and lanterns and cooling off hot rooms before meetings since the weather was heating up.

The other servants ignored him. Some had magical capabilities, but none could match Quint.

After a month of duty, he opened a third-floor door and found a library. It was dark inside, but he lit a magic light and perused the books. There were two shelves with books and folders dedicated to wizardry as well as books in a language Quint couldn't read.

No sign warned him of trespass, so he began using the library at night after his duties when the building was mostly empty. On an off day, he bought notebooks, pencils, and folders to document his reading.

Since the training camp focused on teaching strings, Quint missed out on a good grounding in the philosophy and origin of magic, and Quint started with that. It was quickly apparent that the underlying magic theory was given little emphasis at Fort Draco. Even Pozella hadn't given him the insight he was learning, but then the trainers were focused on teaching strings, not magic theory.

Quint learned that energy absorption was thought to be a critical differentiator between those who could manipulate magic and those who couldn't. Quint wasn't so sure it was that simple, but being sequestered in the basement of the Strategic Operations building wouldn't help Quint gain much power.

After cooling a conference room, Quint began rearranging the chairs when a group of officers filed in. He waited for them to go through the door before leaving. The last one to enter was a familiar face.

Talia Occo, his city guide, walked in carrying portfolios. He noticed lieutenant badges on her shoulders. She stopped and gave Quint a smirk. He hadn't expected such an unfriendly greeting.

"Amaria, bring the handouts," a colonel said.

She lifted her chin and walked directly to the colonel. Quint caught her glancing at him as he left.

Amaria, he thought. Even her name was false. Quint suspected his tour wasn't a success. Other than being released from the service or executed for not measuring up, Quint couldn't imagine a worse outcome after his testing.

At least he still was the only servant with a private room. All the others shared rooms, and Quint was often reminded of the fact. However, he never neglected his duties, and other than his nocturnal self-study, he abided by the rules he was given.

Quint knew he was moving too fast through the magic section, so he branched into military strategy and history. With nothing else to do, Quint was absorbing more than what the books at the fort had to offer, and the library had become his new home.

When he had a day off, Quint walked around Bocarre with his sleeves rolled up to absorb more sunlight. He could feel his magic strengthen when he returned to his building. He approached his superior, the woman in charge of the servants.

"Is there a place on the grounds where I can get some sun rather than wait for my days off?" Quint asked.

The woman worked her lips in thought. "Out the back, there is a courtyard lined with chairs. You didn't hear me mention it. Wizards go there all the time. You might not be welcome, but you have never complained about your situation, and I owe you something for how you've handled your post."

Quint gave the woman a grin and a salute. "Thank you, ma'am."

He expected a frigid response from everyone, and his superior had thawed out enough to make his day. After a short break in his schedule, he stepped out the back door and found the courtyard.

"Corporal," an officer said, "bring me some of that pink punch you people serve."

"Yes, sir," Quint said. He quickly went to the kitchen and had a cook prepare a tray with a snack. The officer was still seated. Quint didn't know the officer's rank since his uniform tunic was off.

"Your drink, sir," Quint said, putting the tray next to the officer.

"I didn't think. Are you here to get some sun?"

"I just found out about this place, sir," Quint said.

"What level?"

"I am a Level 3, sir, but I am too young for a commission."

"Sixteen, seventeen?"

"Sixteen, sir."

"I've seen you around. Why are you doing servant work, Corporal?"

"No one has told me, but I suspect there are two reasons. I am a hubite and too young to lead others, sir."

"And a Level 3. They didn't know what to do with you, so they put you here. Do you know anything about strategy?"

"I read military strategy in training and a little since, sir."

"…and put you in the basement so you wouldn't grow."

"That might be a reason, sir. I can't say I know for sure about anything."

"I might be able to do something about that. Don't expect a miracle, young man. Your name?" The officer chuckled. "I don't need it. I'm sure you are the only corporal-servant in the building."

"Corporal Tirolo, sir. Quinto Tirolo."

"You may leave. I wouldn't want anyone to see you with me now."

"Yes, sir." Quint left, wondering who the officer was. He seemed happy to converse with a hubite and a subordinate.

The following day, Quint was called into his supervisor's office.

"You've had a change in assignment," the woman said. "You will be responsible for the conference rooms and the library on the third floor." She scratched her head. "I've never been asked to arrange the staff that way, but I follow orders, just like you."

"What do I do, ma'am?"

"You'll serve the most senior meetings, and the others will remain behind. You will still clean the conference rooms after each meeting like you have been doing."

"How do I serve in the library?" Quint asked.

"Keep it dusted and orderly. I generally have someone move the dirt around once a week. You can do a better job, I'm sure."

"Thank you for your confidence in me, ma'am," Quint said.

The supervisor scribbled on a copy of the assignment sheet and handed it to Quint. "Today's assignment. Oh, I just about forgot. If you have the time, monitor the sun courtyard and serve drinks occasionally."

"I can do that, ma'am," Quint said.

CHAPTER EIGHT

~

LIFE SHIFTED IN A SLIGHTLY DIFFERENT DIRECTION. Quint checked on the courtyard a few times a day, and when it was empty, he spent a few minutes soaking in the sun with his uniform tunic off.

Quint accepted the instructions from some of the indignant serving staff since he had taken away the opportunity for the staff to rub shoulders with the strategic operations officers, for he had learned that everyone in the division was an officer with one exception: him.

On the fourth day, he was called to bring a tray of punch up to the commanding officer's office on the third floor. In the months he had been working at the division, he had never met the commanding officer, and that fact had always gnawed at him: a display of his insignificant worth.

A clerk helped open the door for Quint.

"You can go right in," the clerk said.

Quint stopped as he passed the door. The officer in the courtyard sat behind a large desk in a large office with its own conference table. No wonder he had never seen the commanding officer in a conference room. The meetings were held here.

"Where should I put these, sir?" Quint asked.

"On the table. You'll be sitting in that chair in the corner listening in on my meetings, Corporal Tirolo. If we need someone to fetch something, you can do an admirable job. We haven't been formally introduced. I am the commanding officer of the Strategic Operations Division of the Wizard Corps. You can call me Colonel Sarrefo."

"Yes, Colonel Sarrefo, sir."

"Good. Go to your assigned seat. The attendees will arrive any time." Sarrefo rose from his chair and came around, holding a portfolio.

Four people walked into the room. Quint recognized Amaria. He didn't know if her last name was Occo or not. She paused as she looked at him. Quint could detect a slight narrowing of her eyes before she turned her attention to the table.

"You can shut the door, Corporal Tirolo," Sarrefo said. "I decided we could use our little corporal for a little more than emptying the trash. He is a Level 3, after all. None of us can surpass him except for me, of course."

Everyone but Quint smiled or laughed softly.

"Tirolo will perform some of Amaria Baltacco's duties, giving her more time to assist the rest of us."

Amaria Baltacco's duties were unknown to Quint, so he had no idea what he was doing there except to take the refreshments away at the end of the meeting and perhaps close the door to the colonel's office on the way out.

The meeting was not interesting. There were no secrets discussed that day. The colonel reviewed the personnel. Quint did learn that there were eight hundred people in the Wizard Corps. There were one hundred and twenty in strategic operations with new orders to procure thirty more. The attendees nodded and were happy about getting more wizards in the division.

Promotions were bandied about. Quint knew none of the names, so the discussion was meaningless to him, except it was clear he knew nothing about the mission of strategic operations and would need to learn more about the Wizard Corps organization to think intelligently about the division's plans.

Sarrefo stood. "I have a meeting at headquarters. You can see your way out. Tirolo, close the door after everyone leaves."

Amaria stayed behind, leaving Quint and her alone in the colonel's office.

"Do you feel triumphant?" Amaria said. Any pretension of being pleasant or personable had disappeared.

"No. Why would I feel anything? I brought refreshments from the basement and then was banished to a corner of the room, listening to everyone talk about something I do not know, and now the crowning moment: I will shut the door after you leave the office, ma'am."

"Are you being insubordinate?"

"Other than mentioning a crowning moment, certainly not, Lieutenant," Quint said.

"We will see if you ever sit in that corner again," Amaria unpleasantly said as she walked out the door.

Quint shrugged and closed the door with one hand, balancing the goblets and the tray with the other.

∽

Three days later, Quint was called to his supervisor's office. The officer who had escorted him to the basement on the first day was chatting with her when Quint rapped on the door.

"Inside, Tirolo. I heard you like the open air. We have a little diversion for you," the male officer said. "As you know, we are fighting border skirmishes with the Barellians. You also might know that wizards in strategic operations must spend some time each year in the field. Since you haven't had any training for the field, you will be assigned to a support company."

Quint's version of the orders is that he was to remain a servant, but that was okay if he could get more fresh air. He would miss the opportunity to work in his new duties, but it looked like Amaria had more influence over his disposition than he thought. It might be some time before he sat in the corner chair in the colonel's office again.

Barellia was south of Bocarre. Barellia and Racellia made up most of the west coast of South Fenola, the continent where Quint lived. He was about to pack his black uniforms when a servant showed up with a package.

"For your field assignment, Quint," the servant, a willot, said and then left. Those were the first words that the servant had ever spoken to Quint.

He opened the package. There were two dark green uniforms complete with wizard corps insignia. He put one on and stuffed the other in his bag with his personal items and civilian outfit. He was about to close everything but thought of his battle strategy notes. He could review them before he fought in a battle.

There were five other wizard corps officers heading to the same destination. Their uniforms looked much like Quint's, but those fit much better than

Quint's "greens," as the others called them. He wasn't ignored as they loaded up a carriage that took them out of Bocarre and into the countryside on the west side of the capital.

It took three days to reach their destination, a temporary camp commanded by Field Marshal Chiglio.

The field marshal approached them. "I always greet my wizard corps troops. I hope my soldiers will treat you well. Your observations as we fight will help us all improve at this."

The officers laughed, but Quint could sense the condescension in Chiglio's words. Other officers took their wizard corps counterparts to their army section, leaving the field marshal and Quint looking at each other.

"You met my old friend, Geno Pozella? We fought together in the early days. We were both in the wizard corps. He became a master, and I rose to Level 3, just like you. Now, he teaches, and I command. I don't know who is enjoying life more. He asked me to keep an eye out for you."

"I'm too insignificant for such attention, sir," Quint said.

"Be that as it may. You have been assigned specifically by headquarters to one of our support companies that support the wizard corps component of this army. We don't move unless there are support troops to keep everyone ready to fight."

"I understand that, sir. I will do my best."

"Since I have a little influence over my army, you will be assigned to protect your company of wizard corps support troops with your magic. Pozella said you know many strings, and he is confident you will figure out how to use them in the field. I'm assigning Specialist Gaglio as a mentor. Both of you report to the sergeant in charge of your company, but Gaglio is an old timer, serving with Pozella and me. Consider your time with us a time to learn. He won't care if you are a hubite or a willot."

A soldier walked up. He was older and walked with a limp, but it wasn't as pronounced as Pozella's.

"Gaglio, this is Corporal Quinto Tirolo. We talked about him yesterday. Make sure he becomes a real soldier when he returns to Bocarre."

The marshal saluted both and briskly walked away.

Gaglio watched the field marshal turn down a lane of tents out of their sight.

"I'll take your valise," the specialist said.

"I can carry my bags."

Gaglio smirked. "You outrank me, lad. Let me do it."

Quint watched Gaglio struggle with his limp for a few steps, but he kept up with Quint, and the man passed him so he could lead.

"What is a specialist?" Quint asked.

"In my case, a former officer who is no longer able to lead."

"Like Master Pozella?"

Gaglio chuckled. "He gets to keep his wizard title. I'm only a Level One, so I'm a specialist. I'm good at what I do, which is drive a wagon and run the company because the sergeant is too lazy to do it."

"Are the rest of the supply company members of the wizard corps?" Quint asked.

"No. The sergeant, the specialist, and now the sucker."

"I am the sucker," Quint said, not entirely understanding why Gaglio made the insult.

"You should have declined this post. It's your right to do so. As a Level 3, you have lots of privileges. We'll talk while we are in the field. Pozella talked to you about threads, weaves, and strings. I'll make you more aware of your surroundings."

Perhaps Quint had been too subservient, but then who was Gaglio to tell him of his faults? He had fallen as far as Quint had risen, it seemed. But then, perhaps Pozella was right, and Gaglio's experience might help. The only reason his strategic operations duties improved was through a chance meeting with the commander, not because of something Quint did intentionally.

Gaglio turned right into a narrow lane of tents and entered one of them.

"We will share this palace for a few weeks," Gaglio said. "I talked the sergeant into having you stay with me. Your other option was to share an eight-person tent with the rest of the Wizard Corps supply company."

"Specialists have the same rights as a Level 3?"

"No. They have the same rights as a corporal, Corporal Tirolo," Gaglio said, grinning.

There were two cots in the tent, enough room for two chests at the ends of the beds, and a table with a couple of mismatched hard chairs.

"Thrilling, isn't it?" Gaglio said with a smirk.

He put Quint's bag by one of the chests and laid on the opposite cot. "I do get tired more quickly than the others," Gaglio said. "Wake me when you've finished putting your things away. The sergeant likes tidy subordinates."

"You don't seem put off bunking with a hubite," Quint said.

Gaglio lifted an eyelid on one eye, keeping the other one closed. "I grew up in the southeast. Probably not far from where you grew up. Being a willot among the hubites made our situations closer to the same than they were different until I was sold to the wizard corps."

"Just like me."

"Just like you," Gaglio said. "I wasn't treated well growing up until I went through training, and suddenly, the shoe was on the other foot. Being a stupid nineteen-year-old, I threw my weight around until it hit me that willots and hubites aren't that different, and most of the perceived differences aren't there once you strip away outward appearances."

Quint pursed his lips. "It doesn't stop those who think hubites are animals from giving me a bad time."

"That doesn't, but you won't get hassled by me, young man. Enjoy it while you can. Wake me when you're done." Gaglio turned over and was soon snoring.

Quint took his time and decided to rest for a few minutes, too.

A bugle woke him up. Gaglio had already left the tent, but he stuck his head inside.

"That's the call you need to heed more than anything else. It's time to eat!" Gaglio opened the tent for him and ran his hand along the edges with one hand while he generated strings with his other.

"No one will steal our things through the tent door. They will have to slice open the tent elsewhere," Gaglio said.

Quint would have to ask Gaglio how to cast the string. It wasn't the same one he would have used.

They walked to a massive tent in the middle of the camp, jostled by soldiers moving faster than them.

If Quint had any worries about not getting a place to eat, they would be erased by all the empty seats.

"Half the camp eats at the same time. There are almost enough seats for the entire camp inside, so there are always places to sit. If we set up a field camp elsewhere, this tent stays up for when we return," Gaglio said.

Quint looked across the tent. He counted six feeding stations. Gaglio led him to the other side, where the lines were shorter. "When the other group eats, the short lines are on our side." He shrugged as he took a beat-up metal tray and a fork.

"No knives?"

Gaglio shook his head. "Everything is cooked bite-sized. It cuts down on the cost. You can use a thread to cut something when you are in the wizard corps."

"One I don't know," Quint said.

"But you are a Level 3."

Quint laughed. "I know how to create strings, but I'm not practiced in their use." Another string to learn, Quint thought.

"Perhaps Pozella didn't have the time to show you how useful they were. We will have weeks," Gaglio said.

After dinner, the camp erupted into different activities.

"We aren't on the march, so we have choices about our evening activities after dinner. I generally read, but with you sharing the tent, perhaps that can be the time we teach each other a few things."

Quint raised his eyebrows. "What can I teach you?"

"I'm sure I'll learn some lessons during our time together, Gaglio said. "Let's go for a walk."

They left the camp and strayed into a meadow. There were burn marks on the short grass, so it had been used by wizards before.

"Show me some useless strings," Gaglio said.

"This one sharpens a pencil." Quint took the stub of a pencil from his pocket and laid it on a dead log before creating the string that put a sharp point on the writing implement.

Gaglio grinned. "Try it on my knife." He dulled the edge of a metal nail someone had embedded on the log and ran his finger along the edge. "Dull."

Quint shrugged. He'd only been taught to sharpen pencils. He thought momentarily to get an image of a knife edge instead of imagining a point on a pencil and used the same string.

"Oh, it worked," Quint said, somewhat disappointed that Pozella hadn't shown him the possibility that Gaglio just did.

"Not good enough?"

Quint sighed. "Does that count as a different string?"

Gaglio shrugged. "I'm not sure, but does it matter if it worked?"

"Not really. How good is that edge?" Quint asked.

Gaglio picked up a fallen leave, slid it along the blade, and it parted easily. "Sharp enough?"

"That works on anything?"

"It won't make a dull soldier sharp if that is what you mean," Gaglio said.

Quint laughed. "I suppose not. But it will sharpen an edge?"

"I know this thread. Only if there was an edge before, it consumes a bit of magic, if you didn't notice."

"I wasn't paying attention," Quint said.

"You'd be out of magic after a lot of sharpenings."

Quint nodded. "I do know that you have to conserve your strength. It's a limitation."

"Get more sunlight. It's the fastest way to recover, but you see what I mean? We can go over your spells and see what we can do to expand their usefulness. You know how to modulate your magic?"

"Something I'm good at, I think," Quint said.

"Then, when we must sharpen weapons, one of our company's duties, you can determine the minimum magic to use. From a practical point of view, wizards waste a lot of their power by applying too much magic," Gaglio said. "I'm a specialist because I was able to figure it out. Not all wizards do. Master Pozella didn't have time for any of that during your training, I suppose."

"We concentrated on maximizing the number of strings I could learn."

"If you are a Level 3, then he did the right thing. I didn't expect you to sharpen the knife on your first try. You must be excellent at visualizing."

"Perhaps another talent that I have," Quint said. "What other strings will work?"

"Let's go back and list your strings, and then we can do some thinking. Most strings aren't as easy as the sharpening one."

They spent an hour working on Quint's list of spells and went through half of them.

"Some of our applications may require different approaches," Gaglio said.

"I'd like to understand better what I can do before I have to return to Bocarre."

"A change of subject. Do you have any personal enemies at the division headquarters?" Gaglio asked. "The Marshal had specific orders for you to be assigned to a support unit. The order suggested the horse groomer company.

Chiglio did some checking and put you with the logistic company."

"Wagon drivers," Quint said.

"And odd jobs when we aren't driving, like sharpening weapons," Gaglio said.

"There is a lieutenant, Amaria Baltacco. She gave me a tour of Bocarre before my final assessment."

"Baltacco? Any relation to General Baltacco, the head of the Wizard Corps Military Arm? His responsibilities don't include your strategic division, but he is very influential."

"Her father is a prominent member of the wizard corps, but she gave me a false name. I found out her real one when I met with the commander of the Strategic Operations."

"I heard she is somewhat willful," Gaglio said with a smile.

"I know what you mean. I think she was responsible for my being assigned to division headquarters as a servant and then convinced her father to put me into the field."

"If I were managing a very young Level 3, I'd put him with the wizard corps soldiers to learn how to fight. You may be right, but don't tell anyone I said so," Gaglio said. "It isn't healthy to express yourself too freely in the corps."

"I was a little too free with my tongue when she took me around Bocarre. Maybe if she wore her uniform, I might have been more circumspect, but," Quint thought for a minute, "probably not."

CHAPTER NINE

~

After ten days of inactivity, Gaglio had gone through Quint's strings. Quint learned three new strings. Gaglio tried, but he couldn't do many of the strings on Quint's list. Gaglio added to Master Pozella's teachings of using power and the difference between power intensity and making weaves more precise. Even after Gaglio's instruction, Quint realized how much he didn't know about magic.

A fellow company member put his head in their tent. "Sergeant is gathering the company at the wagons."

Quint walked with the slower Gaglio on the way to the gathering point.

"We leave tomorrow at dawn. Here are your assignments," the sergeant said.

Quint was a walking guard, the only one.

"What do I do?" Quint asked Gaglio, showing him his order.

Walk by the side of my wagon. I'll give you instructions along the way. The sergeant will be in the front wagon, and I'll bring up the rear. For now, help me hitch the horses to load the travel tents. The horses are in the picket line, and the travel equipment is stored at the back of the camp.

"Corporal Tirolo," the sergeant said. "You are to help Gaglio and stay out of the way. If we are attacked, run under the wagons or something."

Quint watched the sergeant return to his tent.

"He doesn't work too hard," Gaglio said. "Don't worry about him.

Everyone knows their job. We drilled doing this a few days before you showed up."

"But I'm the only guard!" Quint said. "And the sergeant wants me to hide. That doesn't make sense."

Gaglio laughed. "We all know where the sharp end of a sword is. If we get attacked, we will fight."

The wagon drivers took off in different directions toward where their supplies were located. Two wagons were dedicated to the field equipment. The supplies were piled high, with a tied-down tarp covering it all. They put their loaded wagons in a line at the camp's perimeter behind the palisade walls and returned to their tent to pack.

Gaglio took Quint to the mess tent for dinner when they were done. After they had eaten, they collected cold breakfast packets to eat when they were underway.

Quint was surprised at the calmness in the fort when bugles called before the sun was up. They took their bags and their breakfast with them to the wagon.

"You can ride until we get closer to the front," Gaglio said.

"How long will that be?"

Gaglio smirked. "A day and a half or so. They don't give us that information, but I know where the border is. The sergeant will kick you off the wagon if I don't."

When the sun descended into the trees in the woods the army passed through, they turned into a large meadow, and soldiers lined up at the wagon to pick up tents and grab camp chairs. If they were on a campaign, soldiers would carry the tents on their backs, but this time, they were headed to a battle with the intent of pushing the Barellian forces out of Racellian territory with a single battle, and then the army would return to the temporary fort.

"If we are successful, I am sure the fort will be relocated to the border," Gaglio said. "Border incursions happen all the time, so this is nothing new. Sometimes, it's Racellia going into Barellia, and vice versa."

Quint spent most of this time reading the sheet with his extended string applications, practicing the visualizations he wanted for each string.

After lunch on the second day, the sergeant approached Gaglio and Quint.

"Corporal Tirolo, you will walk from here to the battlefield. Gaglio, issue weapons."

Gaglio saluted as the company lined up at his wagon and were issued short spears with wooden shafts.

"Won't swords cut through those?" Quint said after the last spear was issued.

"We've never been attacked before," Gaglio said. "The men, including me, feel better having something to protect them. I can still cast strings, but there is something to be said about hefting a physical weapon."

"It helps the morale in the middle of a battle?" Quint asked.

Gaglio nodded. "We just sit and listen to the sounds of it all," Gaglio said as he handed Quint a spear.

He couldn't do all his strings with one hand, Quint thought, and he handed the spear back. "I'll rely on my hands, both of them."

Gaglio grinned. "That's a good attitude. You are free to roam around but stay close to our part of the wagon train. You don't have to stand by me during the battle. It might be good for you to move forward and see what fighting looks like. I've done it enough in my time."

"Good. I'll see what strategies are employed for real rather than read about them in a book," Quint said.

"Practical training. That's my boy," Gaglio said.

※

"The fighting will begin tomorrow," Gaglio told Quint as they put up the tiny tent they shared.

The wagons were loaded, and the camp left behind as they traveled slowly for a day and a half to the battlefield, a vast meadow surrounded by forests in the hilly boundary between the two countries. Quint counted the wagons surrounding the area. There were forty wagons supplying the army. The wizard corps contributed seven to the forty.

"We will leave the wagons here and guard them from stragglers," the sergeant told the drivers and loaders. He turned to Quint. "Roam around and let us know if you spot anyone. Generally, we get a squad or a few soldiers of the enemy sniffing around for easy pickings, but we aren't easy pickings."

Gaglio gently shoved Quint toward the edge of the wagons. "Make sure there are no monsters in the woods."

Quint shook his head. There weren't any monsters in the woods circling the wagons or any other place in the world. He walked through the trees and then stepped through the trees and undergrowth circling the meadow.

He watched soldiers clumping together in groups, talking to their sergeants and officers. The wizard corps was notable, dressed in dark green uniforms in a sea of the red coats of the regular army. Quint thought that black would be more fitting, but there might be reasons for the difference that he didn't know.

A stream that ran along the edge of the meadow on the other side from where they parked the wagon provided a slight challenge to cross, but he found a tree trunk that had been used as a bridge so many times the bark had worn off the top side.

The forest began to thin until Quint stood on the edge of a plain. He wondered where all the farmers were, but he saw a shepherd and his dog moving a flock of sheep out of tomorrow's battleground. Quint stepped onto the plain. The grass was almost knee high, but as he walked farther away from the wood's edge, he noticed patches where herd animals had eaten the grass to short stalks.

He closed his eyes and put his cupped hands together, extending tendrils that became threads that Quint wove into a portent string. That's what Pozella called it. Quint just thought of it as peeking into the future.

A picture materialized in his mind. The blue coats of the Barellians fought the red coats of the Racellians. He saw the wizard corps fight the wizard corps of the Barellians, who wore their army uniforms with silver-edged black epaulets.

In his mind's eye, the battle would range from dawn to afternoon. The war ended in a standoff. Both sides withdrew, leaving dead and dying soldiers on the field. The wizard corps of both sides fought each other, but their efforts did not affect the outcome, and then the vision blurred.

Quint grunted. He knew enough about portents that the outcome in his vision might not occur precisely as he envisioned, but the chances were good the battle would be inconclusive.

He recalled the wizard corps duel taking place off to the left side of the battle. It was futile for wizard to fight wizard, negating the advantages that wizards had in a battle. Quint would have to review his strategy notes to see if that was a standard tactic.

Quint retraced his steps, and this time, he was surprised by a regular army sentry while he crossed the log bridge and lost his balance, falling into the stream.

Quint sat for a moment, letting the water soak his uniform before he climbed the stream's low bank and sloshed his way back to the wagons, enduring amused looks from soldiers. He avoided the cluster of wizard corps soldiers and sought his bag that contained a small towel.

"You can do better than that," Gaglio said, approaching Quint.

"I can, can't I?" Quint created a string that dried his uniform briefly. He shook his head. He could have dried his uniform right after he fell in the stream.

"Find anything interesting?" Gaglio asked.

"I think it will be a draw," Quint said. "I stood on the edge of the battlefield and invoked the portent string."

"Then it might not happen," Gaglio said.

Quint shrugged. "I've never tried anything so ambitious, so that we will see. There is a chance it won't happen the way I saw it unfold. What do you think?"

"It's happened before," Gaglio said.

"Why? Doesn't Strategic Operations make sure the Racellians win?"

"You have strategies and tactics mixed up," Gaglio said.

"But soldiers will die for nothing," Quint said. "The wizard corps of Racellia fought the wizard corps of Barellia. It was inconclusive, too. Can't wizards be deployed to make regular troops more effective?"

"You don't understand that there are politics involved."

Quint shook his head. "Then politics is wasting the lives of a lot of people."

"It always has," Gaglio said.

Quint left Gaglio, looking at him as he replaced his towel. He was so wet behind the ears he forgot to use a drying string when he fell into the stream, but Quint couldn't understand the cost in money, lives and time of thousands of soldiers without any benefit.

Quint didn't feel like sharing a tent with Gaglio, so he slept underneath the wagon like other servants did. The camp woke to the blaring of bugles. The support soldiers waited until the regular soldiers and the wizard corps had their breakfast.

The meadow was suddenly empty of people except for support personnel.

"Nothing to do but wait," Gaglio said with a short spear in his hand.

Quint was too anxious to do that and used his magic to reshape his spear's head, sharpen the blade, and strengthen the shaft. He walked across the road and through the woods, finding a little clearing. Quint took his uniform tunic off, sat on a warm rock, soaking up the sun,

While nodding off, Quint heard voices. He hurriedly put his uniform on, grabbed his sharpened spear, and crouched down, creeping until he reached the security of the woods.

A few companies of Barellian soldiers stopped when they reached the clearing. An officer checked a map, and they headed straight toward the camp.

Quint followed. These weren't stragglers. He counted about forty soldiers. There weren't that many more support troops at the camp. His spear, as sharp as it was, had a very inexperienced soldier using it. Quint didn't have that much confidence, but he kept in contact with the enemy as they trampled through the forest's undergrowth.

When they approached the road crossing into the meadow, Quint decided to try a potent weakness string that would affect all the soldiers. He had just spent an hour charging his magic and worried he would exhaust it again using the spell.

The Barellian soldiers bunched up as the officer explained that they were to slaughter all the support troops and burn the camp.

Quint took a deep breath, and from behind a tree, he wove the string, stepped out, and delivered the weakness spell with the visualization that the men had no strength and couldn't walk across the road.

The soldiers stopped when the spell hit them, and they fell to the ground on the road. The officer was less affected, and Quint stepped out and swung with his spear at the back of the officer. The sharp blade cut through the uniform as if it were paper and bit deeply into the back of the soldier. Quint stabbed the wounded man a few times until the officer ceased to move.

"Over here! Ambushers!" Quint yelled, running into the entrance of the camp.

Support soldiers ran to Quint and then past, killing the defenseless

Barellian soldiers too weak to fight back. The ambush was thwarted, but Quint stared at the carnage and felt sick. He looked at the back of the officer he had killed and had to run back into the forest to relieve his roiling stomach.

Gaglio spotted Quint walking a bit unsteadily out of the woods.

"Did you see this attack?" Gaglio asked.

Quint shook his head, totally exhausted. "I went to absorb sunlight, and they walked through the clearing I was using. I couldn't think of any offensive spells that could stop so many soldiers, so I wove a weakness string, picturing them unable to move. It worked. The officer wasn't as affected as the soldiers, so I attacked him from behind." Quint shuddered. "I've never killed a human before."

"It won't be your last. You are a soldier, after all. Your business is to kill people and break things. Maybe you might want to keep this a secret," Gaglio said.

Quint sighed. "How can that happen? I was the one who called everyone to the road."

"Then take credit for everything, but don't volunteer the information. No one will appreciate a hubite taking credit on his own."

Quint nodded. "I can agree with that. I need some food and some more sun. I almost emptied my magic."

"Someone else can clear this off the road. I have some food and wine stashed in the wagon."

In an hour, soldiers began showing up from the battle. From the look on their faces, Quint saw a lot of frustration. Field Marshal Chiglio had suffered an arrow in the shoulder and was taken to the medical tent.

The Wizard Corps soldiers looked shocked. Quint probably looked much the same, but for a different reason. He didn't lose friends, but he was responsible for thirty-eight deaths.

Quint was called to the field marshal's tent. Two supply sergeants stood at the campaign desk behind the field marshal who sat with a bandaged shoulder.

"These two men said you were responsible for stopping an attack on our camp. I'd like to hear your version of the story."

Quint explained what happened.

"Why did you desert your post?"

Quint held his breath. "I was told I didn't have to stay with the wagon,"

Quint said. "Earlier, I walked through the woods on the other side of the road to the battlefield."

"You went to the battlefield?"

"I stood on the edge of the woods looking out and imagining what might happen."

"Did you weave a thread? One that looked into the future?" Field Marshal Chiglio asked. The man looked at the sergeants. "You two are dismissed. Thank you for your work today."

The tent held the highest and the lowest in the camp; at least, it seemed that way to Quint.

"Now, did you create a portent thread? You do remember I'm a Level 3, too."

"I did," Quint admitted. "I saw that there would be no victory for either side," Quint said.

He didn't want to admit this, but Quint did not want to lie. If he lied and was caught lying, Quint was sure he'd be executed.

"Did you learn anything from that vision?"

Quint sighed. "I didn't get the sense the tactics were very creative. The attempt to destroy the camp was the only thing that seemed effective, and I didn't look in that direction."

"No creativity," Chiglio said. "How can a person at their first battle come to any conclusion?"

"I hate to say it, but I've read books. That isn't a good reason for anything," Quint said, "but I have been studying military history and strategy, and I saw two forces fighting each other, toe to toe. Forces weren't strategically grouped. The Racellian Wizard Corps fought the Barellian Wizard Corps. Why have two evenly matched groups fought when the wizards have tactical advantages over regular soldiers? Use archers to put down the opponent's wizards."

"What you described is exactly what happened," the field marshal said. "No creativity. I received my battle plans from headquarters. I was told the Strategic Operations plans weren't accepted." Chiglio stopped. "Forget everything I just said. Forget your portent string. I will put in a commendation for your efforts in battle and suggest that Strategic Operations should give you a chance to participate. I know you've been sweeping floors and emptying the trash."

"Thank you, sir." Quint was surprised his plight was known to Chiglio.

"I can see why some jealous wizards are there to put you down, but some of that is the reality that is the Racellian military. Forget I said that, too." The Field Marshal waved his hand and winced from his wound. "Dismissed."

When Quint returned to the wagon, Gaglio asked what happened.

"At first, I thought I would be disciplined for leaving my post. I can see why someone would say that," Quint said, "but it looks like I'll get a commendation. I don't know how that works, but the Field Marshal said he was impressed."

"A different man might have had you expelled from the service."

"And that means executed?"

Gaglio shrugged. "Chiglio isn't one of them. Neither is Pozella nor I. Your girlfriend, Amaria Baltacco, sounds like someone who would."

CHAPTER TEN

~

THERE WASN'T ANOTHER BATTLE, and the army returned to the temporary fort from the meadow. Quint and Gaglio went over more strings, proving that Gaglio knew more strings than he let on.

Quint didn't hear anything more about a commendation until it was time to return to Bocarre. He shared a carriage from the temporary fort to the capital with the same wizard corps members except for one who had perished in the battle.

The others hadn't explicitly heard about Quint's role in defending the supply wagons, but they did mention the action on the way. Quint was fine with that. He returned to his room without any fanfare other than snide remarks about him returning from such a long holiday from the other servants.

Quint was assigned to another conference in the commander's office the following day. Amaria's threat about him never sitting in the corner chair didn't come true.

Most of the same officers showed up who usually attended meetings in the colonel's office, including Amaria Baltacco.

"What are you doing here?" she said quietly with a sneer as soon as she spotted him.

"Following orders," Quint replied, "like you, ma'am."

When everyone was present, the colonel stood and reported on the recent battle with the Barellians. Our battle plans were not considered, again,"

Colonel Sarrefo said. "One of our wizards separated himself with distinction and honor during the conflict, and we happen to have him in the room." Sarrefo looked at Quint and had him stand.

Quint was embarrassed, but his only consolation was that Amaria would have to hear what he did.

Sarrefo gave a reasonably accurate version of what happened without Quint's killing the officer. Quint never mentioned it and so far, it hadn't been mentioned.

"We've all wondered what the wizard corps will do with our Level 3 servant, who used a powerfully cast string on the enemy. Corporal Tirolo will be no more. Our colleague has just been promoted to lieutenant in the Wizard Corps. He will be reporting to me as a strategist."

Amaria stood. "How can you do such a thing? A strategist? When has he even read a book?"

"Field Marshal Chiglio is adamant that he and Tirolo discussed strategy while Tirolo briefed the field marshal on his action. Can any of us claim to have done anything like that?"

"I'm talking to my father!" Amaria said.

"He signed the commission, Lieutenant Baltacco." Sarrefo walked to his desk and showed Amaria the commission.

"How could he do that?" she said, almost to herself.

"With a pen, lieutenant," Sarrefo said.

When the meeting was over, the colonel had Quint stay.

"I am very impressed. It isn't easy to crack through the field marshal," Sarrefo said. "I received a personal letter from him that claimed you told him that the army was using stale tactics."

Quint sighed. "I told the field marshal that I didn't see any creativity. Our wizard corps fought their wizard corps. Why would you fight like that? Where is the surprise? I've read enough strategy to know that predictability leads to defeat. The Barellians weren't any better other than their foray into the supply wagons, which was countered by chance. I was in their path because I had gone to get some sun."

Sarrefo laughed. "I can believe it. I'm assigning you to one of our planning groups. Amaria Baltacco won't be a member of that group. She has something against you."

"I'm a hubite, and she has made it clear she detests us," Quint said.

Sarrefo shook his head. "There is more to it than that. Stay clear of her. You won't be attending my meetings until she settles down. We do show some creativity in what we submit to headquarters, and now you'll get a chance to see it and add a little of your own. You no longer have to sneak into the brigade library. Officers have access, Lieutenant." Sarrefo said with a smile.

"Thank you, sir. I didn't expect any of this."

"You will receive pay commensurate with your rank and level, but you'll have to find accommodation outside headquarters. See my assistant. She will have some ideas of where you can move. You have until the end of the month to get situated, and I'll send more specific orders to your current supervisor. You are dismissed."

Quint saluted and staggered out of the room. The colonel's assistant wasn't at her desk, so Quint descended to the basement almost in a daze. He was a lieutenant. How could that be? After all the abuse he'd been taking, it didn't feel real.

☙

Even with the Level 3 bonus, a lieutenant's pay wasn't a vast sum. Sarrefo's assistant knew of a four-bedroom flat that had a vacant bedroom. The current occupants were lieutenants and senior lieutenants in the Strategic Operations division.

His new flatmates were willots, but they had agreed to let Quint room with them, even after the assistant made doubly sure Quint would be welcome.

Quint found out that he had replaced the casualty from the battle. Hero for hero, one of the three occupants had said when Quint moved in.

The room was three times larger than the closet he was given in the basement of Strategic Operations. If nothing else, Quint had a larger space to hide. The flat was on the third floor and had a balcony with four chairs with exposure to the morning sun.

Quint bought a bookcase the room lacked and was ready to start life in his new role.

"We eat cold breakfasts and lunch at division headquarters, and none of us cook, so we eat out for dinner or have it cooked here. The closest market is a few blocks away for a quick meal," one of the flatmates said. "What will the old man have you work on?"

The other two gathered around Quint. He hoped they weren't going to begin pummeling him with their fists.

"I'll be a strategist reporting to the Colonel and working in a group. I'm afraid I don't even know what the group does."

"Battle planning. I heard you dressed down the field marshal for being too predictable."

Quint sighed. "I didn't dress him down. I pointed out that the strategy employed in the battle was stale. It was easy to see that the battle wouldn't accomplish anything if the forces were evenly matched, which they were."

"If you were with the wagons, how did you see the battle? Did you climb up a tree?"

Quint closed his eyes and realized he'd have to tell. "I cast a portent string. The battle played out in front of me, standing at the edge of the battlefield."

"Portent!" the youngest lieutenant, except for Quint, said. "That's a challenge even for a Level 3."

"I hadn't used the spell like that before," Quint said. "The flaws were easy to see, and as it happened, the vision was pretty much how it happened. Field Marshal Chiglio described parts of the battle, and I would finish with the result. He believed me. Where do you serve?" Quint wanted the subject changed.

"Two of us are in the operations part. We manage logistics. You were guarding the wagons, although we didn't call for a guard."

"Someone did," Quint said, "and I would have done nothing if the Barellians hadn't thought to attack the supply wagons."

Quint looked at his peers, for they really were peers now and didn't see the animosity that usually blossomed when Quint showed up anywhere.

"I'm in one of the five strategic groups," one of them said. "I doubt you'll be working with me. Amaria Baltacco is in my group. She has made it plain you aren't her favorite colleague," the lone senior lieutenant said. "We have learned to watch what we say. Too many comments have made it all the way to headquarters if you know what I mean."

"I think I do," Quint said. "Are there any rules I need to follow in the flat?"

"Don't go into any of the bedrooms unless invited. There is little enough privacy in the sitting room and kitchen. The washroom is first come - first served. We have a housekeeper to minimize the womanly duties of keeping a residence."

Quint pursed his lips, his cheeks getting a little warm. "I am unfamiliar with what womanly duties you have mentioned."

"Oh," the senior lieutenant said, grinning, "Not those kinds of womanly duties. Cooking, mending, and washing clothes is what I meant. Marena generally cooks our dinner twice weekly unless we tell her otherwise."

Quint felt relieved, but the explanation left the subject of letting women into the flat open. He was too young for that kind of thing and was too timid to clarify the rules any further.

"Do you play cards, Tirolo?" the middle lieutenant asked.

Quint shook his head and shrugged. "I wasn't able to learn. My mother wasn't interested, and my father never taught me, preferring to spend his leisure in the village pub."

"So did mine," the senior said. "I learned at the training fort."

"Which one?" Quint said.

"Mine was in the northeast."

"Central for me," Quint said. "Fort Draco."

"That isn't one of the main ones," the middle lieutenant said. "It has regular soldiers mixed with wizard corps recruits. There aren't as many recruits in the southeast since most of that area is settled with…" The lieutenant raised his eyebrows. "Forgive me."

"You were going to say hubites. There is magic among my people, but it isn't a strength. The local hedge wizard called me a wild talent, but I thought he had done that to raise the price he received for selling me to the army."

"Pressed. I see," the senior said. "You've done well for yourself. Talent has a way to emerge."

A curse and a compliment, Quint thought. The curse didn't come with emotion, just a recitation of facts that Quint agreed with.

A woman younger than Quint's mother walked through the door with her arms filled with bags. Quint was the first one there to help. The woman looked cross for a moment but then relaxed. "Masmo's replacement?"

"In the flat, yes," the senior lieutenant said. "Quint, this is Marena, our housekeeper." He turned to the woman. "Marena, I introduce you to Lieutenant Quinto Tirolo, who was on the same expedition as Masmo."

"You look too young to be a lieutenant," Marena said without a greeting.

"He earned it," the youngest of the three lieutenants said. "A hero of sorts. Quint was recently promoted."

"For good deeds," she said. "That would be the only way."

"For good deeds," Quint said. "I am pleased to meet you."

"I should hope so. You won't be eating dinner without me on two days of the week."

"I will look forward to it," Quint said.

Marena snorted and took her bags into the small kitchen.

"You can bring your wash and put it in the clothes sack. Marena will wash tomorrow," the senior said. He leaned closer to Quint. "Marena can be a bit prickly, but she is very good at what she does."

Quint hoped so. He retreated to his rooms, separated the clothes, desperate for a cleaning, and filled the rest of the sack with his washing.

The youngest of the lieutenants was the only one of the group remaining with the others in their rooms. Quint would be more comfortable in his, so he also left the sitting room. He went through his notes on strategy to be better prepared for his first meeting with his strategy group the following day.

Quint had no illusions about being a substantial contributor, so he studied to look less dumb than he probably was.

An hour later, Marena called for dinner. The bedrooms were evacuated, and they sat at the table outside the kitchen. It sat six, and there were five plates set. He guessed Marena joined them.

Once dinner started, Marena looked at Quint and then at the others. "Be warned, I may raise my rates if he stays," she said. "There were bloody clothes in that sack, and I don't like cleaning bloody clothes."

Quint wondered if there was a story behind that. He should have rinsed out the uniform that was splashed with the blood of the officer he had killed at the battle.

"If there is a next time, I'll rinse the blood out. I'm new to being in action," Quint said.

"What action?" the youngest lieutenant said. "You fought the sappers?"

Quint sighed. He couldn't in good conscience hide his actions from his new flatmates. Quint told them about his weakness spell that incapacitated all the men except the officer. Quint said he had to put the man down with a short spear.

"I thought those were worthless," the middle lieutenant said.

"I used three strings to make the spear into a usable weapon. The officer was in a weakened state when I fought him."

That part was primarily true, Quint thought.

"Three strings. You made the most of being at the tail end of the army," the senior said.

Marena narrowed her eyes as she glared at Quint. "I thought your clothes were blooded helping with the wounded. You did well for your first encounter with the enemy."

Quint was surprised to hear a compliment.

"I had to do something, or the wagon drivers would have been killed," Quint said.

"Have a little more of this," Marena said to him. "I may still want a raise."

"I'll pay all of the increase since you are raising your rates because of me."

Marena nodded with her eyes narrowed again. "I expected you would, and I'm sure they did, too."

None of the lieutenants looked Quint in the eyes after Marena's comment.

Quint laughed. "I get a bonus for being a Level 3 anyway."

"You're really a Level 3?" the senior lieutenant said. "I thought you said that in jest."

"I don't feel like a Level 3," Quint said. "I feel like a regular soldier in the wizard corps."

"Suit yourself," Marena said, rising from her place and returning to her prickly ways.

Quint noticed she had eaten everything on her plate. He returned to his room to study for the rest of the night.

CHAPTER ELEVEN

~

QUINT REPORTED TO THE COLONEL'S ASSISTANT when he arrived at the division headquarters.

"Here is your schedule for the rest of the week. You are expected to make your schedule from this point forward. You get a new badge to wear in the building. It will give you greater access. Most people here are commissioned, so that isn't a unique badge."

"Thank you, ma'am," Quint said.

"Flip it over."

Quint turned the blade over.

"You have access to the third floor, including the library. Colonel Seffaro gave you the privilege to remove books from the library. They are expected to be returned, Lieutenant Tirolo."

"They will be, ma'am," Quint said.

She gave Quint a frosty smile. "You no longer call me ma'am. My name is Zoria Gouta. You can call me Zoria if we are alone or Sergeant Gouta if in a group, sir." The smile warmed up a little bit. "You have enough time to go to the mess and review your schedule. The first floor has a supply room for notebooks, pencils, pens, and ink. You will be expected to write proposals and papers."

"I will, sergeant," Quint said as he saluted and left the colonel's office for the officer's mess.

Quint had emptied the garbage and the trash in the mess on his servant assignments and knew where the supply office was. He had used that, too, for cleaning supplies.

The schedule was fuller than Quint expected. He didn't work directly for the colonel. Quint was faintly disappointed that he didn't, but he was still in a state of wonder and confusion.

He withdrew writing materials from the supply room and jotted down his observations of how he should approach his calendar. Quint had seen calendars on desks throughout the division while cleaning and had been nosy enough to know how to set one up for himself.

A staff meeting was scheduled in a few minutes, so Quint left the mess to arrive early in the meeting room. He resisted the temptation to order the chairs and empty the trash.

He expected mixed reactions when the attendees entered the room. Chairs had been set in two sections, and three planning groups were supposed to start their day with this meeting. Quint sat in the back of the room. One of his flatmates entered with two colleagues and nodded to Quint, making him feel less isolated.

"Tirolo?" a middle-aged man with a captain's badge stopped. "Our group sits up front."

"Yes, sir," Quint said, following his new boss to the front room.

"Sit on this row," the captain said before taking a seat in the row ahead. In a few minutes, Quint sat in a group that took up three rows.

"Rise," a voice said from the back as Colonel Seffaro walked in and sat in the front with two officers he recognized, who attended the meetings in the colonel's office.

"Be seated," the same voice said behind Quint.

"Good morning. We have a new face to introduce. Lieutenant Tirolo, would you stand?"

"Yes, sir," Quint said. He looked about the room to a mix of various expressions. He didn't see venomous expressions, but Amaria wasn't in attendance.

"I have given your captains action reports on the recent battle with the Barellians. This week, I'd like you to critique what happened. Most of you worked on our battle plan that was chosen to be ignored, but that isn't the standard to evaluate the battle. I want a fresh analysis. Am I understood?"

"Yes, sir!" the room said in unison. Quint didn't know how to respond, so his reply was a silent nod.

The colonel sat on a short row of five chairs in the front while one of his underlings announced the statistics generated by the battle.

"See if your plans would have worked and come up with suggestions for improvement."

Colonel Seffaro stood.

"Dismissed," came the same voice from the back of the room.

The colonel sat back down and his staff stayed seated as the wizards filed out.

"Room 4 on the third floor in fifteen, Tirolo," the captain said. "I will get you a desk after we meet."

Quint saluted when he saw others doing the same thing. He spotted Amaria walking up. She snorted in disgust as she passed him and proceeded into the same room Quint had just left.

The planning meeting was awkward. The group was evaluating the wizard corps portion of the battle and Quint's action with the sappers.

"It isn't often that we have an eyewitness to help us with our after-action reports," the captain said. "Quint was actively involved in one action and stood on the battlefield minutes before the wizard corps fought. Let's start with the wizard battle."

Quint observed the discussion while one of the group read the official report. Quint's vision of the battlefield had been consistent with the report.

When the recitation was over, Quint raised his hand.

"What did your group recommend?" Quint said. "I'd like to know that so we can compare what was proposed and what was implemented."

The captain laughed. "You criticized a Field Marshal about the wizard part of the battle, didn't you?"

Quint nodded. He admitted he had cast a portent string before the battle and gave his impression of what happened. "It had no impact on the battle's outcome," Quint said. "Unless the intent was to isolate the wizards."

"You are questioning the Wizard Corps headquarters strategy?"

"I suppose I am. Please let me know if I am out of line doing that or anything else. All this is new to me, sir."

"We are allowed to question," the captain said. "That is part of our job. There was no intent to isolate the wizards, but those are traditionally the orders."

"Was that what you proposed?" Quint asked, emboldened since he wasn't told to shut his mouth.

"No. Senior Lieutenant Morioso, please explain in simple terms what our recommendation was."

Morioso was a tall woman with her hair pulled back into a tightly wound bun.

"We suggested, as usual, that the wizards be split into groups of three and used to pierce the front lines with magic, enabling our troops to advance in the field," she said.

"Did you dictate the strings the corps was to use, ma'am?"

"We gave suggestions. Dictate is too strong a word to use on the battlefield."

"Can archers be employed to contain enemy wizards?" Quint asked. "It's been done in battle before."

"A hundred years ago," one of the strategists said.

"And why did that fall into disuse?" the captain asked.

The man shrugged. "We won the war and didn't need to keep the strategy."

"Maybe it's time we tried it again. I see what Tirolo is trying to say. We intentionally put our wizards out to pasture for the duration of the battle," the captain said.

"Isn't that a bit harsh, captain? We lost a wizard in that conflict," another lieutenant said.

"The valor of our troops isn't being questioned," the captain said. "The deployment is. Let's diagram our proposed plan and see what our new lieutenant has to say."

Quint looked on while the group took the Wizard Corps battle plan proposal and their proposal for the entire battle and laid it out with the formations, the movements, and the projected results.

Quint had expected the battle to be run more like their plan.

"Your proposal was pretty much like I suggested," Quint said. "Do your plans ever get used?"

"Not our proposed battle plans," Lieutenant Morioso said. "They are always tampered with by wizard corps headquarters or rejected by the Racellian army planners."

The captain stared at the lieutenant. "That is not to be talked about in an open meeting!"

Morioso took a deep breath and nodded. "My apologies, Captain."

Quint wondered if Amaria Baltacco was involved. That was probably another topic not for an open meeting, so he kept his suspicion to himself.

"Where have you picked up your tactical knowledge?" the captain asked.

"From books. I've been spending the last months since I arrived reading strategy books in the third-floor library and taking notes," Quint said before he realized he probably didn't have permission. "I used to clean the library and took advantage of being there," he added.

"Time well spent. Continue to do that. Do you have recommendations to minimize the chances of an attack on our supply wagons?"

"I'd start by tossing the useless little spears the drivers get. They were useful only because I had disabled the enemy. Real spears might be better, but I'd train the drivers as a fighting unit. Scouts would be useful. The sentries that monitored the battle camp left when the fighting started."

"They left the back door unlocked, eh?" one of the junior lieutenants said.

"Exactly," Quint said with a smile.

"Tirolo, you are assigned to write that up. We will review it as a group and include it in our report."

"Yes, sir," Quint said.

"I think that wraps it up. You all know what to do. We will meet again in two days, on schedule," The captain said. "Tirolo, you stay behind."

Quint tried to smile at his peers, but his nerves were getting to him. He was way over his head.

"Don't feel that you must respond with the others unless you have something to be added. You did well today but knew your part of the action better than anyone. Next meeting, we will talk about other things, which will probably be outside your experience. I'd like you to observe, for the most part, and we will meet after each meeting and go over your notes."

"Yes, sir."

The captain chuckled. "Don't be intimidated by anyone, including me, but this is a learning experience for you and not for the rest of the group. We will proceed with this strategy in your development until it is no longer needed, and as I said, you can contribute if you think your opinion will add or if you are called upon."

"I'm to sit in the corner, sir?" Quint asked.

"No. You are a group member but one in training. You sit at the table with everyone else. Now, you are dismissed."

When Quint consulted his schedule, his next meeting was with Zoria Gauto, Sarrefo's assistant.

"Here I am, Sergeant Gauto," Quint said when he reported to the assessment.

"Good. We don't have much time. I will show you to your desk. You probably were wondering where you were going to work."

Quint grinned. "I was about ready to think about that. I'm trying to absorb everything else."

"Overcome by it all?"

"Almost, sergeant," Quint said.

"Then follow me."

They walked across to the other side of the building into a large room filled with cubicles on the same floor.

"You get this one. There is a padlock on one of your drawers. That is where you will keep your sensitive papers. You don't have any right now, so don't worry," Zoria said.

The cubicle was across from a window on the south side of the building.

"You may be bothered by the sun."

"I don't consider that to be a disadvantage. I can recharge my magic while I'm working."

Zoria laughed. It was almost a giggle. "Uniforms are supposed to be worn in the building at all times."

"My face and hands will be uncovered. Isn't that permissible?"

"It is. This cubicle has been open because wizards are more concerned about their comfort than their power," Zoria said.

"I'll go down to the supply room and get more supplies," Quint said.

"I'll leave you here then. Keep this in the desk. It is your cubicle assignment and may keep others from bothering you about why you are sitting up here."

Zoria left Quint alone. There were others in the room, but Quint's walk between the cubicles didn't reveal anyone he knew.

He didn't have anything for the rest of the day and slipped down the stairs, withdrew an armful of supplies, and trudged up the stairs. He put everything away and looked at the padlock. The key was sticking out the side.

He opened the drawer and withdrew an unaddressed envelope.

Quint stared at this commission as a lieutenant and a new certificate of his Level 3 status. A rating sheet behind it told Quint he needed to learn seven new strings. Two of them had to be psychic. Quint would have to ask someone how he could find an instructor. No one had talked to him about progressing as a wizard.

He already had his library badge, and that was his next stop. The library was close to his cubicle and when he walked in, he produced the badge to the librarian.

"You are here legally this time," the librarian said.

"I was here legally before. I stayed behind longer to dust the pages of a few books."

The librarian cast off her rigid demeanor. "You can continue with your dusting and are welcome any time with that badge. Your rank and rating also allow you to check out books, but any with a red or blue dot on the spine are ineligible to leave the library."

"I can remember that. I wanted to see if my badge works."

"It does, even though you are a hubite."

Quint's breath stopped. "And what does being a hubite have to do with anything?"

"Nothing," the librarian said. "You are the only hubite in Strategic Operations, and only a few are in the wizard corps."

"Should I meet them?"

"That is up to you. The other hubites are senior to you in rank but not in rating; both are Level 2's, as I recall."

"Maybe when my training is farther along," Quint said. "I won't be long."

Quint took a few books from the shelves and sat at a table with the books in front of him. Both had red dots on their spines, and Quint suspected the best books for him were adorned with red dots, too.

After absorbing a few minutes of triumph, not feeling guilty about his presence, he returned the books and took his commission envelope and some supplies to work on his assignment.

CHAPTER TWELVE

~

IT WAS A COOKING NIGHT, and Marena was already in the kitchen toiling away.

"I'm back," Quint said.

"So?" Marena said.

"I wanted to let you know I'm in the flat," Quint said.

Marena gave Quint a cold smile. "I'm aware you are in the flat. If I am about to be abducted by a band of criminals, I will let you know."

"Right," Quint said. He wouldn't tell her again.

"Two and a half hours until dinner," she proclaimed and made a shooing motion with her hand.

"If you need any help…"

Marena sighed. "As I said, I'll let you know if I need you."

Quint put his things on his desk. He'd need a smaller valise and would get one in the market after dinner.

He sat down and stared at the stack of paper. He trimmed his pen, opened his ink bottle, and returned to staring at the paper. Quint didn't know how to open a report. He didn't know how to begin, and he didn't know how to end. The captain hadn't given him any instructions.

At least he could get started. He scribbled out an outline of what he wanted to say and then wrote from that. He was finished by the time one of the lieutenants arrived.

"Writing a letter home?"

Quint's eyebrows shot up. He'd forgotten all about his parents. How could he do such a thing? But he realized he had been very distracted.

"I need help with my first assignment. I'm to make a critique about one action in the last battle, but I don't know how to format it."

The lieutenant pulled Quint gently from the chair and sat down, grabbing the pen.

"This is how you format the cover page. You don't number it, but you number each page with information inside. When you are done, you sign a back page with a certification that you wrote it."

"And what is a certification?"

The lieutenant wrote a few words on the back. "Something like this. Name, date, and what you are evaluating. If your officer doesn't like it, he will have you do it differently, but you will have shown him that you can do the report." He then explained the format of the report, including page numbers, title, author or authors and to whom the report is delivered.

"That is a lot."

"That's the army, Tirolo. Let's see what you've got."

The lieutenant read the report and nodded his head.

"Not bad for a first try," the lieutenant said. "You could be a little more direct. This isn't a storybook, so there are few suppositions and more facts. Don't make anything up. That will almost certainly bite you where you don't want to be bitten."

"I think I can proceed," Quint said.

He made a few changes to his draft. Re-read it for mistakes and rewrote it with the expected title page, report and ending page. He walked into the sitting room and smelled something wonderful.

"Is dinner ready?" Quint asked the senior lieutenant.

"Have I called everyone to dinner?" Marena called from the kitchen.

"Could you look this over while we wait?" Quint said. "I've already had one person look at it."

The senior lieutenant read it and shrugged. "It looks good to me. You must submit this in an envelope, write a title for the report, and address it to your superior officer."

"Dinner!" Marena shouted from her domain.

Two bedroom doors flew open, and Quint rushed to his room to put the report on his desk before returning to dinner.

Marena sat at one end of the table like a queen. She was the commander-in-chief of the kitchen, after all.

Dinner was delicious and uneventful. The other lieutenants stood and gave bows to Marena, thanking her for dinner before each one retreated to their rooms. Quint stood up last, consistent with his strategy for the meal, but he didn't leave.

"Can I help you clean up?" Quint asked.

"I'm paid to cook and clean up, lieutenant," she said.

"And I'm willing to give you a hand. At least let me help clear the table."

Twenty minutes later, Quint dried the last dish and put it away.

"It is I who should thank you," Marena said. "If you wish to help again, I won't resist letting you. You are young enough. You helped your mother with dinner at home?"

Quint smiled. "I couldn't let you clear the table on your own. My mother seems to have taught me well."

"She did. Run along. I'll finish here and leave the evening to all four of you."

Quint did as she ordered and re-read the report. He found some errors that persisted through his first rewrite and rephrased a few rough patches. Although he usually went to bed later, with a full stomach and a full day behind him, Quint retired, feeling good about what he had accomplished, but he never made it to the market and didn't even start writing home.

※

Life was bearable for a while. Quint was accepted as a junior strategic team member, giving his opinions, which weren't always shouted down. His roommates accepted him except for the occasional barb. Just as he felt accepted, he was sent to a magic class taught by wizard corps headquarters instructors.

His first session brought Quint back to reality. The instructor hated him and told him so, holding him back when the first class ended.

"I'll remember you, hubite. Thought you were too good for the rest of the class, eh? I will stop that kind of thinking right now. You are little better than the dirt you walk on. Don't forget that. The strategic people are the best of the best, except for you."

"Why aren't you in the division, sir," Quint said, not enjoying the onslaught of insults.

The instructor turned red. "I am needed elsewhere in the corps."

They both knew the instructor was lying, but Quint knew he had already gone too far and stayed silent after his retort.

"I'll do my best to be a good student, sir," Quint said.

"You better! Dismissed."

Quint had no idea what else the instructor intended to say but left before the man could call him back. When he returned to his desk, he looked at the handout the instructor had handed out at the end of the class.

As it turned out, Quint was the only Level 3 wizard in the class, and none of the Level 2s were even close to Quint's level. After three sessions, it was clear that the instructor was a Level 2, as well. The class was a waste of time.

Quint found magic books in the library that he worked on during the class. The instructor found out.

"You are to follow along with the rest of the class," the instructor said.

"Why should I study spells that I already know?" Quint asked, trying not to be argumentative.

"I'm the instructor. That is all you need to know."

Quint frowned. "What happens if I continue to read books that will improve my magic?" Quint asked.

"I will report you to the commander of the strategic division," the instructor said.

"Then do it," Quint said, hoping that his friendly relationship with Colonel Sarrefo might result in something positive.

When Quint left the classroom, he felt anger and disappointment. The instructor had made no attempt to accommodate Quint, but Quint hadn't been as submissive as usual, even though he was telling himself not to be argumentative.

Quint kept his temper in control during the next class, but at the beginning of the third session, the instructor sneered at Quint while he called Quint to the front.

"This is from the commander. I hope it results in your dismissal from the corps. Leave my class immediately."

Quint saluted and left the room after retrieving his books. The envelope was sealed, but Quint couldn't wait a second longer to read what his fate entailed.

The commander started with a condemnation of Quint's behavior in the classroom. Nothing Colonel Sarrefo said wasn't true, and Quint accepted the criticism, but there was more to read, like the punishment that Quint expected.

I am withdrawing you from the magic class. You probably should have never been put into a class teaching at a Level 2 curriculum. You are ordered not to return.

My old friend, Master Pozella, who taught you before, has been ill and needs a different assignment. I am allowing him to work in the capital of our division. He will be tutoring you in advanced magic, and you will be training him for work in the strategic division, although he may not need the training. I'll leave that up to you two.

He will arrive next week and meet you at your desk. Until then, make some use of the library privileges in lieu of attending your required magic course.

I expect you will resume your proper deportment with the new arrangement.

Quint was satisfied with the new arrangement and headed directly to the library to choose some appropriate magic texts.

※

Master Pozella showed up at Quint's desk on the third day of the following week. There was a communal chair, and with no one else in the office area, Pozella dragged it over and sat beside his new pupil.

"We meet again," Pozella said. "I didn't expect to see you again."

"I understand you are ill," Quint said.

"Sarrefo said I needed to be ill to return to the capital, and here I am. Cough, cough." Pozella smiled and said sotto voce, "As it turns out, I'm chronically ill, but I'd never tell the corps that, or they would retire me."

"So, this inconvenience of yours is actually a convenience."

Pozella nodded and grinned. "We will be a little less, uh, unfettered in our instruction, and I can live with my wife and daughter who live within walking distance. My walking distance."

"When do we get started?" Quint asked.

"What is your schedule like? I'm now working part-time for the strategic operations division, and at this point, your time is my time."

"Where do we meet?" Quint asked.

"Anywhere."

Quint grinned. "There is a garden that we can use since today is nice. We won't be talking about anything others can't overhear?"

Pozella shrugged. "Not that I know of. Today, I want to know what you learned since you left the fort."

"Seven more strings," Quint said. "My list is at the flat, but I am free until lunch."

"Then let's get some sun," Pozella said with a smile.

The master's limp seemed worse than before, but Quint hadn't seen Pozella for months. The garden was empty. Pozella took off his uniform tunic and rolled up his sleeves. He urged Quint to do the same.

"Do you know which strings you want to learn?" Pozella asked. "Perhaps that is where we want to start. The minimum a Master knows is fifty strings, five of which must be psychic. You knew four, so that would be a good place to define more strings."

"How many strings do you know?" Quint asked.

"I used to know one hundred and thirty-two, but," Pozella shook his head, "I know I've forgotten some and haven't learned many new strings. So, you want to learn one hundred?"

Quint blinked. "You think I can?"

"It's a bit more complicated than learning words, but you are young. Why not? Let that be our goal. We can write them down and cross them off when you learn them."

"I've already diagrammed all the strings I know. Forty-two are in my book. Eight more to go before to be a master, but I'm lacking physical strings and another psychic string," Quint said.

"Then tomorrow, we will meet in the library. Sarrefo said there is a good one here."

"On the same floor as my office. You can meet me there in the afternoon."

CHAPTER THIRTEEN

~

POZELLA SHOWED UP AT QUINT'S DESK AT one-thirty in the afternoon, and they found a corner in the empty library. Quint had brought his portfolio of spells. Pozella had seen most of the diagrams since Quint had learned so few while a servant.

"You made progress on how to cast strings. Tell me how you protected the supply wagons. The reports said little about your magic."

Quint explained how he dealt with the sappers and used the strings in detail.

"You told Sarrefo?"

Quint nodded.

Pozella sat back. "I'm sure that is why Sarrefo summoned me. You could be in more trouble if he weren't the commander."

"Trouble?"

"You weren't at your station during the battle. If you weren't working in strategic operations, that might have been an option for an officer who doesn't like hubites," Pozella said. "The colonel likes you."

"Despite my race?"

Pozella smiled and nodded. "Not all willots are bigoted haters, although that group is growing. Anti-hubite sentiment ebbs and flows."

"What am I to do?" Quint asked, wondering how much danger he might face in the future.

"Do what you are doing. You have value to the wizard corps. I think you are safest where you are."

"If Amaria Baltacco doesn't have her father execute me," Quint said.

"And who is Amaria Baltacco?" Pozella asked. His eyebrows shot up. "Not Emilio Baltacco's daughter?"

Quint nodded. "She is in strategic operations."

Pozella pursed his lips. "I see. Emilio is no friend of the hubites. I've known him for many years."

"You will need more defensive strings. While the shield you used when tested remains useful, there are better physical strings you must learn to protect yourself. I'm sure your current magic instructor would find a way to have you out of the classroom when he taught them."

"You mean I could have avoided the beatings I had to endure at the fort?"

Pozella nodded. "Those aren't taught to raw recruits since they would use them to avoid punishment." He smiled. "Punishment hurts, doesn't it?"

"It does."

Pozella spent the rest of the session reviewing Quint's portfolio and stood. "I have homework to do, even if I am the teacher. I will devise a list of physical strings you will begin learning immediately." He looked around the library. "I'll talk to Sarrefo about a different area than this library. You'll be learning destructive strings, and we wouldn't want to damage the library, would we?"

○○○

Pozella and Quint perused the magic section of the library, and Quint came to a section he had ignored before. All the books had blue dots.

"Is there anything worthwhile in these?" He showed Pozella the spine of a book written in a different language. "I don't know the willot language," Quint said.

"There are. Why would you want to learn the language of your kind's enemies?" Pozella said.

"I don't care about the political aspects of willot writings, but I want to learn useful strings. Are these secret?"

Pozella smiled. "Not secret, but generally set aside for willot use."

"So, I'm forbidden to read these? I ignored them when I looked through the magic books."

"Let's say the language is a barrier to entry into the mind and culture of willots," Pozella said.

Quint was disappointed by Pozella's verbal jousting. "If I learned to read these, would my knowledge grow, or can I get the same information in other books written in common language?"

"You might not appreciate all that you read. That is a warning, not a prohibition."

"I think I already know how willots regard hubites. I'm willing to be exposed to willot ideas."

Pozella smiled. "Then I will give you a dictionary and a phrasebook. There won't be one in here." He looked at the bookshelves. "You learn on your own and read on your own. I won't help you with magic usually reserved for willots."

"It is dangerous for you?" Quint asked.

Pozella nodded. "And dangerous for you, too. But you are in enough peril that I don't think there will be a difference."

"Should I kill myself now, or should I wait for a few days or a week?" Quint said sarcastically. "I don't know what else to do. I get the sense that if I leave the wizard corps, I won't last long on the outside."

"A fair assumption. However, if you leave now, your mastery will not be complete, and any escape from the wizard corps will have to be more carefully planned," Pozella said.

Quint looked at his instructor. What he had just suggested could be regarded as a crime. "I assume you don't want me to mention this to anyone?"

"I don't have to answer that question," Pozella said.

No, he didn't, Quint thought. "I'll regard it as a challenge. You can help me with how to speak in willot?"

"In very protected spaces," Pozella said.

Quint stared at the shelves of books with willot titles. "Maybe I can learn independently and not involve you in any way."

"You won't be able to get to the books that will help you learn the language without me. I'll supply that and step away," Pozella said, looking relieved.

"We can talk later. I suppose there is enough to keep me busy learning strings in the common tongue."

Pozella nodded. "Let's find some of those," Pozella left Quint to stare at the titles.

That night, Quint thought long and hard about the bookshelf conversation as he thought of the willot language discussion. There had to be some very uncomfortable things mentioned in those books. With the hate he'd seen on display by many willots, he didn't expect any praise for the hubite contribution to Racellian culture.

※

Over the next few weeks, Quint had learned a string from the list that Pozella and he had devised about every three or four days. The weaves were more complicated than most of the other strings that Quint had learned.

Quint collapsed on his desk after a long meeting with the team about convincing the Racellian army to improve its supply tactics. The army colonel who had joined his strategic group was not open to new ideas, and he clearly didn't like Quint's participation.

"A letter from Colonel Sarrefo," a female sergeant said, putting the letter on Quint's desk rather than giving it to him. It was just another slight out of a day full of them.

Quint opened the letter and sighed. No wonder the colonel didn't call him into his office. Quint was assigned to support another incursion; this time, he was to travel to Gussellia and observe wizard corps troops in action. He was to leave tomorrow.

At lunch, Quint was visited by the colonel.

"I'm sorry about the orders. One of my orderlies removed your orders from my desk and gave them to you. She told me the assignment sounded too important to wait on my schedule."

"You didn't know they were delivered?"

Sarrefo nodded. "My calendar is full this afternoon and this is the only time I must discuss your orders. It came from the corps headquarters. You are one of two members of our division to go. The other is Lieutenant Baltacco."

"Am I being singled out? I don't count the lieutenant as a friend."

Sarrefo nodded. "You are, and I wanted to warn you that you'll have to be alert. I'll be expecting you to return. If your assignment becomes too dangerous, then you have my permission to leave the assignment and make your way back to the division on your own."

"I have friends here?" Quint asked.

"A few. Pozella, myself, and most of those who you work with. You are a promising young man, and I'd like to see you survive," Sarrefo said.

Quint almost remarked on his being a hubite but recognized an outstretched hand when he saw it.

"Make sure you contact Pozella before you leave. I asked him to give you a few maps and suggest you take more money than you need. I'll expect you back in a reasonable timeframe. The operation lasts three weeks, but in an emergency, it might take you longer to return."

Quint's eyes grew. "You expect something to happen?"

Sarrefo managed a weak smile. "I do, so be prepared. I must leave to prepare for my next meeting."

Quint had lost his appetite but knew he'd need the strength for whatever came his way.

Pozella was waiting at their makeshift classroom.

"Our session won't be long," Pozella said. He gave Quint a small pouch and a large, thick envelope. "The pouch has small versions of the books we talked about. Make sure they aren't found on your assignment. I'd put them in the envelope containing the maps and the list of inns and eating places that should serve hubites. You'll be traveling through willot country. Sarrefo said you would be issued a horse for transportation to the army gathering for an incursion into Gusellia."

"I'll try to memorize these," Quint said.

Pozella nodded. "We have our last string to practice, and then we will talk about what to do with what you've learned. You brought your string portfolio?"

Quint nodded. "I did. I also copied down the strings and what they do so we could review what would be appropriate if I'm in danger."

"The best thing to do is remember what you've learned and use whatever applies to the situation. Some of what you learned before won't be very useful in any fight, but I know you are more creative than I, so feel free to cast strings as they come to you."

Quint already knew that, but he nodded. Pozella gave him more uses of some of the more recent strings he had learned that Quint hadn't considered, and Pozella shooed him out of the classroom so Quint could spend the bulk of the afternoon preparing for his assignment.

Quint tied his bags onto the horse and left through the back gate of the Strategic Operations Division of the Wizard Corps after breakfast, heading toward the northeastern gate to the capital. Halfway to the gate, he stopped when he heard his name called.

"Lieutenant Tirolo," Amaria Baltacco said as she trotted from behind to join him. "I left from headquarters and thought I'd be able to catch you before you left the city."

"We are to travel together?" Quint asked.

"Not by my choice," Amaria said.

"By someone's order?"

Amaria frowned. "My father insisted."

It was Quint's turn to frown. "You are my minder again?"

"It appears so. We will be observers together," she said.

Would Amaria stab him in the back at some point? Quint thought. Sarrefo's warnings alarmed him, and Quint's ability to escape from the battlefield just became complicated. He wondered if she would attack him physically or mentally on their journey.

"You know your way there?" Quint asked.

"Someone planned the trip for me," Amaria admitted.

"Then let's follow my plan. We can take a break outside the city, and I'll show you the map Pozella put together for me."

"Master Pozella, your trainer?"

Quint nodded. "He's recuperating from an illness and Colonel Sarrefo has him tutoring me while he recovers. I'm a little ahead of the others in the magic class."

Amaria nodded. "I'm allowed to go to magic class at headquarters. How many strings do you know?"

"Forty-something. I'm still a Level 3. Pozella is somewhere above one hundred."

Amaria scoffed. "And you think you can learn one hundred and become a Master? That's impossible for someone like you."

"Someone like me? What does that even mean? How many strings do you know?"

"Why would I tell you?"

"Because you asked me. It's a common courtesy to reply."

Amaria pursed her mouth. "Not for me," she said.

"Then you are an uncourteous person, aren't you?"

Amaria took an angry breath. "My father…"

Quint held up his hand. "Leave your father out of it. He isn't here, and you are. At this point, I aim to learn the right kind of strings to qualify for a Master rating. Is there anything wrong with that?"

"It's not aspiring to Master that is wrong. You are wrong."

"Because I'm a hubite?" Quint asked.

Amaria raised her eyebrows and turned away as they approached the northeastern gate.

They showed papers to leave and continued, quietly riding through the expanded capital until they finally reached the Racellian countryside.

"I need a break," Amaria said. "Can we stop soon?"

Quint remembered the first stop. "In half an hour or so."

She grunted and frowned and ran behind the open roadside stand after asking where she could wash up. Quint tried to keep from smiling while he spread the map of Racellia on the rickety table.

Quint ran his finger along the route to the border where his other map would take over and refreshed his memory of their route when Amaria returned.

"That's the map?" she asked.

"Does it look like the map? The capital is labeled Bocarre."

"I know," she said brusquely. "Why are we going a roundabout way?"

"Pozella has traveled widely, and he chose a route where there are inns that aren't hostile to hubites," Quint said. "I might as well restrict being in danger to the battlefield."

"You are afraid?" Amaria mockingly asked.

"Concerned that if I'm not careful, I won't be able to complete my orders," Quint said. "I've been beaten up by soldiers in the Wizard Corps annex and know how that feels."

"You aren't accusing my father of anything!"

"No, but I'm not safe there like I am within the Strategic Operations division, not that everyone is a friend. For example, you have often exhibited hostility," Quint bluntly said.

"I suppose you can look at your situation like that."

"I appreciate your permission," Quint said. "We can make our journey more pleasant or less pleasant, but it is up to you, not me."

Amaria was interrupted by the proprietor taking their snack and drink order. She looked at their horses, tied at the same post. "I suppose a truce will make life better for me if we have some conditions."

"I could agree to adhere to something benign as long as we travel on my route."

Amaria thought for a few moments after their quick meal was delivered.

"We don't share a room. We stay together while riding, but you always ride in front."

Quint smiled. It was as if she was escorting him somewhere. He knew enough strings to leave her at any time, but Pozella had told him he must arrive on the battlefield to fulfill his assignment.

"I can do that," Quint said. He was more comfortable traveling with someone since he had never gone on a journey as long as this one by himself. If a willot accompanied him, the reactions to his light skin color and eyes might be mitigated by Amaria's presence.

She extended her hand across the table. "Shake to seal the agreement."

Quint didn't put much stock into shaken hands. Customers had stiffed his father after shaking hands, so he didn't put much faith in others.

"That's fair," Quint said, repressing a smile. "Do you need to go over the map anymore? We can get going now."

They mounted and continued their journey. The inn Pozella suggested was a few hours away, but Quint thought they should reach the village before sunset.

⁂

Amaria kept her mouth shut and her temper hot. She snapped back at Quint when he asked her questions about their assignment.

"I hardly know myself!" Amaria said. "I was told to pack up and requisition a horse this morning. My father said I was to babysit you, but I'll be damned if I'll do that." Amaria said. "You behave yourself."

Quint wondered how she expected him to misbehave, but he had detected a faint odor of fear in her voice. Was Amaria afraid of him? She had to be a few years older, and Quint was still a gangly sixteen-year-old whose male hormones hadn't quite kicked in yet.

He wouldn't be a threat, even if he met the physical requirements. He had no interest in a snappy, ill-tempered young woman older than himself. He had enough of those in the school he had graduated from not long ago.

"You are letting your imagination get ahead of yourself," Quint said.

"Not me! I'm an educated woman!" she said.

Amaria was losing her grip with each league from Bocarre.

"Do we need to make a more specific handshake agreement?" Quint said.

"Stop, right there!"

Quint stopped his horse and let her ride up behind him. He didn't know if she was going to attack him. He didn't think she was currently very stable.

She rode to his side. "I can't stand riding with you. I think we should split up," she said.

"I don't mind, but I don't think it would be a good idea for you to ride alone."

Amaria snorted and blinked her eyes. "You don't think I can protect myself?"

"Do you want to get in a situation where you must fight off brigands or drunk farmers?" Quint asked. "If there are two of us, there will be less temptation. Rural people don't always act rationally."

"You know that from personal experience?"

"As a matter of fact, I do. My father has returned from his trips delivering and repairing wheels after being beaten up. He's a handy man with his fists, too. It's worse at night."

"Hubites!" Amaria snorted.

"At night, brigands don't care if you are a hubite or a willot," Quint said.

"You don't look like you could protect anyone," Amaria said.

Quint shook his head. "I'm a Level 3. I won't admit I'm proficient at all the strings I've learned, but I know enough to make a few robbers think twice about attacking me. Are you proficient enough to be confident in a fight?"

Quint almost winced when he said that. He might have laid out a challenge Amaria would feel she'd have to take.

If she hadn't readily agreed to follow his route, Quint might have suspected she was part of a plan to attack him, but she wasn't reacting the way he would have expected.

Amaria held out her hand. "Give me your map. I don't care what Father asked. I'm not going to travel another step with you. Promise you'll find me when you get to the camp."

Quint chuckled. "I can do that as long as you remember that splitting up was your idea."

"Do you think my memory is that faulty?" Amaria said with eyes flashing.

"Not at all," Quint said, handing over the map he memorized. "I'll be using the same route."

"Then go ahead of me. I don't want you following."

Quint moved ahead and took off at a gallop to get some distance, but he hid until she had passed him. He could not be honorable and have her proceed behind him.

※

CHAPTER FOURTEEN

~

Two days later, Quint followed Amaria's tracks on the dirt roads that Pozella suggested. One of her mount's horseshoes had an end missing. Better roads were more dangerous, but he still worried about Amaria.

After a quick lunch at a roadside stop in the middle of an expanse of woods, Quint stopped at a crossroads. The server at the stop said a solitary woman had been at the same stop less than two hours previous. Amaria was to go straight ahead, but there was a cluster of recent horse tracks, and Quint sighed. He hadn't read tracks since he worked for his father and played with his friends back in the village.

It looked like Amaria had been stopped and led in a different direction. After he followed the tracks, he could identify three horses and Amaria's.

He looked around the woods to make sure he wasn't being followed and continued until a track showed all four horses moving east. Quint rode along the track until he couldn't be seen from the road and stopped.

He heard nothing besides forest sounds: No horses, no talking. He continued until a horse neighed to his left, followed by another. Quint dismounted and found a small clearing to tie his horse. He reviewed his spell list and cast two shield spells to calm his nerves. The weakness spell was still his best alternative. He was tempted to cast a portent but didn't have the nerve.

The forest wasn't thick enough to impede his progress toward the horses in a straight line off the track. In about one hundred yards, he stopped at the edge of a meadow. A stream curved into the meadow, closer to a log cabin, and then out again.

Four horses were tied underneath a lean-to away from the stream. A tiny curl of smoke wound into the sky from a low chimney. Quint didn't hear any screaming as he continued to observe the scene, seeking out the best way to approach the cabin unobserved.

He moved toward the stream and saw the back of the cabin didn't even have a window. Quint stepped into the stream and crouched down, following its course to the back of the cabin before running through the grass to the wall. The logs were in terrible shape and there were gaps in between. He couldn't see through the chinks, but he could hear what was said.

"He will follow you, right?"

"I told him not to," Amaria said. "Quinto Tirolo is an idiot. Of course, he said he would follow me, but Tirolo wouldn't know how to find his way out of headquarters if he wasn't shown."

"So, we won't be able to complete our job. Is that what you are saying?" a man's voice said.

"He will follow my horse," Amaria said. "He could be out there now, listening to us."

The men laughed. "No one knows you are here, then?"

"Of course not. I didn't know anything about this," Amaria said. "Is this my father's doing?"

Quint heard laughter.

"It doesn't matter who hired us. A pretty young thing like you disappearing in the big bad forest. That means we can do whatever we want with you."

"No! No!" Amaria said. "Stay away from me!"

Quint heard struggling. "You'll pay for this," Amaria said.

"Where are you going to go? You are all trussed up like the holiday goose, little girl."

Quint put his back against the cabin wall and took deep breaths. In a sense, Amaria was part of this, and she was about to pay an awful price. He took another deep breath and thought of the strings he would use before creeping to the front door.

He stepped on the cabin's porch, but a creaking board destroyed his stealth. He wove his tendrils into a weakness string and kicked the door open, except his kick didn't open the door.

Quint pulled down on the latch, and the door swung open. Three angry thugs stared at him. One had his hand on Amaria's shoulder as Quint flooded the room with weakness.

Just like during the invaders of the camp, one of the men still stood. He had an evil grin on his face.

"You showed up after all. She didn't think you had it in you, and I wouldn't have thought a hubite could muster that much ability, either." He looked down at his sleeping companions.

The thug began to weave a string and tossed a string against Quint's shield. The string died in a cloud of sparkles.

"What?" the man said with his mouth open.

Quint wove a distraction string, which worked despite the bandit's shield. The man looked around, dazed. It was enough time for Quint to take a club and hit the bandit over the head. The man crumpled to the floor.

Running to Amaria, he tried to shake her awake, but his weakness string was too strong. He ran to the horses and grabbed hers, leading it to the porch. Quint dragged Amaria's bound body out of the cabin and draped her body sideways on the horse, leading her through the forest to his horse, and then he took Amaria out of the track and onto the road.

Quint looked both ways, wondering how the bandits knew where they would be. Was there a tracking string cast on Amaria? He shook his head. Quint didn't know. He found the map he had given Amaria and traced a new path to the invasion camp just inside the border of Racellia and set off heading north instead of returning to the crossroads and turning back to the east.

Amaria didn't wake up until they approached a small village. Quint stopped and let her struggle with her bonds for a few moments before he cut the ropes and helped her stand. She was still woozy from the spell.

"What happened? You broke through the door on your second try," she snorted. "I do remember that, and then I fainted,"

"They were about to do their worst to you," Quint said.

"Don't remind me," Amaria said, rubbing her forehead.

"You asked me what happened. How were you involved in all this? I heard some of your discussion with the kidnappers."

"It sounds like something my father would have arranged," she said.

"How did they know where we'd be?" Quint asked.

Amaria shrugged.

Quint wasn't going to let that gesture slide. "Is there such a thing as a tracking string where a person can be found?"

Amaria shook her head, but the blush on her cheeks told Quint she lied.

"I'll talk to Pozella about it," Quint said.

"If you make it back to Bocarre," Amaria said.

Quint sighed. "Why attack me? I'm just a boy."

"It isn't who you are but who you might become," Amaria said. "That's what my father told me. He wouldn't say anymore."

It was Quint's turn to shrug. "Even if he used a portent spell, they don't always speak the truth in a way you can understand. Why would anyone waste a spell on me?"

"You are a Level 3 at sixteen and could be a Master before your next birthday. Given time and practice, you could become a threat to Racellia."

Quint had to laugh. "A sixteen-year-old is a threat to a country? I'm as much a Racellian as you are."

Amaria narrowed her eyes. "But you are a hubite."

"That doesn't make me an enemy of the people."

"No, an enemy to the willots," Amaria said. She rubbed her shoulders, and tears began to flow. "I don't know what I'm thinking."

"Shock, most likely. Let's get to the next village and get you a good night's sleep if you promise not to kill me," Quint said.

"Were they going to violate me?" Amaria asked.

Quint nodded. "It sounded like it to me, but I wouldn't let them."

"Why? I'm your enemy," Amaria said, trying to blink away the tears.

"Maybe I'm your enemy, but you aren't mine. You are very irritating, yes, but I wouldn't attack you or let anyone else do it," Quint said.

☙❧

They had to share a room in the tiny pub, the only place available in the village. It wasn't as small as Quint feared, and there were four beds in the large room.

"I'll sleep here, and you can sleep across the room," Quint told Amaria.

"I've paid for one bath, and you are the one that needs it. I'll sleep in my uniform."

Amaria nodded and left with one of her bags. Quint could tell she hadn't recovered from the shock of her experience. He had no idea what was happening inside her head, but Quint had already decided to report to his assignment and then return to Bocarre alone.

He half expected there to be a few companies of soldiers assigned to kill him if he stuck around. Quint made a few notes about the tracking string and looked through his list to see if anything was close to that, but he didn't see anything. He documented the effects of the distraction string.

Quint would have named it Disorientation rather than Distract, and that was how he would think of it in the future. He quickly concluded it wasn't the best string under the circumstances, but it was the weapon at hand, and it worked this time only because it broke through the kidnapper's shield.

If he ever became too proud of his Level 3 ranking, he only had to remember the day's mistakes. There were too many of them. Quint had so much to learn. He had a toolbox of strings but little skill in their use.

He removed his shoes and stockings and lay on his bed after invoking another shield thread. He stared up at the ceiling in the candlelight and wondered if Amaria spoke the truth about a portent string identifying Quint as a person of importance. He had no idea how that could happen in Racellia. Quint would be happy if he could survive the next week.

Amaria walked in, rubbing her hair with a towel. She looked clean and more in possession of herself.

"Impressed with my lies about you?" she said.

Quint noticed the blush but said nothing.

"I'm sorry I put you through all that," Quint said. "The kidnappers were serious about having a little fun at your expense."

"They even made sure to bind my hands," Amaria said. "I don't know what my father will make of all this. We must return to Bocarre."

"It wouldn't have happened if he left me alone," Quint said, thinking he might try a different tack with Amaria. "Let's continue our mission. You won't have to ingratiate yourself, and I can still see the wizard corps in action."

"That isn't going to change. You are still fulfilling your assignment, aren't you?"

Quint nodded. "We will arrive a day or two late with our detour."

Amaria narrowed her eyes at Quint. "I hate to feel beholden to you, but thank you for saving me today. You could have just continued to the camp. I didn't know you could track people."

"A boyhood talent that came into use today. A simple thank you is all I need," Quint said.

"Thank you," Amaria said in a small voice. Her cheeks blushed again, but Quint didn't think she was lying. It was her embarrassment doing all the coloring.

CHAPTER FIFTEEN
~

THE CAMP WAS MUCH LARGER THAN THE FIRST one Quint had visited far to the west. Amaria said that all Racellian camps had their commander in the middle, so they rode down a lane of tents and ended up in a training ground. A large tent faced them as they rode through the square.

"Lieutenants Amaria Baltacco and Quinto Tirolo from the Wizard Corps Strategic Operations Division reporting for their assignment," Amaria said to the officer, who left the tent's door to face them after they dismounted.

"You were expected two days ago," the officer said, initially looking at Amaria, but his eyes slid to Quint.

"We were attacked along the way and had to take an alternate route, sir," Amaria said.

"Orders." The officer extended his hand.

Amaria and Quint put their orders on the officer's outstretched palm.

"Very well," the officer said, quickly looking at the orders. He crooked his finger, and an orderly rushed to the officer's side.

"Take these two to the Wizard Corps section." The officer's eyes never left Amaria and Quint as he gave his instructions. "Dismissed."

"Walk your horses," the orderly said.

As they strolled through the camp, Quint could see it was organized by squads with tents surrounding a fire and a temporary worktable and chairs.

Soldiers were checking their weapons or playing games.

They walked over a vacant strip of land and saw their first wizard corps soldiers.

"This is where you will be staying. It is at the edge of the camp, but the wizards know how to protect their little corners."

Quint didn't see any evidence of protection in his last field experience, but he was mired with the supply wagons, and others could have cast threads to protect their camp. The other camp put the wizards in a corner just like this one.

The major in charge of the corps greeted them, although Amaria got the warm welcome, and Quint felt the typical coolness willots gave hubites.

"We didn't know who was being sent, so only one tent was open. You will have to share," the major said.

"That can be modified," Amaria said. "We can be split up."

"But you are both officers, and the hubite Lieutenant is a Level 3," the major said.

"I'll share a tent with anyone," Quint said. It would be easier to escape if he stayed apart from Amaria.

The first day was interesting enough to prompt Quint to remain in the camp for at least another day. He had never seen wizards train for battle before and he wrote notes about it for a report to the colonel to prove he had observed the camp.

The food was awful. They had arrived just before lunch, and Amaria almost gagged on the thick soup served with a tiny, stale loaf of dark bread. Quint shrugged. Food was food in the outdoors. The soup was probably made up from previous meals. He guessed if it were dinner, the soup would be called stew.

After lunch, the wizards took off their shirts and sat in the sun. Their brown skin was even darker with daily sunbaths. The women had their area to sunbathe. Quint wasn't exactly white since he used the little park to catch sunlight, but he was paler than anyone else. No hubites in sight.

Practice made up the rest of the afternoon. Half of it was physical, training with weapons, and the other concentrated on offensive spells. The physical part was fun for Quint. He hadn't had much training with real weapons at Fort Draco and none when he reached Bocarre. Quint knew the strings, but he hadn't practiced them, intending to kill someone.

"Your orders said you were a Level 3. Is that correct?" the sergeant in charge of string training asked.

"It is," Quint said.

"Then act like one. Your strings are too tentative. This is an army, not a cloister, sir."

Quint pursed his lips. "I was never given a chance to enter a cloister," he said.

"Few are, and none of them hubites. Then cinch up your breeches and try harder." The sergeant walked away to berate another soldier.

Quint put more power into fire, lightning, and wind strings and had no more comments from the sergeant. Using more of his power while he casts a string was fun. He had always held back since he didn't want to stand out. There were plenty of good string casters, but Quint knew he had more in reserve.

"I didn't think hubites had that much magic in them," a lieutenant ten or fifteen years older said, eating dinner that, as expected, tasted much the same as lunch. Quint's idea that lunch and dinner varied only by the thickness of the liquid sludge they had to ingest was verified.

"Your companion is adequate, but your strings had some punch. Have you been in the field before? You look awfully young."

"I'm a lieutenant in the strategic operations division. I have a good head for strategy, as it turns out," Quint said, "but the corps doesn't know quite what to do with me."

The officer shook his head. "And they sent you here on your own? That's a risk for you, isn't it?"

Quint nodded. "We were attacked on the way from the capital, but we repelled whoever our attackers were."

"Did you tell anyone?"

Quint looked across the mess tent and then shook his head. "There are some things better left unreported. It was a lonely stretch of woods, and we were on an alternate route."

"Did the girl help?" the officer said.

"She did her part," Quint said, but he didn't elaborate about what that part was. He was about to say he was thinking about leaving early, but upon consideration, Quint figured it would be better to leave that unsaid, too.

A higher-ranking officer stood behind them. "Lieutenant Tirolo will share your tent while he is in the camp. His traveling companion will take the extra tent. Are you okay with that?" the officer turned to Quint. "We know you are a Level 3 and can demand the unoccupied tent. "

The lieutenant sputtered into this cup. "A teenager Level 3? No wonder your division doesn't know what to do with you." He looked at Quint but spoke to the officer standing behind them. "I don't have an objection."

"I'm fine with sharing," Quint said. "You have to sacrifice a few comforts when in the field."

"Then that's taken care of. I'll leave him to you," the officer said, walking away.

"What is after dinner?" Quint asked his new escort.

"We meet for an hour to review strategies, and then it's free time."

After rearranging the tables and chairs, the strategy session occurred in the mess tent. Amaria sat next to Quint, with the lieutenant on the other side.

"Do you expect to learn something here?" Amaria asked.

"Isn't that what we are here for?" Quint said.

"You are from strategic operations. How can you expect to learn something from these people?"

"And you know it all?" Quint asked Amaria.

She folded her arms. "*Enough.*"

Quint shook his head. He was smart enough to know that he knew next to nothing about magic and about life. His experiences in the Racellian Wizard Corps were distorted because he was a hubite, sixteen, and gifted wizard.

An army colonel and two staff stood in the front. A large map was unfurled and hung behind them.

"This is the map of the incursion into Gussellia. As you know, the army's job is to penetrate the blue line and hold the territory for up to three months," the colonel said.

"Why don't you head to the capital and force the Gussellians to surrender?" Amaria asked.

"That is not our question to ask, Lieutenant Baltacco. We do what we are ordered. There are reasons for our orders. As soldiers, we follow them and do whatever our next orders tell us."

Quint was surprised he knew Amaria's name. He leaned over to his new tentmate. "Did you know Amaria's name?"

The tentmate shook his head.

Amaria's name and rank were on the orders, but he doubted if the colonel knew his name, just that he was the hubite Level 3 from the capital, if that.

The rest of the session dealt with positioning as a group. Quint was struck by how the Wizard Corps was still positioned as a single, large group. Any competent commander would isolate the wizards and focus on regular soldiers. It was the same strategy employed in fighting Barellia, and in Quint's mind, it was still wrong.

One of the subordinates took over and drilled the wizards in what strings they would use under which circumstances. Everyone was to use the same strings. Quint wondered if the Gussellian wizard corps would fight the same way.

"Now, the information that you've been anxious to hear. We fight tomorrow!"

There were cheers in the room.

"Split into your units and discuss your deployments."

Quint walked up to the map after everyone was dismissed and examined the positions written on the map. Everything was down to company level, but everyone stood in a block, and Quint didn't know what would happen as the enemy began to chip away at their formation.

"You look disappointed," Quint's tentmate said.

"I expected something more creative. We just stand and trade blows with the enemy."

"Until someone breaks. Once that happens, we follow them into battle, and it's every soldier for himself," the soldier said.

"You must be a company commander," Quint said.

"I am over three companies. A sergeant runs each company."

"Do you follow them when the formation is challenged?"

"I follow my company and will get my chance to fight."

"Where is the strategy in that? Why don't you pretend to break and then collapse as you bring soldiers from the back or sides to bottle the enemy up or something like that."

The lieutenant laughed. "Why would we do that? We are superior to the Gussellians in every way. We will not break. We will succeed."

Quint wondered if the awful stew had been laced with hubris. He thought that was the right word. Overconfidence. The last battle against the Barellians had resulted in a draw. Did this lieutenant know that?"

"Were you involved in the Barellian battle a few months ago?" Quint asked.

"Another glorious Racellian victory," the lieutenant said.

Quint kept his mouth shut from that point on. He was stuck with observing the battle, but he would do so from a distance, and he'd suggest Amaria do the same.

The rest of the evening consisted of listening to the lieutenant's companies tell stories of previous victories amidst a lot of bragging.

"Do you have these incursions often?" Quint asked.

The lieutenant shrugged. "All the time. They usually end with both sides claiming victory."

"Do the boundaries ever change?" Quint asked.

The lieutenant looked confused. "Of course not. They keep our enemies from invading. We spank them, or they spank us."

Quint was surprised by the results of keeping soldiers in camps for no visible results. How did the strategic operations division deal with a lack of success?

Amaria stopped Quint as soldiers finished their day by checking the equipment they would bring into battle.

Quint would bring the practice sword he'd been given at the beginning of the day. It didn't have much of an edge, and Quint was competent at sharpening if nothing else.

He placed the sword on the ground outside his tent while his tentmate snored inside and cast the sharpening string at the sword. A mist enveloped the weapon and drifted away with the breeze.

Quint lifted the sword and grabbed a broken rope tossed into a box of broken things. His face brightened into a smile as the sword's edge had no trouble cutting the rope in two. He wasn't much of a swordsman, but if he lost his magic, Quint had a backup plan, and from what he saw in the morning, wizards weren't great swordsmen.

❦

Amaria stood in the back of the wizard corps lined up in their designated section on the left of the battle line. Quint was farther back, sitting on his horse to the left of the high officers mounted on the rise on the edge of the Racellian side of the field, directing the battle. His eyes were on the wizard corps, but then his eyes kept moving over the battlefield.

Trumpets blared and the Racellian army took a step forward and then another until drums picked up the cadence. The enemy on the other side of the large field began to advance. Their cadence differed, but Quint could see the Gussellian wizard corps facing their Racellian counterparts.

Quint suddenly felt exposed, mounted on his horse with no one around. He cast a shield thread with as much power as he dared and felt more secure. As the inevitable clash was still minutes away, Quint wove a portent string and looked at an overlay of the battlefield. Two large contingents of Gusellian soldiers appeared on either side of the battleground and overcame the Racellian army. The scene shifted to the Gussellians ordering their troops and marching into Racellian territory.

His vision wasn't one of a draw but of a stunning defeat. Quint didn't trust the string but couldn't ignore what he saw and urged his horse onto the battlefield.

"It's going to be a rout," Quint told Amaria. "Racellia loses, and we are exposed. I'm leaving, and you are invited. We don't have to throw away our lives, not here and not now."

Amaria's eyes widened. "You cast a portent?"

Quint nodded. "I trust it enough to take precautions. Come back up with me to the battle commanders, and if Gusellian soldiers appear on both flanks, we must flee."

"Your cowardice is showing," Amaria said, but Quint could see her blush. She was thinking.

"I'll be up there. We probably won't have time to get our bags."

"I didn't bring anything that can't be replaced except for me," Amaria said. "You really saw defeat?"

Quint nodded. "Doesn't the wizard corps cast portent strings for the army?"

"They don't believe them," Amaria said. "Father has said portents aren't accurate enough and have cost lives in the past."

Quint thought that was interesting since Amaria said her father had cast a portent string into Quint's future, and the general seemed to believe it.

"I'm not going to ignore what I saw, at least not yet. I learned that portents get less accurate over time, but I'm only looking an hour or less into the future," Quint said.

Amaria looked at the wizards in front of her and then back at the row of officers on the slight rise that led into the woods.

"It won't hurt to observe the battlefield better from up there," Amaria said.

Quint nodded. They watched the developing battle for half an hour, and then there was yelling to their right. Gusellian soldiers emerged from the woods.

"Time to leave," Quint said.

Amaria's eyes grew as her gaze was transfixed on the attacking enemy. Quint took her reins and led her away from the battle.

"Have you seen enough?" one of the officers said.

"I don't think you will win the day," Quint said as he trotted past them back toward the camp.

"Give me the reins," she said.

Quint tossed them to her. "Do you want to split up?"

"Perhaps," Amaria looked back, and then she gasped. "They are coming from the rear, too!"

"Follow me," Quint said. "Keep your head down!"

She did as he commanded Amaria to do as he plunged into the thickening forest. They heard enemy soldiers running down the road toward the line of officers.

"They must have three times the soldiers that Racellia brought," Quint said.

"If you say so," Amaria said.

They encountered a thicket of bushes. Trees were on the other side, so Quint dismounted and urged Amaria to do the same.

"Inside!"

"Where are we going?"

"Into someplace safe until dark when we can continue our escape."

Quint used his sword to cut an angled entrance into the thicket that opened into a protected copse. The thicket surrounded the trees within. There was room for the horses and themselves.

"In our forest back home, there are thickets like this. I don't know why, but I used them as hiding places when I played with my friends. The secret is how you get inside. The Gussellians will only go around the thicket, not knowing there is a small clearing inside."

"You hope," Amaria said.

"Do you have a better idea? The forest is full of Gussellian soldiers," Quint said.

"What are we going to do until it's dark?"

"We aren't going to be singing, and we shouldn't get into an argument and raise our voices."

Quint reviewed his strings and then wrote about his experiences on the trip. Amaria grumbled to herself and eventually fell asleep. He had brought his notebook, the only irreplaceable thing. He cast a string for water to fill up his water jug, and he did the same for Amaria, who had forgotten she had a jug in her saddlebags. It was empty when Quint found it.

As the sun went down, voices were heard in the forest. The enemy came closer, but they were speaking willot. Quint heard someone rustling the thicket, but he could tell by the sound of their voices they didn't find anything, and the sounds faded away.

He sat against a tree facing Amaria. She opened her eyes.

"Do you want to know what they said?"

Quint nodded. "All I could tell is that we weren't discovered."

"They were looking for the Level 3 wizard who had deserted in the middle of the battle. They didn't even mention me," Amaria said, sounding disappointed.

"Why would they want me?" Quint asked.

"Level 3s and Masters are always in high demand by an enemy. Often a time for hostage exchanges."

Quint laughed softly. "Who would want a teenage hubite?"

"I was asking myself the same question."

"Will your father's people be able to sniff us out with the tracking spell on your clothes?"

Amaria sighed. "I left that tunic in the tent."

Quint looked for the telltale blush and didn't see one, but the light was dimming. He hadn't expected her to admit she knew about the spell so easily.

"Do you have any idea where we are?" Amaria asked.

"I have a string for that," Quint said. He wove the tendrils and cast the string. "North is that way. I think we are still north of the border. So, south,"

Quint pointed in that direction, "is where we need to go, but we will head west since the camp was directly south, and the capital is southwest of here."

Quint led his horse and relied on Amaria to follow him out of the thicket. Quint still sensed direction, and they headed away from the camp. They passed over a few roads and then Quint guessed they were back in Racellian territory.

CHAPTER SIXTEEN

~

IN THE DARK, QUINT STILL LED AMARIA SOUTHWEST, having had to pause a few times and backtrack into the woods or move across a road ahead of them until they reached the main road.

"Can you sense people?" Quint asked Amaria. "There is a string for that."

"A psychic string. I haven't been able to learn any yet."

Quint was surprised she admitted a weakness, but psychic strings were beyond most wizards. Pozella said that any wizard could learn a psychic string or two if they spent sufficient time. Sufficient time was gauged in years for common wizards, Pozella claimed.

"The road heads west. This was the route we were to use per Pozella's map, which is back at the camp. We can follow this most of the way to Bocarre," Quint said.

They didn't meet another soul on the road for half an hour, and then a company of Gusellian soldiers burst onto the road behind them.

One of the soldiers shouted in Willot.

"He told us to stop."

"I didn't understand a thing," Quint said, "so I'm going to ignore them, and they can try to get me. Our horses should be more rested than theirs."

They kicked their horses and galloped into the darkness with the Gussellians in pursuit. Quint discovered that weaving strings was not possible on the back of a galloping horse.

A flash of light sped past Quint's right ear, illuminating their escape. The globe splashed on the ground, and the spell looked like liquid light. Quint stood in his stirrups and made sure his horse jumped over the pool of light. Having the light stick to the horse's hooves wouldn't do.

"Left!" Amaria said.

Quint blindly followed her down a track only wide enough for one rider. She slowed down and lit a magic light barely bright enough to pick their way through the twisting and turning of the trail.

Another light globe hit Amaria squarely in the back. She grunted and tore off her tunic. However, some liquid light spilled onto the back of her horse.

"We are going to have to leave the trail," Quint said.

They grabbed their bags as they dismounted and ran into the dark woods. Quint stopped and cast wind to cover their tracks before continuing. Quint found another thicket.

"Through here," Quint said, pulling a branch aside and letting Amaria through before slipping past the branch while he gently moved it back so it wouldn't shake when their pursuers reached them.

They heard the Gussellians talking in willot.

"They are about to give up," Amaria whispered.

"They are speaking willot?" Quint asked although he didn't admit he knew that was what they spoke. He wanted more information about the language.

"We can talk about it later. I'm all turned around," she said.

"South is that way," Quint said, pointing farther into the woods. "We will head south for an hour before deciding what else to do.

Quint pulled an extra tunic from his bag and gave it to Amaria. The rest of his clothes were at the camp. "There are a few specks of light, but this should cover them."

"What about the horses?"

"They will probably put a watch on them or take them away. Would you try to retrieve your mount and get caught or walk through the night and find a way to return to Bocarre?"

She grunted her assent. "I will follow you."

Quint walked around her to see if there were more light spots, but he couldn't see anything. He barely used his power this time when he created a light string, and they followed the dim light through the woods.

After stopping, he extinguished his light, determined his direction, corrected, and cast another light before continuing toward the darkness. They traveled for two hours before crossing another road and plunged into another part of the forest.

In less than an hour, they saw lights to their right, away from the Gussellians, and entered a Racellian village. They were far enough south to be sure they weren't close to the Gusellian border.

They entered a half-full pub.

"Do you have any rooms tonight?" Quint asked.

"Not for you, hubite," the woman at the bar said.

"I'm not a hubite," Amaria said. "I'll take a room if you've got one."

The woman frowned, and her face hardened. "You came in with him," she said, shaking her head.

"Can we have something to eat and drink?" Amaria asked.

"You'll have to consume it on the porch." She glared at Quint. "I'd like you to leave our establishment now."

"I'll leave you here," Quint said.

Amaria didn't say a word to Quint. "I'll take the room," she said with steel in her voice.

Quint left the pub and sat on a bench, trying to sort out what to do. A server brought out a bowl of stew, a small loaf of bread, and a mug of ale in a few minutes. He lit a magic light and looked at the ale. Someone had spit in it, but the stew looked fine, although the pub hadn't supplied a spoon. He sopped up the juices with the bread and picked out the resulting chunks with his fingers. He left a few coins on the bench with the mug and bowl and began to walk toward Bocarre.

Quint reached the end of the village when he heard riders stop at the inn. The light from the pub revealed three soldiers wearing Gussellian uniforms. They tied up the horses and entered the pub.

Quint stared at the scene from the middle of the street, struggling with what he should do. He sighed and ran out of the street and along a parallel lane to the main thoroughfare. There was shouting inside.

He stepped through the back door. The frightened kitchen staff was huddled in a corner. Quint put a finger to his lips. "Don't worry," he said quietly.

The scene in the pub was what Quint expected. A Gussellian wearing a uniform that would have suited a Racellian general held his hands together with a green swirl of threads. The customers were backed against the wall, and the other two soldiers had already caught Amaria.

"Where is the Level 3?" the wizard said, letting the string float in the magic above the man's palms.

"He left," the woman at the bar said. "And good riddance. He's a hubite, and you are welcome to him as long as you leave us alone."

"I'll take her with us." He pointed at Amaria with his chin.

Quint spelled a double shield and stepped into the room with a swirl of red in his hand, holding a strong wind string. Quint didn't like the look of the other wizard's string, so he cast his string. "No, you won't."

The wizard, Amaria, and her two guards were pushed into the wall. The wizard went through the window, Amaria was blown out the door, and the two soldiers slammed against the wall.

"Take care of those two," Quint said.

"Who are you to order me around?" the barkeep said.

"I'm the Level 3," Quint said.

The woman shrunk and ducked behind the bar as a few patrons dragged the regular soldiers away as Quint ran out the door. He ignored Amaria's groans and cast a weakness spell at the wizard, who fell back, senseless.

Amaria struggled to her feet. A few of the patrons poked their heads through the broken window.

"Tie his wrists to each leg and wrap his hands tightly. He's dangerous if he gets loose."

"Why don't we just kill him? He's the enemy, isn't he?"

Quint sighed. "Whatever. He's yours."

He helped Amaria mount a horse. Quint took the best mount and rode out of the village toward the capital.

After a few minutes of riding, Amaria stopped and dismounted. "I might have broken something," Amaria said.

"What did you break?"

"A little bit of my pride," Amaria said. "I thought I could handle them, but…" She shook her head and went silent.

"It's hard to think what to use against someone like him," Quint said. "I'd guess he's at least a Level 3 and more likely a master. At least he didn't have the time to cast a shield."

"We should have taken the third horse," Amaria said.

Quint shook his head. "If he's a Master, he could easily extract a mount from someone in the village. If they don't kill them, the villagers will have their hands full with the three of them as it is. We need to get out of here," Quint said as he remounted.

They rode for a few hours, stopping at a sleepy village to rest and water their horses. It wasn't a time for stealth but time to put as many miles between the Gussellian soldiers and them.

☙

It was dawn before they arrived at a large town. Quint and Amaria were exhausted from the night ride, but Quint wasn't refused a room at a busy inn. He took the bags from the wizard's horse into the room. Amaria said she would sleep a few hours and acquire more appropriate clothes.

Quint sat on the bed, staring out the little window at the front of the inn, not seeing anything. His life had been a nightmare once he had cast the portent string at the battle. The Gussellian officer's bag caught Quint's gaze.

There was a razor, a bar of soap, a tiny towel in an oilskin pouch, a spare tunic, dark green underwear, and a notebook. Quint's interest level increased as he opened the first page. The wizard had left his book of strings.

Did the Gussellians have different strings than the Racellians? Quint wondered as he tried to make sense of the notes in the willot language. A quick count revealed sixty-seven strings, all diagrammed, including the weaves. The wizard's work was like Quint's documentation of his strings.

The notebook was a treasure! He couldn't wait to show it to Pozella, but Quint wondered if an etiquette was attached to another wizard's work. Quint wasn't a big fan of being polite to someone intent on capturing him.

He transferred the book to his bag and slept the morning away.

Amaria knocked on the door just before lunch. She wore an attractive riding outfit. Quint thought she would be considered pretty if her personality wasn't so abrasive.

"We should be on our way. Bocarre is still a day away, but we can spend tonight in a big village I've visited."

"I'm all for that," Quint said. "The farther away from the Gussellians, the better."

They ate lunch at the inn and tackled the road again. No one had seen Gussellian soldiers among the people that Amaria talked to. Quint didn't engage with anyone after his experience in the pub the night before.

They rode through mainly cultivated land, which didn't provide hiding spots for Gussellian soldiers to ambush them. They arrived at the village Amaria mentioned before dinner.

While Amaria composed a message to her father with a preliminary report about the battle, Quint found a general store, bought a notebook and a tube of pencils, and began copying the wizard's book of strings.

It was twilight when she knocked on the door to her room.

"I've sent a messenger to the capital. They will be there hours before us," Amaria said. "You should read this copy to know what I sent. We should have similar stories."

Quint looked at Amaria before taking the paper and reading the report. Not surprisingly, she led their 'retreat,' and Quint's role was following her like an obedient dog. She did give him credit for enabling the escape from the pub, probably because there were plenty of witnesses.

Amaria's version was fine with him. Quint wasn't looking for credit and was glad she hadn't mentioned his using a portent string to identify the battle's outcome.

"I'll back this up," Quint said, "although my recollection differs slightly from what you wrote. I don't mind if you're not mentioning my foretelling string. It is better left unsaid, although it was accurate in this case."

Amaria blushed. "I'm sure you don't want too much credit."

"You are right about that. Are we going down for dinner?"

Amaria's face remained flushed. "I will eat by myself, but I'll have your dinner brought up to you. I already asked them to do that when I sent the message. It would be better for both of us for you to remain in your room."

Quint gave Amaria half a smile. "Of course. My presence makes others uncomfortable."

Amaria cleared her throat. "Something like that."

"Fine," Quint said.

He let her go and began gathering his few things. He was back on the road, alone, and riding toward the capital in a quarter-hour.

Amaria could enjoy her meal without the complication of a hubite, but Quint had little appetite for being shuttered away like a crazy aunt.

CHAPTER SEVENTEEN

THE FLAT WAS DARK WHEN QUINT ARRIVED early the following day. He collapsed on his bed after tucking his bags underneath the bed. Quint woke mid-morning to an empty flat and wrote a different version of his experiences fleeing from the defeat for Colonel Sarrefo's view only. Quint wrote a note at the bottom to the effect that he was comfortable with Amaria's account for official purposes.

"I'm surprised to see you," Colonel Sarrefo said when Quint approached the strategic operations leader just before lunch.

"Amaria and I fled from the battle just before being overrun by the Gussellians. That was consistent with our orders to observe but not join the fight."

Sarrefo nodded. "You did the right thing. The Gussellians continued invading Racellia and took over the battle camp inside our border."

"What happened to the army?"

Sarrefo shook his head. "There weren't many who survived. The Gusellian army was three times our size, and invading with an army that size hasn't happened for a few centuries."

Quint nodded. He had learned about the stability of the borders in his classwork at the fort.

"This is my report," Quint said. He explained that it would read a bit differently from Amaria's report to her father. "It is for your eyes only, sir. Perhaps we can learn something from it."

Sarrefo brightened. "Good thinking. I'm afraid our approach will have to change in response to the newly aggressive Gussellians. I'll read this," he flicked the envelope containing Quint's story, "this afternoon. You are dismissed."

Quint sat by himself for lunch. The refectory was buzzing with rumors about the Gussellians. Few knew he had been assigned to observe, so even those friendlier to Quint didn't talk to him about the battle.

He sat at his desk, continuing to copy the string book, when Pozella walked up.

"Sarrefo said you'd returned. Did you have an interesting trip?"

"Can we talk somewhere else?" Quint said, looking at the other wizards in the office area.

Pozella took Quint to a small office with a table, bookcase, and two chairs.

"I've come up in the world. Welcome to my domain," Master Pozella said. "You can shut the door, and we can talk all we want."

Quint tossed the Gusellian wizard's string book across the desk. Pozella picked it up, and after two pages, his eyebrows rose.

"This is a valuable item," Pozella said. "Where did you get it?"

"I know what it is, and I recognize that everything is written in willot," Quint said, "but I wanted to know if there is some kind of hidden etiquette demanding I return this to the wizard."

Pozella nodded. "There is. You should send this through diplomatic means to the owner. His name is on the inside front cover."

"I'm going to copy it first," Quint said. "I'm half finished."

"Another reason for you to learn the willot language?"

Quint nodded. "I needed some motivation, and now I have it. Perhaps you can help me understand parts of it."

"I can do that, but I said I wouldn't be responsible for teaching you willot."

"I remembered our conversation. There are sixty-seven spells; I'd first like to know what they are. When we escaped, the wizard cast a liquid light that splashed on Amaria's clothes."

"You were with Amaria?" Pozella asked, astonished.

Quint told him the story of their escape and how the wizard's string book fell into Quint's hands.

"I haven't used a light string very often since it is easier and less costly to my power to cast fire or a torch for my light," Quint said.

"We can talk of that later. Finish your copying first. We should get that book out of your hands as quickly as possible. From what you've told me, it is something that the wizard might kill to retrieve."

Quint didn't want that. The Gussellian wizard had seen Quint and knew he was a Level 3, so locating him in Bocarre wouldn't be difficult for a trained wizard or his subordinates.

"I'll return to the flat and do just that," Quint said.

"Let's meet here tomorrow an hour before lunch," Pozella said, and I'll show you how to put the pouch together that will send that journal back to Gussellia."

☙

Quint spent his lunchtime putting the wizard's effects in a box that went into a diplomatic pouch that Pozella brought to their meeting. Quint had already asked one of his roommates to deliver the pouch addressed to the wizard to the Gussellian embassy.

Master Pozella quickly checked the notebook with the copy Quint had made.

"This should take some pressure off you," Pozella said. "Colonel Sarrefo secured the pouch and verified that the Gussellian embassy was still open."

Quint found the roommate and fervently hoped Pozella was right about reducing the likelihood of Gussellians sending agents into the capital to retrieve the wizard's possessions. The two Gussellian horses were also returned to the embassy after Amaria was notified she had to give up the horse by Colonel Sarrefo.

The early meeting didn't release Quint from spending the afternoon with Pozella labeling the strings in the common tongue. As expected, most of the strings were ones Quint had already learned, but there were plenty left, with a surprising amount that Pozella had never learned.

"As you know, the ability to weave a certain thread is different among wizards. With only one hand, my current repertoire is limited. Here is the light spell that was used. The wizard calls it light paint. It is very advanced. Let's go through some of the easier ones. I'll take this home with me tonight," Pozella said.

Quint took a deep breath. "No. I'll make another copy first. This," Quint poked the pages of the copy with the tip of his finger, "is too valuable to have only one version."

Pozella chuckled. "I totally agree. Then try the liquid light string tonight. Cast it into a waste bin in an alley so the light won't be detected. I would guess the light has a lifetime. If you can master the string, see how long the effect lasts."

☙

Quint spent the rest of the afternoon in his flat making the second copy. It wasn't that he didn't trust Pozella, but he never liked Pozella's refusal to teach him willot directly, and the unwillingness limited his reliance on the master.

He copied a third of the book before Marena cooked dinner. She didn't ask him to help clean up, so Quint worked on mastering liquid light. The string was made by very complicated weaves that were based on the light string, but then there were three other weaves that Quint spent two hours mastering, but he finally succeeded and walked into the building's back garden. There were three trash barrels, but they were all full.

Quint looked around, found a spade, and dug a hole in a vacant flowerbed. He'd cover the light with dirt. It took him another twenty minutes to duplicate the threads and the string, but he succeeded and attempted to cast a tiny amount of liquid light into the hole. Part of the weave gave the string's magic the ability to project the light toward a target. Perhaps that was written in willot in the notes.

He used very little magic and liquid light, not as bright as what hit Amaria's back, dribbled into the hole. That was enough. He'd need a lot of practice to control that string anyway. Tossing it as far as the Gussellian wizard had to have taken a toll on the officer's power.

Satisfied that Quint could perform the spell without reading willot boosted the value of the book of strings in his estimation. He spent the rest of the night finishing the second copy.

Morning came too early. One of his flatmates woke Quint and said he was expected to be in the colonel's office first, which gave Quint barely enough time to wash and dress. He'd have to eat something on the way to the strategic operations building.

Colonel Sarrefo was alone in his office when Quint arrived and was invited in.

"Shut the door and take a seat," the colonel said. "I have received a formal copy of Amaria's report. There are a few accusations inside that I'd like to clear up."

"Yes, sir," Quint said. His nerves just increased.

"She said you deserted her during the escape."

"She changed the report after she returned to Bocarre, sir!" Quint shook his head. "I left her after she refused to eat with me. I asked her if my presence made her uncomfortable, and she admitted it did. I couldn't trust her then, and since we were half a day away from Bocarre, I decided I would go ahead without her."

"She also claimed that you convinced her to desert the field of battle, claiming that you knew how to cast a portent string."

"And she denies that I described to her how the battle would unfold before it happened?"

"Something to that effect. I can't let you read it. Her father slapped a restrictive cover on her report."

Quint frowned. "I've cast a portent string three times in my life, twice on the battlefield. The one I did in my first taste of battle was done the day before the battle, and it was generally accurate. The second one was at the Gussellian fight and cast at the beginning of the battle. It was accurate since I abandoned it when I realized the officer corps would be attacked from both flanks, sir."

Sarrefo knit his brow. "And you warned the officers?"

Quint nodded. "I did, sir, but they ignored me. Amaria didn't have a weapon, so I told her what would happen, and she agreed to leave with me. We were observers, not fighters, if you recall, sir."

"I recall, Lieutenant Tirolo. The rest of her report puts her in the position of leader. The only time that changed was at the pub. She claimed she had the situation in hand until you attacked the Gussellian soldiers and forced her to run."

Quint found it hard to control his temper, but he had to in front of his commanding officer. "You read my account. I swear mine is correct, sir."

"I believe you, but few will fervently want to believe otherwise. Along with the report came a note saying that you may be reassigned because of Amaria's account."

"But I like it here, sir. I'm almost accepted."

Sarrefo chuckled. "I believe you are, but if a reassignment comes from headquarters…"

"Signed by Amaria's father, sir?" Quint asked.

"Signed by her father or any of his peers, I will be bound to comply, and you will, too. I will recommend that you continue receiving training and counsel from Master Pozella, but I can't promise anything."

"I'd appreciate that, sir. Am I still assigned to my group until I'm ordered to leave?" Quint asked.

"You are, and I understand they will be meeting soon. You should prepare. You are dismissed, Lieutenant Tirolo."

Quint stood and saluted. "Thank you, sir."

He left feeling greatly disturbed about Amaria's duplicity, which was worse than he had anticipated, and his inability to dispute her description of what happened. Quint's time once he had been promoted to lieutenant was better than any other time while he was in the Racellian Wizard Corps.

He entered the conference room where the rest of his strategic group met. The leader was the only one in the room.

"Where are the others?" Quint asked.

"I wanted a personal debriefing on your assignment to the Gussellian border. Colonel Sarrefo and Master Pozella thought a less restrictive environment might be better than to present your story to the group."

"So, everyone wouldn't get into trouble, sir?" Quint asked.

"That is an element that went into the decision, but Master Pozella said you had a perspective on the battle that might be useful for me."

Quint thought for a minute and then sat down. "Shall I begin, or do you want to ask me questions?"

"You begin. I want your side of the story. The colonel said there was an official version, but official versions are often edited to remove certain aspects of the report."

Quint nod. "I may be frank?"

"I encourage it!" the leader said.

Quint gave the leader every bit of information that Sarrefo had received. "I didn't report my opinion of the strategic aspect of the battle," Quint said.

"Go ahead. I'd like to hear your views."

Quint explained his viewpoint on the continued lack of creativity and use of strategy on the Racellian side of the battle.

"There have been two enemy flanking maneuvers in each of the battles I've experienced. There were no defenses laid out to counteract those kinds of attacks. Do strategic operations review battles and make recommendations?"

The leader asked Quint some points and explained that the regular army didn't always respond to strategic operations suggestions.

"Do they ever?" Quint asked. "The army seems to be very predictable in their tactics."

"That is correct, but the generals traditionally use the wizard corps to fight the wizards in the other army," the leader said.

"Then we should mix our wizards with the regular units to use magic throughout a battle. I've proposed that before."

"Our group can develop new suggestions, but you can't initiate the topic. I will have to do that. Be careful how you present your case. Accepting a teenage hubite into the group could be threatened if you become too strident."

"Message received, sir," Quint said.

"Return to your desk and return at the mid-morning hour."

Quint had almost an hour and a half to himself before the group met. He spent the time reading one of the library books on battle histories. The tactics hadn't changed since the battles described, reaching back four centuries. If everyone on the continent used the same thinking, no wonder the borders had barely changed.

He returned to the conference room and took his seat at the table. The leader walked into the room with an envelope in his hand.

"I just received this a few minutes ago," the leader said, holding the envelope. "These are new orders for one of our group, a promotion to the military ministry."

Quint didn't like the way the leader's eyes were fixed on him. His new orders had come too quickly.

"Our newest member is the first to leave our group," the leader said, "but before he goes, perhaps he can describe the recent battle on the Gussellian border."

Quint stood and gave as neutral a presentation as he could. He left out portents, liquid light, and desertion but talked about magicians fighting magicians and flanking maneuvers.

"Our forces were overrun. Why?"

The discussion began. Quint was careful not to say too much, but he said enough to point out that the Gussellians tried something new, fielding an army three times the size of the Racellian forces and surrounding a feckless opponent.

Talk began to move toward obtaining intelligence on the opponent rather than assuming what tradition dictated. Flanking tactics were never used to such an extent as the Gussellians employed, but in a hostile fight, it seemed the world might be changing tradition.

Quint was encouraged by the ideas thrown out, but the time went quickly, and the meeting ended.

"Was that more to your liking?" the leader said after holding Quint back.

"It was more of an exploration of the problem. The kind of thing that's done before you work on a solution. Right, sir?"

"That is what we do in strategic operations," the leader said. "I'm sad to see you go. Now is the time to read this."

Quint stared at his new orders. He was to be posted to a diplomatic post representing the wizard corps at the Ministry of the Military. Quint had worried about returning to Wizard Corps headquarters, where Amaria's father was in charge. Still, he was assigned to the Racellian military ministry, a large building next to the Council Palace in the exact center of Bocarre.

He couldn't help but wonder what kind of punishment this would be. Quint had liked being immersed in strategic operations. The discussion was terrific, but he was now removed from that environment and promoted to senior lieutenant.

A message from Pozella told him to meet in his office after lunch.

"Sarrefo told me about your new assignment. You are being promoted to an even more useless position."

"At least when I was first here, I was productive," Quint said. "I was a servant. The strategic operations group tolerated me, and I felt I could contribute, but before I can there is this," He lifted the envelope with his orders inside.

"You get a pay increase," Pozella said.

"To spend on what?" Quint asked irritably.

"How did your morning go?"

Quint told him about the string book copy and his success with liquid light.

"At least you understand that you have barely tapped into the string. Many of the strings you know are like that, and if I'm not to follow you to army headquarters, and I'm almost certain I won't be allowed outside the wizard corps, make sure you practice what you know. When do you report?"

"Tomorrow morning. As far as I can tell, my flat is between the army headquarters and this building," Quint said.

"I'm not sure what kind of assignments you'll get in the diplomatic organization. I don't even know what they call themselves," Pozella said. "I'd appreciate a letter occasionally, and hopefully, we can still meet for lunch occasionally."

Quint was touched that he had made a good enough friend to invite him anywhere in public. "I will. I'll work on the string book tonight and deliver it here tomorrow."

"Have them send it in care of Sarrefo. I've been inactivated for the next three months for health reasons, I've been told," Pozella said.

"Is that because of me?" Quint asked.

Pozella nodded. "I was assigned specifically to you, remember? Don't worry. Sarrefo said he'd find something for me to do."

CHAPTER EIGHTEEN
~

QUINT WORE HIS BLACK UNIFORM on the first day of his new assignment. He expected an office the size of Pozella's tiny workspace. He wasn't very disappointed to have an office a little bigger and with a window looking out of a window well in the basement of the military ministry instead of a desk in the middle of a room full of them.

After reporting for duty at the front desk, an orderly took him down a narrow set of stairs and deposited him in his office.

"You'll be summoned when you are needed, sir," the orderly said as he saluted.

The salute surprised Quint. He hoped that wouldn't get the orderly in trouble, he thought sarcastically.

Quint looked through the empty desk drawers and concluded the office must have been set up just for him. He walked out the door into the empty corridor. The rest of the doors were closed, and the few Quint tried were locked. At least he wasn't executed, at least not yet.

A young officer ranked lower than Quint but at least a decade older showed up after an hour or so.

"You will meet your commanding officer now. Follow me."

They stopped at an office on the third floor. It said Military Diplomatic Corps on the double door. Quint's escort opened the door, walked in front of him, and looked behind as he walked to the office in the corner.

"You may be seated. The commander will be here shortly," the escort said before doing an about-face and walking out of the offices of the Military Diplomatic Corps.

Quint waited for his escort to leave before taking a few steps into the office. Desks filled the area with a row of offices, some with open doors, and some doors were closed.

He attracted unfriendly stares, so he returned to his seat. Quint waited half an hour before a woman rushed into the office dressed in a female army uniform with designations of colonel on her uniform.

"I like the black," she said. "Make that your standard uniform at headquarters."

Quint scrambled to his feet. "Lieutenant Quinto Tirolo reporting for duty, ma'am," he said saluting.

She returned his salute with a casual wave and gestured that Quint sit back down.

"I'm aware who you are. The question is, how can I use a teenaged Level 3 hubite wizard?"

"You don't know, ma'am?" Quint asked.

"I'll be honest; I'd rather you not be here. I'm responsible for making my people productive, but you were assigned to me without a personnel request."

"I know military strategy and history. I'm a wizard, but then that's hardly unusual."

"It is around here, Lieutenant. I don't suppose you know willot?"

Quint shook his head. "I was told I was forbidden to learn."

"Perhaps at the wizard corps. I'm a little more flexible. Some of our internal communications are written in the willot language. I don't want to have to translate everything you write. Find some texts and spend the next few weeks learning the basics. The grammar is identical to the common language."

"I can do that, ma'am."

The colonel grimaced. "I don't know what to do with a wizard, but maybe you can help me figure that out. I will want to meet with you weekly. You will be on your own to stay busy, but I suggest you also start reading newssheets and periodicals. I'll send down the previous day's sheets, and you can read those to start."

"What about writing supplies, ma'am? I'd like to take notes."

"There is a cabinet against the corridor wall when you walk in. You'll find what you need there. You shouldn't force yourself on anyone in the office. Hubites are…" She peered at Quint. "You know how things are. You'll be the only hubite under my command and the only wizard. There will also be escort duty from time to time. You'll get notice for any assignment."

The woman brushed her uniform off and looked out the window. "That's all for now. Don't bother to salute, just get started."

Quint grabbed some supplies from the cabinet and headed down to his office. A female clerk came out of one of the doors in the basement corridor and scurried in the other direction. Quint couldn't see much difference between his time as a servant and working for Colonel Julia Gerocie other than a better title and better pay. Something to keep the hubite wizard occupied, Quint thought.

His office door latch didn't have a lock, so Quint decided he would use a wood-binding string to bind the door to the doorframe. Something a wizard could do, he thought with a smile, and since he was the only wizard in the diplomatic corps, his office was secure.

A uniformed servant brought a basket full of newssheets. Quint sighed and began reading. He hadn't done much reading of current events since a class on the subject when he was twelve. The world had seemed so remote then, but he had experienced more of life than he had wanted to, and even that was a tiny shred of what people lived every day.

He took notes as he read, but Quint decided he would concentrate on military and world affairs. With that as a filter, Quint dived in and spent the rest of his day perusing the information. Quint's tiny shred of knowledge quickly became smaller as his exposure to external events grew.

Quint noticed the window's light dimming, and it was time to return to the flat. He had arrived in time for dinner and reunited with his flatmates. He told them about his new assignment, and even Marena, the housekeeper commiserated with him about his position.

"At least you don't have to empty trash and deliver snacks to your fellow officers," one of his flatmates said.

"I think I will like learning all about the newssheets," Quint said. "I'm hoping to explore other subjects in my free time, which at this point seems substantial."

"Keep up with your strings," another flatmate said. "Practice, practice, practice. We are told that in our magic instruction, but you have time to do that."

Quint nodded. "Maybe I can ask to leave my office occasionally to become proficient at offensive spells. I need more black uniforms for the headquarters. My commanding officer likes our black uniforms."

"I can take care of that," an officer said.

"And if you need alterations, I know my way around a needle and thread," Marena said.

Quint smiled. At least the people in the flat tolerated him.

※

Quint had learned to eat his lunch at his desk. He quickly realized he wasn't welcomed in either of the two restaurants in the large headquarters building. The Racellian army had no tolerance for hubites, which was no surprise.

Colonel Gerocie, the leader of the military diplomatic corps, tolerated Quint enough to make their weekly meeting every week.

"What have you learned this week?" the colonel asked as she crossed her legs in the hard chair facing Quint's desk. It seemed she liked to get some exercise and visit him most of the time.

"There are indications of a crop failure along the Racellian and Barellian border. No one knows what is causing it," Quint said.

"I'm aware of the situation," Gerocie said. "Any ideas as to why?"

Quint showed a hand-drawn map of the area. "There has been a rush to mine gold in the Levino mountains. The water source for the plains comes from the mountains being mined. Could there be some kind of water contamination? I don't have enough information about the areas affected, but that is possible. According to other articles, it hasn't been a lack of water."

Gerocie stared at the map and raised her eyebrows. "That could alter our relationship with Barellia, making it a diplomatic matter. I'll get this investigated. What else have you noticed?"

Quint gave her a few more observations, but they didn't apply to Gerocie's corps. She added some comments, and Quint felt like she valued his opinion.

"Are you practicing magic?" she asked.

Quint nodded. "Yes, ma'am. I don't practice the dangerous threads in here, of course. I try to get out of Bocarre to practice those."

"There is a practice yard on the other side of the headquarters bordering on the council's gardens. I'll write out a pass so you can practice there. I was told that a wizard needs to practice to improve."

"We do," Quint said. "I may know a lot of strings, but I'm not as proficient as I should be."

"I read your reports, Tirolo. We mustn't ignore your talents, although I still don't know how to use your magic. For a young man, you have a good mind on your shoulders. I can see why Colonel Sarrefo was reluctant to see you reassigned," the woman said.

"I didn't know."

Garocie raised her eyebrows. "I should have known better not to have let that slip." She winked. "I'll get the pass sent down. I'm afraid there isn't anything I can do about your lunches."

Quint smiled when the colonel left. She was another willot officer who Quint regarded as something close to a friend.

When she left, Quint pulled out his willot materials and continued his studies of the willot language. He had translated half of the willot notes in the Gussellian officer's strings book, but some words didn't appear in his materials. He wondered when Colonel Garocie would help him with a more comprehensive dictionary.

His other problem was that he didn't have an ear for the language. He didn't know if any pronunciation was correct, but that was a problem for another time.

Quint heard steps and quickly shuffled his willot material into a drawer before the door opened.

"Yesterday's newssheets. The colonel is adding three more newssheets for you," the servant said. "She must like your opinions."

Quint shrugged. "Like isn't a word I would use. Perhaps she wants a different view. I have nothing to do but write reports on what I read."

"Whatever," the servant said dismissively and left.

The new newssheets were in the middle of the stack. They were more like opinion journals. Quint read a few articles and frowned. He didn't like what he read. They promoted the glories of the central council and boasted about the greatness of the willot race.

He would have to be careful about reporting on opinion journals. There were always asides in the newssheets that boasted about Racellian life, but the bias was never as strong as in the new readings.

Quint found that half of the articles were written in willot. He tried to translate, but there were too many words that he couldn't find. Perhaps this was the reason he needed some willot textbooks.

Quint opened a message from the colonel included in a delivery of newssheets the following week to meet in her office for their next meeting after lunch that day. After securing his office, he wrote up his observations and emerged from the basement.

"I thought you might like a break from living in your little space, Lieutenant Tirolo," she said as she closed the door before their meeting.

Quint brought up his observations which weren't different from the previous week, although he hadn't reread about the crop situation in western Racellia.

"Your thoughts on the new newssheets, Tirolo?"

Quint nodded and gave the colonel an awkward smile that probably looked more like a grimace.

"I call them opinion journals. They don't reflect current events as much as attitudes about current events." He gave her another two pages of observations. "My background is a barrier to understanding," Quint said. "They promote willot culture and ideals to the exclusion of all else, it seems."

Gerocie smiled with a twinkle in her eyes. "I want your opinion, but I won't appreciate defensiveness in your analysis. I'll be sending you journals from our neighboring countries for you to provide me with feedback."

"But there are articles in the willot language," Quint said, his heart rising in his throat as he said it. "I…"

She held up her finger. "I know you are studying willot, Lieutenant Tirolo. You aren't as careful to hide your materials as you think. I want you to learn since I need your analysis on our friends across the border, and some of them speak willot more than they do the common language. I want you to keep up your discretion."

"My books aren't sufficient to translate all the words," Quint said.

She nodded. "I have a valise for you. It is our secret," she said as she lifted a valise to the top of her desk. "This is as much as I will give you. It is up to you to fill in any more blanks. South Fenola has become unstable, as your newssheets have revealed. We still haven't recaptured the land that Gussellia grabbed in the battle you observed. My job will get harder since Racellia has exposed a weakness that others wish to exploit."

"But don't you have diplomats feeding you information?" Quint asked.

"Military diplomats, yes. Many of them are bought off by our neighbors just as we have their people in the pay of Racellia." She grinned. "You know nothing of this, correct?"

"A little of that is revealed through what is reported in the newssheets," Quint said.

"Continue your work, Lieutenant, and I may let you off your leash in a few months," Gerocie said.

CHAPTER NINETEEN
~

QUINT CELEBRATED HIS SEVENTEENTH BIRTHDAY WITH MARENA. The other three officers in the flat had been assigned to the army in another battle with the Gussellians.

"I invited someone over," Marena said. "He said he doesn't mind hubites."

She answered the door and in walked Master Pozella.

"How has the senior lieutenant been?"

"I've been okay," Quint said. "I thought I'd be put in the basement and left to rot, but I've found a niche, thanks to Colonel Gerocie."

"Happy birthday, too," Pozella said. He tossed an envelope on the table. Quint picked it up. "This is my mother's writing."

"I would hope so. She gave me the letter," Pozella said. "Go ahead, read it. Don't save it for later."

Quint felt lightheaded. He hadn't communicated very much with his parents since he was drafted into the Racellian wizard corps. His parents were fine. His mother didn't have much to say except she was surprised he was an officer in the wizard corps. Neither Quint's father or mother thought that would be possible for Quint, but Master Pozella had told them about Quint's talent. She wished him well and said he didn't have to respond to the letter.

Quint looked at Pozella. "They really are all right?"

"As right as any other hubite in the southeast. They are among their kind, unlike you."

"I'm enduring," Quint said, realizing that his statement was truer than he had intended. "Colonel Gerocie has me learning willot on the sly. I'm reading newssheets and opinion journals and giving her my analysis. It's like what we were doing in strategic operations, but it's mostly political, I think. I give her the analysis and then she does what she wants with it."

"You have started analyzing willot articles?" Pozella said, pursing his lips.

"My vocabulary is growing, but I can't speak the language."

Marena snorted. "It is just as well. For some, hearing a hubite speaking the mother tongue would be too much to bear."

"I shouldn't have admitted it," Quint said.

Marena laughed. "I'm not one of those people and neither is the master, I'm sure."

"You're right," Pozella said. "My concern is what you will read. Willot articles are blunter about foreigners."

Quint was going to say he wasn't a foreigner, but Pozella was right about the general attitude.

"I've met friendly willots and unfriendly willots," Quint said. "If you read as many articles as I have, you'd know that the antipathy is always there, beneath the surface of the majority of willots in Racellia. I'm finding that the rest of the countries on South Fenola feel the same, but they don't have sizeable hubite populations."

"Then I don't have any objections," Pozella said. "Is this the extent of your birthday celebration?"

"Most of the strategic operations officers are in the field this week," Marena said. "Our dinner will be good tonight, but quiet."

"Quiet can be good," Pozella said.

Quint smiled. "A letter from my mother and two of the few people I can count as friends is enough for me. I've learned to temper my expectations.

They had dinner. Pozella offered some war stories and Marena talked about her life in the capital. Quint was happy to listen.

"I'll visit you soon in your basement palace," Pozella said as he left.

Quint helped Marena clean up, despite her protestations. He was soon alone in the flat. He sat on the couch and smiled, thinking of good food and good company, something that was in short supply in his life.

He thought of working on the Gussellian string book but ended up going to sleep early. Quint thought he'd have a hard time going to sleep, but morning came soon and his life in the basement resumed.

∽

"Colonel Gerocie wants you upstairs and make sure you are presentable and wear your cap," an orderly said.

Quint nodded. "Thank you," he said as he straightened his tunic and grabbed his hat after he cleared his desk and secured his office.

"Colonel, ma'am," Quint said saluting, his cap underneath an arm. "You summoned me?"

"We are going to a meeting in the council palace," Gerocie said. "We will be meeting a foreign delegation. Watch yourself and only speak when you are spoken to, and I'd advise carefully framing your responses."

"Yes, ma'am," Quint said.

Quint felt exposed as he walked through the Racellian Military Headquarters and out the door. He put his cap on just before he exited the building to hide his light-colored hair.

They were let into a side door to the palace grounds and through another side door to the inside of the palace. The colonel knew her way around, and they stood in front of a guarded set of doors on the second floor of the ornate building.

"You may have met one of those we will be meeting," the colonel said.

They entered and there were a few military officers dressed in a familiar uniform and Quint recognized the wizard officer who was after him months ago.

"We are having talks with a Gussellian delegation," one of the civilians said to Colonel Gerocie. "One of our guests asked to meet with Lieutenant Tirolo. I'd like you to meet General Pacci Colleto."

Quint looked at the wizard officer and gave him a slight bow, which was returned. He didn't think Colleto was a general when the Gussellian officer chased Amaria and him through the forests of northern Racellia.

"I want to thank you for returning my possessions and my horse. Some of them were very valuable to me. I hope you understand that I was operating under orders."

Quint looked blankly at the officer since the man had spoken to Quint in the willot language. Quint looked at Colonel Gerocie. "He said, ma'am?"

"He appreciated your returning his possessions to him, lieutenant."

Quint nodded and pretended that he suddenly understood. "I don't like taking things that don't belong to me, and once I used them to avoid harm to myself and my fellow officer, I felt they needed to be with you," Quint said in the common language.

The wizard officer smiled and nodded. "I understand. It gave me a greater appreciation for Racellians."

"That is all, Lieutenant," the same civilian said. "You may take him back with you, Colonel Gerocie."

They left the room after saluting.

"You performed magnificently. You didn't expect to see your enemy, did you?" the colonel asked.

"Not in a civilized setting. I returned the wizard's possessions since I didn't want him hunting me down on the streets of Bocarre," Quint said. "He knows I defeated him. I truly didn't know why he was hunting me. He didn't care a bit about Amaria Baltacco other than using her as a lure to get me back to the pub where we had our encounter."

"That wasn't in the official report," Colonel Gerocie said.

"I didn't dispute anything in the official report, but that doesn't mean everything happened exactly as written," Quint said.

"I understand that." She smiled with an amazed look on her face. "What really happened when you left the battle?"

"Is this an order, for if it isn't I'd rather remain silent."

"An order, lieutenant. I want to know what happened during the pursuit."

Quint told her the truth, but he didn't mention the string book. "I know they spoke willot amongst themselves and I didn't want him to know that I learned how."

"Not to mention letting my superior and a council member know a hubite had the temerity to learn the mother tongue. Had you answered the wizard, I would have gotten in trouble, too," Gerocie said.

"The thought crossed my mind, ma'am," Quint said.

"That wasn't what I had in mind when I said you might be let off your leash."

Quint stopped to pick up dropped papers when he heard two officers speaking willot in a hallway. He listened and picked up many of the words, just enough to make sense of their discussion on where to eat lunch.

Over the months since his meeting with the Gussellian wizard, his mastery of willot had reached a plateau. His vocabulary was enough to understand the wizard's string book. He no longer had to translate it in his mind but understood as he read. However, he recognized that he needed to listen to the language to increase his knowledge.

He was able to read and understand most of the newssheets of the other South Fenola countries and had begun to provide reports in the common tongue to Colonel Gerocie. Quint didn't know if his observations were useful since the articles were cultural discussions that were beyond his ability to analyze.

Quint's only diversion from solitary life in the basement was living in the flat with the three strategic operations officers. Since everything he read was in the public domain, he didn't mind joining in discussions with his flatmates about current events.

Quint was constantly surprised at how much more he knew about what was going on in Racellia and in South Fenola than they did. Quint still didn't join them in public settings, but it was enough to keep him sane and the discussions reminded him that he could be contributing to the military diplomatic corps in his own way.

That was his life until one of the officers told everyone he was marrying his girlfriend and would be moving out. The three knew another officer who wanted to live in the flat and Quint was home when the new flatmate came by to look over his new lodgings.

Quint walked out of his bedroom to meet the newcomer.

"You're the hubite!" the new tenant said. "You'll have to leave. I won't be living with a sub-human."

The three officers tried to stand up for Quint, but the new person was adamant. "I was promised a room in a nice flat and this isn't it. I'm going to complain to the personnel officer." He looked at Quint with disgust. "You better start packing now!" the new tenant said as he stalked out of the flat.

"That was unexpected," the lieutenant that was leaving said, plopping down on the couch. "I said we had a special flatmate, a senior lieutenant."

"What's going to happen?" Quint asked.

"The division owns the flat. You've been allowed to stay since you worked with us, but now that you are at military headquarters, the personnel officer could make you leave."

Quint sat in one of the easy chairs. "What are the chances?"

The three of them looked at each other and shrugged.

"It isn't up to us. You could appeal to Colonel Sarrefo, but he is traveling and won't be back for two more weeks," one of them said.

Marena walked in. "Where is the new officer?" she asked.

"He took one look at Quint and left in a huff. It looks like he will fight for his spot," a flatmate said.

"And Quint will be kicked out." she said, "since the flat is your organization's."

"Likely," another officer said.

"Not to worry. I know of a place closer to the council palace that is open. I work there, too." She looked at Quint. "You wouldn't be sharing, but there might be other benefits, being in the international quarter."

"What is the international quarter?" Quint asked.

One of the officers said, "It is where foreigners live, like ambassadors and their staff. I understand you need connections to live there."

"I'm the connection," Marena said. "I'm keeping that place clean, too. How much are you paying for the flat?"

Quint gave her what he was paying for rent. The other three whistled.

"We are paying two-thirds what you are," they said.

"But you will have to pay a little more than what you are now. Can you afford it?" Marena asked.

"I can. I have nothing else to spend money on other than food and clothes."

"Let's see what happens, first," one of the officers who remained said,

"Then you can make a good decision."

"In the meantime, you can see the flat. Here is a key and the address. When you've seen it, give the key back."

"I'll do that," Quint said. "In fact, I'll take a look now."

"I'll come with you," Marena said. "I only came to meet the new tenant. Now, I'm not so sure I'll like him."

Quint wore his uniform and his cap to hide his hair. Marena walked faster than Quint usually did, but she was in a good mood despite the circumstances in the flat.

"We will see if I continue to work at your flat," Marena said. "It depends on the new tenants. I think you will be asked to leave. The personnel officer seems to be a stickler for rules from what I've heard. If the other three were honest they would tell you the same but cheer up. This flat is much nicer."

They talked about Bocarre and the tension building up in the city. Quint was aware of it, but Marena gave some common examples of her contacts expressing their uneasiness. Her perspective would make it into Quint's reports.

They came to what Marena called the international quarter. The buildings looked the same, but there was a different feel to the place. For one, there were other people mixed in with the willots. Dress styles were occasionally different, and the names of the stores weren't always written in the common tongue or in the willot alphabet.

Quint stared at the mix. "I never knew this existed."

"To most willots, it doesn't. They ignore the place, but I work here as well as other places," Marena said. "In here."

She opened a door next to a lady's hat and shoe store and led Quint up a set of stairs to corridor with two doors on either side.

"There are two more floors like this above this one," Marena said. "The empty flat is on the top floor."

The building was in very good shape. He wondered if the previous tenant didn't like the stairs.

At the top there were three doors, and Marena used her key to open the only door on the side facing the back.

Quint walked in and stopped. The living area was huge. There was a set of windows that looked out over some rooftops with the dome of the council palace poking up in the near distance with a shadow of the Fenola Sea on the horizon. The furnishings were used, but better quality than the old flat.

"This would be mine?"

Marena nodded. "It has a full kitchen, indoor plumbing, and you will share it with only one flatmate."

"When do I meet him."

"Her. I live here, and I'm rarely home. You are already approved by the owner, me."

"I'm not comfortable living with a woman," Quint admitted.

Marena laughed. "Think of me as your mother or your older sister. Don't you think you are too young for me?"

"I am," Quint said.

"There. I charge a little more, but you get housecleaning and kitchen privileges. If we are home at the same time, I'll even cook for you. However, unlike any other part of Bocarre, you can walk the streets and not fear attack. You can walk into any of the restaurants and be served. That is different, isn't it?"

"I'd have to get used to it," Quint said.

"I was going to suggest your moving here at some point, but I needed a good excuse, so it didn't look like I was luring you away."

Quint smiled as he looked at his prospective bedroom. It was as large as the sitting room in the flat and the furnishings was surprisingly masculine.

"Did a man live here before?"

"I will admit it. My son lived here. He's been gone for a year. He is a year older than you."

"He might come back," Quint said.

"He is half polens. My late husband was from Slinnon on assignment to Racellia. We met, married, and had Horo. My husband died on a voyage to his homeland. My son decided life would be better in his father's country, and I agreed with him. Letting him go wasn't easy, but he won't return. If anything, I'll leave Bocarre and join him. Until then, we can be flatmates."

"So that is why you live in the international quarter," Quint said.

Marena nodded her head. "Even now, my life is easier in the quarter. When people find out I married a polen, they shy away."

"You secret is safe with me."

Marena laughed. "It isn't a secret, but a little discretion is appreciated."

Quint looked through the window. He could see the sea above the distant rooftops. He could learn to like it here.

"I won't desert my flatmates," Quint said, "but if the personnel officer supports the new tenant, consider me in."

Marena smiled. "I'm glad you feel that way. It's not that we don't know each other. I'll be looking forward to the company."

CHAPTER TWENTY

Q UINT'S FLATMATES APOLOGIZED ABOUT THE DECISION of the personnel officer. Quint had a week to vacate his room. Another officer was invited to live in the flat, and he was as angry about living with a hubite as the other. Marena gave her notice.

"Won't you lose a job?" Quint asked as he arrived at his new flat.

Marena smiled. "I can work as much as I want. I've already replaced the officer's flat with a client in the international quarter. There is a waiting list for my services."

"How many jobs do you have?"

"Right now, three including my new one. I'll be cooking one more night per week," she said.

"I can cook for myself," Quint said, knowing that his cooking was substandard at best.

"Then feel free."

Quint put his clothes in the large wardrobe. They seemed lonely hanging by themselves. The desk was a nice table sitting next to a chest of drawers that could be used for papers and writing supplies.

He was finished in less than an hour and walked out into the sitting room. Marena had already gone to a client's flat. Quint sat in a comfortable easy chair. Everything was superior to the other flat. He knew he'd miss the acceptance by his old flatmates, but continuing to live with even one angry officer was too much.

Quint didn't feel like working on his day off, so he strolled along the streets of the international quarter. He quickly found that the district was seven blocks long and four blocks wide. It was easy to know where the quarter ended because the signs in the shop windows stopped being diverse.

There were a few stares, but Quint guessed it might have been because of the wizard corps uniform as much as his hubite characteristics. He walked into a restaurant and was shown a seat.

Quint soon found that he was in a gran establishment. Grans looked more like hubites with lighter colored eyes and hair, but their skin was almost as dark as willots. The food was different than any Quint had eaten and consisted of small dishes that were scooped onto small flatbreads, rolled, and then eaten. The food was spicy, but no more so than normal for willot cuisine.

He paid more than he expected, but Quint guessed that everything in the international quarter was probably more expensive. He could afford it. Since he was promoted to lieutenant, he was saving half of what he was paid and that didn't include his senior lieutenant bonus.

Returning to his flat, Quint smiled. There was more to explore in the international quarter which would expand his horizons. It could help his analytical work, too.

❧

"I've moved," Quint told Colonel Gerocie.

"Oh?"

"One of my flatmates left to get married and his replacement couldn't tolerate hubites. The strategic operations personnel officer said I'd have to leave since I was no longer a member of the division."

"Are you living on the streets?" the colonel asked with a smile.

"I've secured a room in a flat in the international quarter," Quint said.

"You need to have international connections to live there."

"My landlady married a polen from Slinnon. He was killed in a shipwreck or something. Her son left for Slinnon, and she had a room available. She was the housekeeper at my former flat."

"Is it much closer than your old flat?"

Quint nodded. "Less than half as far. It's better for me."

"I would think so. Everyone has to be tolerant there," the colonel said. "Are there any other advantages?"

Quint smiled. "I can get impressions from people. My landlady talks to lots of residents."

"You put her observations into one of your reports? She is a source?"

Quint nodded.

"Good. You need to inform our personnel officer about your change in residence. Don't say it's in the international quarter, just list the address."

"I understand," Quint said.

"Have you learned anything from your first few days? You have moved already?"

"Two days, ma'am," Quint said holding up two fingers.

"The food is different, and to me, that means the culture will be different. I ate at a gran restaurant yesterday."

The colonel smiled. "Interesting. I have an assignment for you. I want you to spend time in the quarter. You do not have to wear your uniform, in fact, I'd rather you went as yourself."

"Like a spy, ma'am?" Quint said, getting to the point of her assignment.

"No specific assignment but consider it an extension of what you've been doing with the newssheets and the journals. I don't want details on everyone's opinions, but we are always interested in trends and anything that support those trends, lieutenant."

"I can do that," Quint said. "Can I let my landlady know I'm doing that?"

The colonel shrugged. "Since you aren't targeting anyone, I don't see why not. You be the judge. I think I'll have some news for you in the next few days. It's developing. Dismissed, Lieutenant Tirolo."

Quint returned to his office. It seemed dingier after his move. He looked around the small room and decided he'd ask Marena's advice to make it look better.

He reviewed his meeting with Colonel Gerocie. He decided she was too agreeable. To him that meant his assignments were meant to fill time. He was sure he was doing some good. At a minimum, he had learned the basics of the willot language and was becoming well-read in current events, but he had realized that all the information he read was filtered to some degree. The forces making things happen were often not talked about, but merely alluded to.

Quint was surprised she agreed so readily when he characterized himself as a spy. But in truth, he was as much a spy as a person doing research in the strategic operations division, which was a far cry from the kind of spies he pictured from reading novels in his village not that long ago.

The day's basket of newssheets showed up with yesterday's publications. There was only one foreign journal, one from Gussellia. It didn't take him long to identify the articles that might mean something. He saved the Gussellian journal for last. It was written in willot.

Like most articles in this particular journal, there were bellicose calls for rising to the call of their new leader. The name of the person, Pacci Colleto, was familiar. Quint closed his eyes to remember where he had heard the name and then it came to him. The wizard officer who had sought him almost a year ago had just risen to lead the Gussellian government.

It took a minute for the shock to wear off. He carefully read the articles again. The bellicosity was different from the previous Gussellian publications. The call to patriotism was stronger and the identification of Gussellia as a motherland showed up for the first time. The two speeches by Colleto transcribed in the journal were just short of a call to arms.

Quint wondered if the colonel had read this. It was an important change and Quint pointed out deeper meanings in the speeches along with a list of willot words he couldn't find the meanings of.

He didn't wait for the next meeting and returned the basket and his reports to the colonel's office. She was in and granted Quint's request for a quick meeting.

"I think I found something important."

"You did?" the colonel asked. It was as if she was humoring him. Maybe she was.

He presented his reports but went through his opinion on the Gussellian journal articles and especially the wizard's speeches.

"If this is how he really thinks, the armistice with Gussellia means nothing," Quint said.

The colonel's eyebrows rose. As she read the report on her own, she rubbed the back of her neck, focusing on what Quint said.

"I didn't think you would catch this."

"The journal was a test, ma'am?"

"I really wanted to see your opinion, but yes. You passed in an extraordinary fashion. Your wizard has been actively presenting these principles after he visited Bocarre."

She looked at the last sheet of the Gussellian report. "What are these words?"

"I didn't understand those. They weren't in my dictionaries," Quint said. "Since they are willot words, I didn't want them attached to the report."

"I'll get you a more current dictionary, but it may take a few days." She handed the sheet back along with the Gussellian journal. "Keep this, you'll be analyzing more. Do that wood joining thing to keep them from casual view."

"You know about that?" Quint asked.

"I do and I agree with the need to protect the work in your office. I'll get a proper lock installed as well. I have an engagement to get ready for, Lieutenant Tirolo. You did the right thing by bringing this to me this evening. If you don't mind…"

Quint took that as a dismissal and returned to his office. The day was over and he would visit the personnel office another day. After securing his office, he left, thinking it was a satisfying day. If the colonel was giving him a lock for his office, perhaps he wasn't being given make-work after all.

❦

Marena was out and Quint changed into civilian clothes before finding a Narukun restaurant. Many Narukuns were hubites and there were a few in the restaurant, but they weren't dressed like Racellian hubites.

The food was not what Quint was used to. It was very spicy with thick sauces. A bowl of rice was served with bowls of the sauces along with cut vegetables and meat.

"You don't eat the dish directly. You dip the vegetable or the meat in the sauce and put it on your rice bowl and eat rice with the dish," the server said.

The spice wasn't as strong and Quint could get to the taste of the dish with something to lower the intensity of the sauce. He hoped they had food less strong the next time he visited.

Fighting the food kept Quint from talking to anyone. He bought a jar of fruit juice from a street vendor and returned to the flat. His stomach was complaining, but the fruit juice seemed to settle everything down.

With nothing to do, Quint perusing the bookcases in the main room.

He found a shelf of willot language books including a few dictionaries. The newest looking one had most of the words that had stumped Quint earlier when he read through the wizard's speeches.

Marena walked in with a few bags of groceries. "You've already eaten?"

Quint nodded. "I experimented with Narukun cuisine. I'm not sure I'm built to enjoy it."

Marena laughed. "You're a hubite. It's not a racial thing?"

"No. The Narukun culture is much different from Racellian hubites. If anything, our food is like any other food working people eat in Racellia."

She smiled. "What are you reading? A willot dictionary? You know how to read books in our mother tongue?" Her smile faded. "That's dangerous knowledge."

"My commanding officer knows. I read opinion journals from the other South Fenolan countries that are written exclusively in willot. The one I read today had words I was unfamiliar with." Quint held up the dictionary. "Most of them were in here. Are these books restricted?"

"No, but like my background, I ask you to use discretion."

"I've been using a lot of discretion. There are three people who know my secret, Master Pozella, Colonel Gerocie, and now, you."

Marena curtseyed. "I feel honored to be included in such august company. We are taught at an early age that willot is reserved for people from our race. Others who know it are heretics of a sort," she said.

"It is part of my job. So I suppose I am a heretic in many people's eyes, however, I am mostly a heretic because I am a hubite."

"Probably just as much a heretic," Marena said, "to some." She smiled. "I'm on your side, Quint. Don't forget that."

"I won't," Quint said.

CHAPTER TWENTY-ONE

QUINT WAS CALLED INTO THE COLONEL'S OFFICE. An army general sat in the seat Quint generally used.

"Come in, Lieutenant and sit next to General Obellia."

The general turned to Quint. "So you are our Level 3 research assistant."

Quint recognized that he was not called out for being a hubite.

"We are cognizant that you have a relationship of sorts with Pacci Colleto."

"The Gussellian wizard soldier?" Quint asked.

"The current leader of Gussellia."

"I do. It really is an 'of sorts' kind of relationship, sir. He was hunting me after the Gussellian border battle."

"He never told you why?"

Quint had specifically written his conclusions in his report. He wondered if General Obellia had read Quint's version.

"All I know is that he was looking for the Level 3 wizard. Amaria Baltacco is not a Level 3 and I think she is barely a Level 2. That made me his target," Quint said.

"And you were called to meet him because you returned his possessions including the horse you rode to escape from him?"

"That is my understanding, although there might have been other reasons for him to meet me."

"Such as?" the general asked.

"Knowing me by sight. It wasn't the best lit inn, and everything happened quickly after dark, sir," Quint said.

"Quite so. We have an operation that you might be suited for."

Quint looked at Colonel Gerocie. "The general is over what unit?"

"You can ask that question directly, soldier," Obellia said. "I am over Racellian Military Intelligence Services. The colonel reports to me, Lieutenant."

Quint had exposed a nerve, but since he wasn't dismissed, he leaned forward for more information.

"Since Colleto knows you as a Level 3 wizard and a hubite, I want you to join a delegation to Nornotta, the Gussellian capital. We don't have any Masters or Level 3 people to spare."

"The wizard corps, sir?" Quint asked.

"Is not under my jurisdiction. I doubt if Baltacco would lend me any of his people for this operation."

Quint sighed. That would let Amaria off the list. "I may still be in danger?"

The general chuckled. "You are always in danger, hubite."

"But they speak willot exclusively in Gussellia," Quint said.

The general smirked. "Colonel Gerocie has told me you have a working knowledge of the language."

"I know a few words, sir."

"Keep your language capability a secret. Being underestimated is a definite advantage for you, Tirolo."

"What am I to do?" Quint looked at the general who nodded at Colonel Gerocie. Quint had run out of objections.

"Observe. Do exactly what you do every day. Observe and analyze, and when you return, report. You will be the military representative of the delegation. We are giving you a provisional promotion to Captain. It is the minimum rank for this kind of operation."

Quint didn't quite know what to do, so he stood and saluted the Colonel and the General and said, "I will perform whatever assignment you ask."

"That's music to my ears, Captain Tirolo. You'll receive specific orders later today." The general turned to the colonel. "Do you really think he's up to it?" He spoke in willot.

"He does a remarkable job of analysis, General Obellia. He won't disappoint, if he returns. We don't know what is behind the Gussellian request for a delegation." The colonel spoke in willot to the general and then turned to Quint, still standing. "You are dismissed, Captain." Gerocie had the ghost of a smile on her face.

Quint saluted again and left for his office.

What did he get himself into? He couldn't reject the assignment, or he would forever be stuck in the basement of Racellia's military headquarters or worse. Perhaps a rejection would lead to a demotion. He remembered the willot recruit who refused to obey simple commands when he was first pressed into the army.

Was the willot discussion at the end of the meeting a test? Quint shook his head. He told himself that all he had to do was observe and then report. How much easier could an assignment be?

But then again, the general said the wizard corps wasn't about to waste a Level 3 or a Master on the delegation. Did they assume the delegation would run afoul of the Gussellians?

Quint shook his head. He didn't have a solution to his dilemma since he didn't have enough information.

His orders were delivered to his office by one of the colonel's orderlies, a sergeant. The man sneered." You're no captain, hubite."

"End that with a 'sir,' soldier."

"You're no captain, hubite, sir," the orderly sneered before leaving Quint's office.

Quint shook his head at the anger the man must live with. He opened the sealed orders. The first page was a certificate promoting him to Captain in the Wizard Corps. Two sets of captain's badges were pinned to the certificate.

He thought he'd be transferred to the regular army, but then he read further where it said he was permanently attached to the military diplomatic corps, a division of the Racellian Intelligence Services, whatever that was. All Quint knew is General Obellia was running it, and Quint's life was now the General's responsibility.

The orders were simple enough. A delegation to discuss a truce with Gussellia would be leaving in three days from the council palace courtyard. Quint, Captain Tirolo as Quint was referred to in the orders, would be assigned as a military advisor. He was to observe and report his findings to Colonel Gerocie upon return. Quint would be expected to protect the delegation along with the other military personnel should there be a need.

He was afraid there would be a need.

~

Quint showed up at the courtyard half an hour early. Coaches were already lined up. A few of the delegates had arrived before Quint. Quint had never met any of them, and they were speaking willot to each other.

Quint ignored the rude comments that were made about him, but he wasn't the only point of complaint. The men spoke unkindly of Gussellian food, lodgings, and the people in general, even though they were willots like the Gussellians, Quint was surprised by the expressed hatred.

He knew all willots weren't like that, but Quint wondered about the true percentage. Was it a willot thing? He stood looking in a different direction until he heard his name called.

Quint turned and looked at Amaria Baltacco.

"My father couldn't stand General Obellia having a person on the delegation that wasn't a true wizard corps officer."

Quint didn't fail to notice the senior lieutenant badge on her uniform. She probably thought she would be outranking him. He wasn't happy she was going to Gussellia.

"I thought you had enough of the Gussellians," Quint said.

"The greater good of Racellia is more important."

Quint laughed. "The greater good of Amaria Baltacco. I'm going to file my own report on this trip," Quint said. "I'm not into fiction like you are."

Amaria blushed. "I wrote the report the way my father wanted it," she said. "That makes it the truth."

"In your dreams," Quint said.

"I see you have found each other. I read Senior Lieutenant's report, Captain Tirolo. You two should work wonderfully together in Nornotta," a white-haired man said. Quint remembered him from his meeting with Pacci Colleto.

"Captain?" Amaria said. "You?" She looked at his uniform collar and finally spotted Quint's captain badges. "How did that happen?"

"How did you get your promotion?" Quint asked.

"I earned it."

"So did I," Quint said.

The man introduced himself. "I am Henricco Lucheccia. I am the foreign secretary. General Obellia reports to me for non-military matters." He smiled at Quint. "Your observations find their way to me from time to time. I'm impressed that someone as young as you are, and with your, uh, rural background has such insight."

Quint was generally surprised. "I am humbled by your compliment, sir," he said.

"Observations?" Amaria said, obviously not knowing what Quint did at the diplomatic corps.

"Captain Tirolo is an analyst for the Military Diplomatic Corps."

"I thought you were stuck in a basement, somewhere," Amaria said.

"It's easier to concentrate that way," Quint said, enjoying the little lie.

"I came over to tell you personally, that you will be riding behind the coaches on our trip. It is your background. I hope you understand."

Quint smiled at Lucheccia. The secretary was honest about his compliment and under other circumstances, Quint felt he could be rational, but others in the entourage weren't.

"I do understand. May I ride in the front instead?" Quint didn't want to eat dust all the way to the Gussellian capital.

"Whatever you wish. Colonel Gerocie sent the horse to us for your use," the leader said.

"Perhaps some of my bags can be carried on the coach," Quint said.

"A reasonable request and one that I will personally make sure is fulfilled. It looks like everyone has arrived. We will be leaving in a few minutes."

Quint carried his string book that he hid in a hidden compartment in his bags. Marena helped him with it. She was convinced it would be detected. He kept a change of clothes, some dried food, maps, and a canteen, as well as a few personal items. The rest of his clothes and an analysis he had made of Gussellia a few months ago after his meeting with the Gussellian wizard were in the heavier bag carried on the roof of one of the coaches along with the rest of the luggage.

Quint brought up the rear while they clattered through the morning traffic in the Racellian capital. Once they departed from a cobbled road, Quint moved to the side of the front coach whose coachman grudgingly had revealed their route to Nornotta where Pacci Colleto waited for them.

When the coaches rested at roadside stops, Quint was ignored other than a nod from Henricco Lucheccia. The nod was enough to get Quint served if the staff at the rest stop ignored him. Amaria noticed him, but her recognition consisted of dirty looks and lifting her chin with disdain on her face.

The first night was repeated every time. Quint was given a room in servant quarters. He shared his room with those drivers and attendants that didn't walk out when they saw him in the room.

The last night was a little better as the attendants and drivers could see that Quint wasn't a threat.

Once inside the castle at Nornotta, Quint was shown to a decent room. He ate his first meal in the dining hall with the rest of the delegation, although he was directed to the far end of the table, sitting ahead of Amaria.

When he went to his room, a servant was waiting at his door.

"Dictator Colleto would like an audience," the servant said.

Quint followed the servant to an upper floor and into a large study. The wizard officer, now wearing an ornate uniform with gold epaulets stood to greet him.

"Sit over here," the wizard said. "We should get a few things out of the way before the others meet."

"I'm only an observer," Quint said.

"I see you were given a promotion to make you an official member of the delegation. Congratulations, if that is in order."

"Thank you, but I think it is a rank given for my commanding officer's convenience."

"It is unfortunate that you come from a hubite background. You would go far in any South Fenolan country with your facility for strings."

"You overestimate my capabilities, sir. I require years of practice before I'll be truly proficient at all the strings that I know."

Colleto raised his hand. "I know all that. I was a young master, myself, but not as young as you. You should know that I wasn't trying to capture and kill you, Captain. I wanted to offer you a position in the Gussellian army, once I was told that you used a portent string during the battle."

"How did you know?" Quint said.

"I have an associate who can sense psychic strings. It is a rare gift. Once one of my magicians noticed two wizard corps officers leaving the battle, I did some quick checking and discovered your names. The girl had a tracking string on a uniform tunic she stuffed in her bags."

Amaria still had the tunic with the tracking string. Another one of her lies, Quint thought.

"We followed it to the village pub. We couldn't penetrate farther into Racellian territory and had to give up the chase."

"The tracking spell. I thought I had fixed that."

"Not good enough for a seasoned Master," Colleto said. "I requested that you accompany the delegation."

"Who did you ask?"

Colleto smiled and slowly shook his head. "I keep my own secrets. Think about my offer."

"To become a traitor?" Quint asked.

Colleto shrugged. "A traitor to whom? A traitor to a nation that reviles you and your kind. I know how hubites are treated in Racellia. We don't have hubites in Gussellia, but I suspect we would do the same. Think about my offer. It will stand until you formally accept or reject. If you want to mull it over in your mind for a period, do so."

Quint didn't know what to say.

"Do your job of observing. I suspect you have learned to speak willot since we last met or you would be useless as an advisor, if anyone would listen to you. I will tell you that I intend to rule all South Fenola," Colleto said. "Who knows what opportunities may arise after that. You may use that as an observation. I don't intend on keeping it a secret for very long. I find that rule suits me."

"But why be so interested in me?"

"Do you believe your portent strings?"

"I believe in them enough to know that if you look too far into the future that the portent becomes uncertain," Quint said.

"You are unique. Some people never realize that. You have shown up in more than a few castings, Captain Tirolo. Your roles have changed as the portents have been cast, but there is no denying, you will be an important figure in the future. I'd rather you be on my side than on another's. Think about my offer. You can have any rank you wish along with vast wealth. You can go back to your room and think, think, think."

Quint stood and left the dictator's study. He followed the servant back to his room. He was in such a fog that he would have never remembered the way.

The offer seemed too good to be true, but if Colleto had wanted him killed, he could have easily done it somewhere to or from the meeting. It was clear that Colleto had his own intelligence services embedded in Bocarre. Quint guessed that it was reasonable that Colleto knew he would be able to speak willot, one of his secrets.

His head began to slow down, and Quint decided to record his impressions as they became more organized in his mind. He didn't see himself standing next to Colleto in any scenario, but he couldn't bring himself to cast a portent for himself. Those were always notoriously inaccurate no matter what the timeframe. It was too dangerous for a wizard to put himself into a portent string.

General Baltacco had inferred that he thought Quint was special. It would make sense that if Colleto's portent string predicted a rise in status that a portent sting cast by one of Baltacco's masters would reveal something similar. Quint didn't feel very special and didn't take much time thinking about himself.

CHAPTER TWENTY-TWO

THE FIRST DAY WAS TEDIOUS. Quint sat against a wall, away from the negotiating table, while parties on both sides went about defining terms and rules for a negotiation. Colleto was absent and probably some of his senior advisors. Amaria and others didn't show up to this phase.

Henricco seemed in his element as was his counterpart on the Gussellian side. When they broke for lunch, the Racellian delegation was ushered to another meeting room.

Quint saw screens, drapes and cloth paintings around the room and thought they were under surveillance the whole time. He decided to walk around the room and look behind things. He found a screened square in the wall and pointed to it when he caught Henricco's eye.

The leader pointed to Quint and put his finger to his lips.

"We should keep our ideas about the rules of the negotiations close to us. Perhaps we can stroll around the grounds after lunch and talk," the leader said.

Quint didn't say that there were strings that could aid one's hearing. He would try to get that across to Henricco at another time.

The servers set a place for Quint at the same table and those close slid their chairs away from him. Eating at the same table was a victory as far as he was concerned, and Quint had no doubt that Colleto was behind it.

The afternoon session involved compromise, but it was a set of compromises of inconsequential importance to Quint's mind, especially since Quint knew Colleto's grand ambition.

Even if a treaty was negotiated, it was clear that the dictator would have no qualms breaking it. Quint's interpretation of Colleto's comments indicated that everyone was a tool to gain power, and that included turning him into an ally. Quint was just as much a tool as the others in the room.

He returned to his room and napped. When Quint arose, he wrote a benign account of the negotiations. In his estimation no side prevailed, although he felt both sides would consider themselves the winners of the preliminary talks.

Quint was moved up a few places among the Racellians at the dinner table with those who didn't participate in the day's negotiations.

After dinner, Quint sat on a patio, eyes closed, soaking up the energy from the sinking sun. Someone sat down next to him.

"You are coming up in the world," Amaria Baltacco said. "Lucheccia was overruled on the arrangement of diners."

"I'm following orders, Senior Lieutenant Baltacco. I sit where I'm told to sit."

"Do you have a sponsor in the Gussellian court?" she asked.

"The only one I know in the court is the dictator. I suppose it is the same with you."

"It is, but knowing is one thing and getting special privileges is another."

Quint frowned. "What special privileges have you gotten?"

"I met with Pacci Colleto and a few members of his staff this afternoon."

"And that was the special privilege, an audience with Gussellia's leader?" Quint said.

"He asked questions about you, unfortunately," Amaria frowned right after. "What is his fixation on you?"

"I'm a young Level 3, I suppose," Quint said. "A person of promise in his eyes. If I am, he's the only one who thinks so."

"But you have risen to captain."

"With a basement office? A captain who only interfaces with his commanding officer but none of her staff? I'm not treated as a person of promise. I wasn't even allowed to ride in the coaches on the trip," Quint said. "But I suspect I'd be treated no differently here," Quint said waving his arm.

"Except Colleto offers me a taste of respect in a country that has no hubites."

"Why don't you defect to the Gussellians? Would he give you a position?" Amaria asked.

Quint wondered if Amaria got her idea from her father's spies or from Colleto.

"I'm afraid I have no affinity for Gussellia. Not that long ago Colleto was out to capture us," Quint said. "If you don't remember, I do."

"I remember," Amaria said as others came onto the patio. "You shouldn't forget what you just said."

The newcomers were Gussellians, strangers to Quint. They moved chairs away from him and whispered amongst themselves. That was confirmation there would be no difference in Quint's day-to-day life in another willot country.

☙

The following day, Quint assembled with the rest of the delegation for a joint breakfast with the Gussellian negotiators. Both Pacci Colleto and Lucheccia attended the meal. When breakfast was cleared, the dining room became the negotiation hall.

Colleto welcomed the Racellians and asked what they had come to negotiate.

"Peace," Lucheccia proclaimed. "Withdrawal from Racellian lands and a pledge not to invade Racellian lands."

"I seem to recall that at the time, you had invaded Gussellia. The battle that Lieutenant Baltacco and Captain Tirolo witnessed was fought on Gussellian territory. We didn't bring the war to you, but you brought your warring ways to us. I think it would be appropriate to claim reparations for Gussellian lives lost. A tiny slice of your country seems inadequate to what Gussellia suffered."

Quint was surprised that hard lines were being established so early in the meetings. He didn't know if that was standard practice in a negotiation of this kind.

"Our army was wiped out, almost to the man," Lucheccia said. "If we wish to talk about reparations…"

Colleto held up his hand. "I do wish to talk about reparations, but not about defending ourselves against Racellian aggression."

The opening statements were the most benign of the interchange. The participants on both sides looked on with surprise on their faces. Quint wrote a few notes. It was clear to him that Colleto wasn't serious about negotiating, and Lucheccia was taken aback by Colleto's stance. It seemed to him that Colleto's pressing the invasion in every response was consistent with his desire to invade Racellia. Why were they even meeting if there was no hope of an agreement? Was Quint missing something?

"I will reserve the right to seek redress for your invasion in any way I see fit," Colleto said.

"But we both desire peace," Lucheccia said.

Colleto gave the foreign secretary half a smile, almost a smirk. "It is you who desire peace. It is you who have come to Nornotta, not the other way around."

"But your embassy indicated a few months ago that you were willing to talk," Lucheccia said as if he had been knocked backwards.

"I was not the Dictator of Gussellia at the time. I make the decisions for my country, and I only recognize acts by the previous government that I agree with. I didn't agree with what they said at the time." Colleto smiled again. "But you wouldn't know that. I will allow you and your delegation free passage to the Racellian border." Colleto looked around the room. "I think the negotiations are over."

Colleto bowed to the negotiators and nodded to Quint before walking out of the room followed by the Gussellian contingent.

"Is that it?" one of the negotiators said to Lucheccia.

The leader looked at the door that Pacci Colleto had used. "It is, for now. We've been asked to leave. The next step for us will be up to the Council. I will make sure Colleto knows we are interested in opening negotiations at any time."

"Doesn't that make us look weak?" Amaria asked.

Lucheccia glared at her. "It makes us appear to be respecting the wishes of the ruling sovereign of Gussellia. There will be another opportunity. There always is."

Quint wasn't so sure the next opportunity would be a negotiation, but he kept silent. Amaria blushed like she always did when embarrassed or caught in a lie. There was no lie this time.

Quint returned to his room and found an upheaval. Someone had been busy searching for something. As Quint put his things together, he was glad no one had discovered his hiding place for the string book.

He packed and the negotiating party left before lunch. Quint was specifically ordered to ride to the rear of the coaches with the prospects of life returning to the way it was before he was made Captain.

The party finished their journey in the courtyard of the Council Palace mid-morning. Lucheccia nodded to Quint.

"Make sure you truthfully put everything in your report. Don't hide anything," Secretary Lucheccia said. "Be on your way. You can keep the horse. Your time back at the diplomatic corps starts tomorrow."

Quint had never owned his own horse before, and he wasn't sure what Lucheccia had meant about keeping it. He tied his bags to the horse and rode to the flat in the international quarter.

"You are back too soon," Marena said when Quint walked through the door.

"The negotiation never really happened. We spent a day defining how the negotiations were to be conducted, and then the Gussellian dictator sent us home after insulting the delegation," Quint said.

"That isn't good."

"Not for Racellia," Quint said. "I seem to have acquired a horse, at least temporarily. Is there a place nearby to keep it?"

Marena beckoned him to join her at a window. "That building is a stable. They give good rates for people living on this block. I'll write a letter of introduction."

Quint changed into civilian clothes, unpacked his bags, and removed his string book from its hiding place in the bag. When he flipped through the pages of the book a page fluttered to the floor. Quint picked it up.

> My dear Captain Tirolo,
>
> You did a masterful job copying my string book. As a measure of the trust I have in you, keep what you have essentially taken from me.
>
> I look forward to our next encounter.

With my warmest regards,
Pacci Colleto

Quint stared at the note. Was he responsible for the termination of negotiations? It certainly wasn't clear in the note. In retrospect, Quint wondered if the torn-apart room was a diversion. Amaria complained that her room had been upset, as well. The others didn't talk to him.

Writing a purely objective report was more difficult than Quint anticipated. He spent the rest of the day blending his opinion with the events as he perceived them until he pondered what to do about his meeting with Pacci Colleto. With all the spies on both sides, Quint would be better off mentioning it.

He began writing and found he could make a credible report by telling most of the truth. The intention to take over South Fenola would stay as an aspirational statement and the offer would make a brief appearance, although to Quint that was the entire purpose of the meeting. He left off the part about the portent because he could make a case that was speculation.

Quint wrote that he didn't give Colleto an answer as it might color the negotiations. As he reviewed his work, Quint was more comfortable adding this to the report.

With his work done, he went into the living room. Marena had gone, and it was time to find a place for a horse.

The stable was run by a willot who was friendly enough. He recognized the horse as one from a government herd bred for officers.

"You are in the army?"

"Wizard Corps, but assigned to military headquarters," Quint said.

"Show me a string," the stableman said.

Quint smiled and cast a liquid light string, letting the light drip onto the straw in front of the stall.

"What is that?"

"Liquid light. I can't say what will happen to it, but it will continue to light the stable up for a while. Is that good enough?"

"Good enough for me." The stableman wanted a month in advance and Quint paid it, thanking the man for making room for his animal.

Marena had returned when Quint returned.

"You didn't have to go in today?"

Quint shook his head. "Will you read the report I wrote? It doesn't have any state secrets in it, but it is confidential. I want to make sure it makes sense. Until I visited Nornotta, I thought no one read my reports."

"And that isn't true?"

"Someone reads them," Quint said.

Marena took the offered report. It was four pages long, and Quint looked at his landlady while she read.

"You are moving up in the world," Marena said. "You even had a personal audience with the head of Gussellia. I didn't see anything wrong with what you wrote, but it is almost unbelievable. Does the Gussellian dictator really want to take over all of South Fenola? It's been centuries or more since it's been done and the unified continent didn't last long."

"You know your history." Quint said.

"I had a good education," Marena smiled "I think your report says what you want it to say. You deserve a good dinner. I'm free tonight, so let me cook."

CHAPTER TWENTY-THREE

~

COLONEL GEROCIE READ THROUGH THE REPORT TWICE after calling Quint to her office first thing in the morning. "Lucheccia won't dispute any of this?" she asked.

"I was careful to combine my opinion and my observations."

"Then I will forward this to General Obellia."

Quint fidgeted in his chair. "Will I remain a captain?"

The colonel laughed. "You will, but your office will stay in the basement."

"Can I freshen it up?"

"How?"

"Paint the walls, buy a bookshelf and maybe a new chair."

Gerocie leaned forward. "I'll give you an allowance to make your office more presentable. You deserve it after your trip to Gussellia."

"Thank you, ma'am."

"Now that the formal report is out of the way, what did you leave out of the report?"

"I hate to share this with you, but Colleto had a colleague cast a portent and it said I would become an important person in the future. He didn't share with me how that importance was valuable to him, but Colleto wanted me to join him in Gussellia."

"You mean turn your back on Racellia? He was serious about taking over South Fenola?"

"I didn't emphasize it in the report, but yes. Even if he agreed to negotiate, he would have no intention about keeping his pledge," Quint said.

"You were tempted?"

"Gussellia has no other races in their country, just like the other South Fenola countries except for Racellia which is almost as bad. I've found a place where I can live in relative comfort in the international quarter. I am not motivated to leave."

"He would have offered you a higher rank and wealth."

Quint laughed. "What do I do with wealth if I can't share it? I save half of what I make, anyway."

"I'm glad you told him no."

Quint swallowed. "I didn't tell him no. I told him I'd think about it. If I rejected his offer outright it might have jeopardized the negotiation."

"He rejected it anyway, but you did the right thing, which you usually do." The colonel leaned back in her chair and thought for a moment. "What will Lieutenant Baltacco say in her report?"

"You mean Senior Lieutenant Baltacco, ma'am," Quint said.

"She can't blame the failure on you, can she?" the colonel asked.

"She met with the dictator the same evening I did. She told me that Colleto asked questions about me. I wasn't a party to her meeting. She may make a big deal out of it. It might be what she said at her meeting that turned Colleto away from a peace agreement."

"You can't claim that," the colonel said.

"And I didn't, ma'am," Quint said. "All I did was mention the meeting as an aside in my report."

"Then we will wait and see. General Obellia thinks she will create something to undermine you and the diplomatic corps."

"I think that is a good assumption. I didn't talk to her at all on the trip back, ma'am, but I know there is no limit to her ability to lie."

The colonel changed the subject, "You have a backlog of newssheets and journals to catch up on. Was your willot language skills tested?"

"Colleto knows I can speak some willot. He figured out my presence didn't make sense otherwise. However, he did intimate that he had some influence getting me on the negotiating team. I'm not sure about the Racellians."

"There was a request, but you must keep that knowledge close, captain. If the wrong people find out, you won't be the only one in danger. You are dismissed."

Quint entered his office and soon he had six baskets of publications to review. He couldn't do a thorough job and keep up, but he had some ideas about what to look for.

By the end of the day, he had gone through three days of materials without finding a lot to report on, but he would take a Gussellian journal home with him to review.

The colonel wanted to meet before Quint left.

"Baltacco didn't take much time to get his little one to write her report. I just got this from General Obellia. It is his personal copy."

The report was only two pages long and even at that, Quint was surprised Amaria had that much to write about. As he had expected, most of it was an attack on Quint.

She accused him of knowing the mother tongue, of committing to join the Gussellian forces, and that he and he alone was responsible for scuttling the mission. On the other hand, Amaria praised herself for meeting with Colleto on her own to pry this important information from Gussellia's leader. She was a model of courage, in her own words.

"And what proof do we have that she was told those things?" Quint asked the colonel.

"Is proof needed to compare the word of a hubite to the word of a general's daughter?" Colonel Gerocie asked.

"Yes," Quint said, but he knew the correct answer. Probably not.

"What will happen?"

"Separately, General Baltacco has recommended stripping your rank to sergeant while charges of treason are being evaluated," the colonel said.

Quint sat back, amazed. "Are they forcing me to join forces with Pacci Colleto?"

"You tell me, Captain." The colonel put emphasis on his title.

"No. Why would I jump from the frying pan into the fire," Quint said. "The Baltaccos, father and daughter, hate me personally. I don't think their attitudes would change if I was a willot. Amaria sees me as competition, although I don't know why." Quint hadn't mentioned Baltacco's portent in his report.

"You are rising in the wizard corps despite being a hubite, and she is relying on her daddy's largesse. General Obellia said he would transfer you from the wizard corps to his division if a demotion was in the works. He believes your report and properly sees Amaria's as the words of a jealous woman. Any sane person would see it the same way unless she had proof. Don't worry about your knowledge of the willot language. General Obellia sees that as an asset in your case."

"Thank you, ma'am," Quint said. "What do I do now?"

"I'd say you have a large backlog of work since you were gone. Get to it, but before that, go home and get a good night's rest. Dismissed."

The Gussellian journal was fascinating after Quint's recent assignment. After his brief conversation with Pacci Colleto, he could more easily pick out propaganda from certain articles. The journal was full of indicators about the war footing in Gussellia.

The other countries were turning into enemies. The Racellian incursion was mentioned in three different articles including one on crop irrigation. He still had a list of words he didn't know, but the context clarified many of the meanings.

His report was eight pages long which was exceptional for a single publication. Quint didn't have access to previously reviewed journals, but he wondered when the slanted articles began. Did they predate Colleto's rise to power?

"Do we have a Gussellian expert anywhere?" Quint asked the colonel when he submitted his reports from his work the previous day.

"Access would come through General Obellia's office." The colonel looked down at Quint's Gussellian journal analysis. "You want verification of what you found?"

Quint nodded. "I may be missing something."

"I'll take this to the general today and see what he has to say. On first glance it seems you have connected a lot of strings."

"I don't want them cast in our direction," Quint said.

☙

Two weeks later an orderly was waiting for Quint to arrive for work.

"Colonel Gerocie wanted you to read this and then come to her office, sir." The orderly struggled saying the honorific.

It was a newssheet with the day's date. Quint read the first page and could tell why it was suddenly a priority.

A herald arrived from Gussellia for the council. Gussellia had just announced an alliance with Vinellia, whom it shared a border on the southeast side of the country. The king of Vinellia recognized Pacci Colleto as the emperor of a united Gussellia which included his country. The king would continue to administer Vinellia, subservient to Gussellia.

Quint sat back in his new chair and smelled the fresh paint of his office. He had to do the work himself, but his space looked much better even if it was the only office in the basement of the building.

He hoped thinking about his freshened environment would help cushion the blow, but it didn't. Gussellia was now an empire consisting of almost half of South Fenola. One down and two to go for Pacci Colleto, thought Quint.

He analyzed the article as he usually did and read the rest of the newssheet, looking for related articles and spotted one that discussed the usefulness of a council style of government. The article was ostensibly for the council model, but Quint identified a few paragraphs that cast doubt on the model in favor of a stronger executive, like a kingdom or an empire. He didn't recall an article like that before and included it with his analysis of the article on the formation of the Gussellian Empire.

The same orderly showed up and asked Quint to accompany him to the Colonel's office.

Quint was astounded to greet General Obellia and Henricco Lucheccia. That was three levels of the diplomatic corps.

"Sit, Tirolo," Lucheccia said. "You have an analysis of this morning's article?"

Quint saluted and handed his work along with the newssheet to Colonel Gerocie. She read it and handed it to Lucheccia.

He nodded as he read. "This is consistent with your other reports on our delegation to Nornotta."

"It is. The dictator is no more. Pacci Colleto now styles himself as an emperor," Quint said. "He said he has taken a liking to ruling."

"And Baltacco's daughter had come up with a different view of Colleto, if you sifted through all the insults to you, Captain Tirolo," the general said.

"What do you suggest we do?" Henricco said.

"Fight or capitulate," Quint said. "I'm sure that was the alternatives that Pacci Colleto gave the king of Vinellia."

"It was," Henricco said. "I don't think the council has an appetite for capitulation."

"Then you have to fire some generals." Quint looked at Obellia. "That doesn't include you, general."

"Good. How gracious of you, Captain," the general said tugging on his tunic. "What kind of position are you in to suggest something as drastic as that?"

"Because they aren't good battle strategists. If Racellia uses the tired old tactics I've seen on two occasions, we will lose as we did when we last fought Gussellia and Barellia."

"We didn't lose in Barellia," General Obellia said.

"Did we win?" Quint asked.

"Uh."

"He has a point, general," Henricco said.

"And how would we prosecute a war?"

Quint laughed. "I'm not the one to ask. You should talk to Colonel Sarrefo of the Strategic Operations division of the Wizard Corps. Let him be honest. The wizard corps leadership and the army leadership are not serving the country well, in my opinion."

"And you'd be executed if you voiced that opinion anywhere but here, Tirolo," Obellia said. "Grand Marshal Guilica would be the first to plunge the blade."

"Quint gives us accurate information without thinking about the consequences. See why I like his analyses?" Colonel Gerocie said.

"I'll get together with Sarrefo this afternoon. I think I've heard enough." The general turned to Quint. "In this case I think the objectivity of a hubite gives me hope that we won't be swallowed up by Gussellia."

"You are dismissed, captain," Gerocie said. "You still have catching up to do."

Quint stood and saluted before leaving the office. When he was alone in his office, he put his head in his hands and took some deep breaths. The comment that rolled through his mind was the one about being executed for his opinions.

Colonel Gerocie had all the proof she needed if someone wanted to execute him. To a reasonable person what was proven was analysis, but to someone like General Baltacco, the truth wasn't necessary.

CHAPTER TWENTY-FOUR
~

For a week, life returned back to some semblance of normal. There were articles about the Vinellian Capitulation as the newssheets were calling the creation of the Gussellian Empire. There was talk of enlisting allies from off the continent of South Fenola, and Marena said there was talk of the international quarter expanding with an expected influx of foreigners. Marena's rumors made it into Quint's reports.

On top of the periodicals, Colonel Gerocie had placed a thick book written in common. The book was an analysis of empires that had come and gone in the last two thousand years, and it was written by a diplomat from Narukun in North Fenola, the continent to the northeast of South Fenola.

Gerocie had slipped a note into the book. All it said was "Read this. High priority."

Quint flipped the pages. It looked like a textbook. Too many pages were his first thought, but after he quickly went through the periodicals, he opened the book and began to read.

What he thought was dry and uninteresting was the opposite. The author, Fedor Danko, a professor at Narukun University, made the historical events read like fiction. As Quint read on, he wondered if it was fiction.

Quint began taking notes to remember all the empires. Danko had a master list at the beginning of the book. There were twenty-three that Danko identified, and at two times in two thousand years there were empires that embraced the whole world.

The book had a list of the empires and the dates of their beginning and their end. None lasted more than three hundred years, and most didn't make it past fifty. That was enough for one, two, or three emperors.

The worldwide empires lasted less than one hundred years before they crumbled.

Now it was time to read the details. Quint was fascinated by the reasons for the empire, the assimilation of cultures, and what factors led to the end. With his experience analyzing hundreds of publications, Quint knew how to pull the pertinent information out of Danko's writings and after notes for the first three empires, he knew what notes to take.

He worked late at his desk and then took the book home, working through the night. Quint asked Marena to deliver a message to Colonel Gerocie that he would be absent for two days and return with the book report.

Quint spent lunch and dinner as a break from his reading and used the time to think about what he had read. His concept of the world began to change.

There once was a hubite empire that spread from North Fenola to South Fenola. The empire was built by an emperor with a thirst for power and blood. The hubites treated their willot subjects no differently than the willots who currently hated the hubites.

Quint wondered if that hatred for hubites had been the result of the subjugation.

Like most empires, it started to crumble with power struggles within and revolts externally. As Quint read on, it was the most common cause for most of the empires.

The powerful emperors typically wanted their progeny to rule, and the descendants were never the equal of the first emperors. The longest lasting empires did not permit relatives assuming the imperial throne, and when times changed that rule, the empire inevitably declined.

Quint had first wondered how empires failed. As he finished the book, his viewpoint changed to wondering how an empire could ever succeed in the long-term. There were too many factors to overcome that could result in a long-lasting government. Were monarchies like that? He wondered about a council model. He found that he would like to spend time with Fedor Danko to answer his questions.

His book notes covered forty pages before Quint replicated the chart of empires. He spent the night of his second day away from work distilling his studies to a ten-page summary for Colonel Gerocie.

He waited for the colonel to arrive with his report in a portfolio. The book was still at home along with his book notes. While he waited, he reread the page that characterized what he thought Pacci Colleto was about. It was unclear if Colleto was really interested in expanding out of South Fenola as it was too early in Colleto's empire-building to determine that.

The colonel arrived and let Quint follow her inside.

"You've finished that thick thing?" the colonel asked.

"It was enlightening," Quint said.

Gerocie smiled. "When are you starting your own empire?"

"I don't think I would make a suitable emperor. There is a certain ruthlessness that I do not possess," Quint said, "and every successful emperor had a streak of that in their personality."

"I can breathe easy then?" the colonel asked.

"You can, ma'am. Here is my report. My book notes are more comprehensive, but this tells the story." He gave the portfolio to the colonel and sat down.

"Can I read this in front of you? I might have questions as I go."

"My time is your time, Colonel Gerocie," Quint said.

The colonel asked a few inconsequential questions before sitting back. "Your usual incisive job. What you are telling me is that if Racellia is patient enough Colleto's empire will fade away."

"Guaranteed, ma'am, but we may all be dead by the time that happens."

"Maybe me, but certainly not you," the colonel said.

"The factors of decline vary all over the place, but decline there will be, according to Fedor Danko."

"Yes, Fedor Danko. He is coming to Bocarre at the end of this week with his daughter, Calee Danko. The council has given him a one-month contract to analyze the current situation on South Fenola. That is why I gave you the book to read."

"Aren't I doing that?" Quint asked.

"You are, but the council has less faith in a teenage hubite from an obscure southeast Racellian village. That is why Henricco Lucheccia requested you for another assignment. You are to escort the Dankos if they are in Racellia. They are hubites, like you, captain."

"Do you want someone to check on Danko?"

"We do and there is no one more qualified to do that now that you've read his seminal publication on empires."

Quint had no reason to object to the assignment, and he was excited to be able to talk to Danko about his book and other political organizations.

"I will be happy to fulfill the assignment. What will I need to do?"

"You've done it. Read his book, talk to him about it, verify the references he has made, and see what his true opinions are about the survival of Racellia."

"You want me to cast a non-magical portent?"

"And you are just the wizard to do it, captain."

"You've never asked me to cast a magical portent."

Colonel Gerocie looked out the window for a moment. "I've asked General Obellia, who admitted he doesn't believe in them, especially for something so involved as Colleto's empire."

"Do you want me to try?" Quint asked.

"Have you already done it?" Gerocie asked, almost breathlessly.

"I'm more in the general's camp on the matter. There are too many factors that can pull the visualized portent away from certainty."

"Obellia put it almost in those exact terms."

"In the meantime, I continue my periodical work?"

"Yes. I have more journals from Gussellia coming in. You'll get them as soon as they arrive."

"More propaganda, ma'am," Quint said, "but we need to keep looking for trends. As I have noted, even propaganda can reveal hidden truths."

The colonel smiled. "I like that. Can I use it with my peers and the general?"

"Of course, but I'm sure you've realized that already."

"But the important thing is that you discovered it on your own, captain. You are my hidden weapon."

"Not so hidden," Quint said. "Colleto knows what I do, and he probably has spies everywhere, and he isn't the only one with spies," Quint said. "Baltacco has his own, I'm sure."

Gerocie smiled. "Spies keep you on your toes."

"May I ask if anything has happened on the battle management front?" Quint asked.

"A difficult question to answer. Unfortunately, it is hard to satisfy all the council members at once and Lucheccia is still collecting sponsors."

"I'll not ask again, but keep my nose in the newssheets, ma'am."

"You do that, Captain Tirolo. Dismissed." She held up the portfolio with Quint's analysis. "I can keep this?"

"You can. I have a copy, and the book, and the book notes."

"You may keep them at least for the time Fedor Danko is in Racellia."

~

Quint stood at the flat's large window looking over Bocarre toward the sea. The colonel's comment on spies to keep him on his toes disturbed him. Quint was getting too exposed as a magician and an analyst. No one really cared about Quint the hubite, but Colleto was intensely interested in him when they met in Nornotta.

He looked around his room to decide what was most important to him. The string books, his own and the copy of Colleto's, topped the list. The problem wasn't making duplicate copies, but where to keep them.

Quint decided to put a false bottom in one of the drawers of his new desk and the other, the backup, needed a hiding place outside the flat. The first thing was to make the copies.

After a busy weekend, Quint accomplished the first step. He measured one of the drawers and found a woodworker in the international quarter to build a box that would slip into the largest drawer in his desk.

The job took to the end of the week and Quint went into work when most others were off and installed the false bottom. It fit well and the wood was a good match with the existing drawers.

With his primary copy hidden at the diplomacy corps offices, Quint decided to ask Marena.

"I want some documents kept outside the flat," Quint said.

"Secret documents? Are you afraid we will be invaded by burglars?" Marena said with a smile on her face.

"Actually, yes," Quint said. "My room was gone over when I stayed at the Gussellian palace. It's probably called the imperial palace by now. I don't expect to be burglarized, but I don't want to leave my documents exposed."

"Give it to me. Put a six-figure number on the top page and on the envelope that you will remember so they can know it's you if you come to retrieve your documents. I'm still thinking of a good place, one that isn't connected with you and barely connected with me."

Quint grinned. "That's the spirit. Spy protection."

Marena smiled. "Something like that."

Two days later, Quint felt relieved when Marena gave him an address. "Just tell them the number," she said.

"You know them well?"

"No. That's the point. But I have known of them for a long time," Marena said. "They will be safe."

☙

Colonel Gerocie called Quint up from the basement.

"Sit, Captain."

"Yes, ma'am," Quint said.

"There is a reception tonight at the Council Palace for Fedor Danko. General Obellia has designated you as an attendee. Secretary Lucheccia and the general will also be in attendance. As will be Grand Marshal Tracco Guilica, the head of the military and a council member. Avoid him if possible. Your role as aide and escort begins tonight. Are you ready?"

"As long as my black uniform is presentable."

"It is. Arrive at the Council Palace fifteen minutes before seven-thirty."

"Yes ma'am."

"And captain. Look smart. Dismissed."

Quint furrowed his brow on the way out. He didn't know if the colonel meant to look orderly and well-groomed or look like an intellectual. Quint couldn't go back and embarrass himself by asking, so he would do his best to do both.

Marena helped Quint with his appearance. His uniform needed brushing, which he had missed. She made him shave, a weekly occurrence, and helped him with his hair, although Quint always wore his uniform cap when he was away from the international quarter.

The time had come, and Quint headed over to the palace. He arrived a few minutes early and was shown into a large dining room that had the tables removed.

"Don't drink yourself into a stupor, captain," one of the servants said as Quint was ignored by the attendees, as usual. "The liquor is free."

Quint wasn't a drinker and asked for fruit juice as he waited.

Ten minutes before eight o'clock, people rushed into the reception. Henricco Lucheccia spotted Quint and motioned him over to him.

"The Dankos have just arrived. Stay with me so I can introduce you."

"Yes, sir," Quint said.

Two hubites, a middle-aged father and a much younger woman, presumably Danko's daughter arrived. They were announced. Henricco shuffled over to them.

"Fedor, this is your escort while you are in Bocarre. He even lives in the international quarter where you will be staying. Fedor, this is Captain Quinto Tirolo of the wizard corps. He is a Level 3 currently working in the military diplomatic corps as an analyst."

"A pleasure to meet you, Doctor Danko," Quint said. "I've read your book on empires." They shook hands.

"You've read all of it?" Danko asked. "What did you do to merit such a severe punishment?" Danko curled his lips.

It was a joke, Quint told himself and he took it as that he shouldn't gush about the publication. "I'm keeping an eye open on the emerging Gussellian Empire," Quint said.

"Henricco said you've met Pacci Colleto."

"A few times," Quint said.

"We will have to discuss it, but not here," Danko said.

The reception had devolved into clusters of people who knew each other. A few had come over to Fedor Danko to introduce themselves. A few appeared uncomfortable. Quint was used to the look.

"I'll take you around and introduce you to the council members and a few others whom I know," Henricco said. The secretary of foreign affairs looked at Quint. "Why don't you accompany Calee? We will find you."

Calee gave Quint a pained smile as she watched her father ushered to meet another embarrassed willot.

"I knew South Fenola countries didn't like hubites, but it comes through loud and clear. Are the other countries like Racellia?"

Quint nodded. "I'm afraid they are."

"How do you stand it?"

"The antagonistic attitudes? There isn't much I can do about it. I was pressed into the army two years ago. I can't leave the wizard corps for another three years."

"How old are you?"

"Seventeen," Quint said.

"One year older than I am, and you are a captain? How did that happen."

"Evidently, I have a talent for magic. They couldn't restrain my learning and by the time I was trained, I was almost a Level 3 wizard, which I am now. They put me to work with a mop, a bucket, and a dusting cloth for my first assignment because they didn't know what to do with me."

"How did you become an analyst? What do analysts do?" Calee asked.

"My superiors didn't know what to do with me, so I was assigned to strategic operations in the wizard corps and did fine with what I was given. I can provide some insight into problems. I ran afoul of General Baltacco's daughter. He is one of the leaders of the wizard corps. They put me into the military diplomatic corps, which works under Henricco Lucheccia. I was assigned to a delegation to Nornotta, the Gussellian capital. I had to be a captain to become a military advisor in the group. So that is why I am a captain."

"What do you do, though?" she asked.

"I read through periodicals and journals and give my opinions on events that might have an effect on military operations."

"The building of empires? Is that why you read father's book?"

"It was an assignment. Twenty-three empires and a new one being born as we speak."

"There are always empires being born, but not many of them actually come to maturity."

"You know your father's works?"

"Intimately, I'm afraid. I'm the victim that has to listen to his ideas before he publishes them. My mother used to do it, but she's gone."

"I'm sorry."

"Thank you. It was a few years ago."

"What is Narukun like?" Quint asked, desperate to change the subject.

Calee shrugged. "I can call it beautiful, but everyone calls their home that. The university where father teaches is nestled in a little valley that it shares with a village full of craftsmen of all types."

"My father is a craftsman. He makes wagon and carriage wheels."

"A wheelwright?"

Quint nodded. "He makes the best in our district."

"What comprises a Racellian district?"

"A few villages and a town. We can't go outside our district without permission, and for hubites, that means you can't go outside your district. The town intersects with two other districts, so my father has a larger market for his wheels."

"But he is suppressed by the government?"

Quint looked around to see if anyone could hear. "You might say that, but the system makes things orderly."

"We will have to talk about that system with my father, sometime. He has a different vision for working people, let us say."

"I got glimpses of his attitude in his writings on empire, but he hid his biases well," Quint said.

"On purpose," Calee said. "What do you do for recreation?"

Quint shrugged.

"Diversions. Plays, restaurants, readings, walks, those kinds of things," Calee said.

"I learn magic strings," Quint frowned. He didn't want to tell her he had no one to spend time with. "Sometimes I sit out in the sun and absorb its energy."

"In other words, you don't have a life."

"Under your terms, no," Quint said.

She grinned. "If you will be our escort, then you'll have to live a little different while we are here."

"What specifically did you do in your university town?"

"The university put on plays, but," she shrugged. "We don't have to attend any plays. Father likes them better than I do. We did attend music and poetry events."

"There isn't much interest in that in the wizard corps and I don't socialize with Colonel Gerocie's staff," Quint said.

"We can walk around the international quarter. Perhaps I can find out what other people do," Calee said.

"Isn't that what the escort is supposed to do?"

She laughed. "I doubt if you can do a good enough job."

PAGE 192 | The Wizard Corps

"Maybe not," Quint admitted.

CHAPTER TWENTY-FIVE

"How did the reception go last night?" Colonel Gerocie said on one of her occasional visits to his office. She looked around the redecorated office. "This is much better, by the way."

"My landlady helped with the concept. Not that there is much of a concept."

"Matching office furniture is a concept, captain," Gerocie said.

"In my opinion, they were taken aback by the cold attitudes of the attendees. I think quite a few of the people who showed up were attracted by the free alcoholic drinks," Quint said. "They were careful not to complain, but there might be some observational bias on my part."

Gerocie laughed. "Observational bias. You are reading some of the books I've given you."

Quint could have told Calee that he read books on observations and argument, but he didn't think that would impress her.

"Did they discuss when they would need you?"

Quint nodded. "They move into their provided flat tomorrow. Then we will get together. I'm going to talk to my landlady about what they can do in the international quarter. I don't think willots will care that they are foreign dignitaries outside of the quarter."

"I'm afraid you're right. I can set up another office in the basement for

Fedor Danko if he's looking for a more professional environment than a kitchen table in his flat."

"I'll ask him. Perhaps the foreign secretary has something arranged."

Gerocie pursed her lips. "I was told to be ready to set something up by General Obellia."

"Then will it be ready in time?" Quint asked.

Gerocie gave Quint a sick smile. "Actually, I was thinking of giving him this office while you perform your decorating magic on another room down here. There is a larger storage room with a window two doors down."

Quint closed his eyes and then popped them open. He didn't want to show the colonel how irritated he was.

"Of course. When I finish with the other office, he can choose which one he likes better," Quint said.

"Good. I'm glad we think so much alike," the colonel said. "You can get started immediately. The storage room has a key." She pulled it out of a pocket and put in on Quint's desk.

The storage room made a better office in Quint's eyes. The window well was deeper and that brought more light into the room. He didn't know where to put the old cabinets, shelves and files, but he dragged them out into the hallway and told the orderly who delivered that day's publications to get someone to find a place for the displaced items.

Quint knew how to order everything and requested the same office furniture as his with an extra set of shelves and two more side chairs for visitors. He measured the room again and ordered a table, with the intent to move Danko into the new office when it was done.

Two days later, Quint was called to the colonel's office and met Calee and Fedor Danko.

"Captain Tirolo begins his assignment today," Colonel Gerocie said. "You will take the Danko's down to the basement and show our guest his new office."

The large office was getting prepared to paint and the furniture wasn't due to arrive for another week. Quint had to figure out what to do during that time.

"As you can see, we are building a new office for you down with me."

"In the basement," Fedor Danko said.

"Yes, the basement," Quint said. "I'll take back my office when yours is ready sometime next week. The office was a last-minute decision. We didn't want you to have to use your flat."

"But I like my flat," Danko said. "I can get up, walk around and chat with my daughter when I need to. Are you required to give up your working space?"

Quint nodded. "I get your new office when you leave," Quint said.

"That's fair enough," Danko said. He looked at his daughter and winked at her.

Quint wondered if they already had other arrangements.

Danko clapped his hand on Quint's shoulder. "I'll show up when I need to, how is that?"

"Perfect," Quint said. At least Fedor Danko showed some reasonableness.

"Why don't we walk to the international quarter. I'll let you see our flat and we can get something to eat. There is a North Fenolan restaurant in the quarter, although it is run by willots. We can try that."

"Great," Quint said.

He left a message at the front desk for Colonel Gerocie and joined the Dankos for a stroll to the international quarter. Quint wore his cap, but the Danko father and daughter were bareheaded. Their light hair fluttered in the breeze bringing stares from passersby.

Quint was used to it, but he doubted if Fedor and Calee were. He relaxed a bit when they crossed the street into his neighborhood.

Calee laughed. "It's as if the pressure of life dissipated as soon as we came here."

"It is like that," Quint said. "I used to live in barracks, and it wasn't easy."

"Are you the only hubite in the army?" Fedor asked.

"There are a few others, but they are common soldiers, the basic level. I imagine they have it tougher than I do. Being a Level 3 has certain advantages and a tiny bit more acceptance with certain people. Others will never give a hubite a chance."

"We are through this alley, I believe," Fedor said.

Quint took the same alley to his flat. He wondered if the army had put up the Dankos in the same building, but no. Fedor passed the alley gate to Quint's building and walked through the third gate along the way into a nicer building.

"I live back there," Quint said, "four stories up."

"Then you get more exercise than we will," Fedor said. "We are on the second floor."

Quint followed them up the tenant stairs. There was a leather shop on the ground level.

"I'm afraid there might be some extra sounds during the day, but I didn't hear anything yesterday and last night. Did you, Calee?"

She shook her head as she took out a key and let them in.

The flat was as big as Marena's, maybe a little bigger with an extra bedroom.

"You can use the third bedroom as your office," Quint said as he noticed fancier furniture in the Danko flat.

"That's what we intend doing," Calee said, "but father can visit the council palace from the closer office."

"Whatever works at the time," Fedor said.

The pair was apologetic about it. Quint wasn't used to so much politeness.

"Now that you've seen our lodgings, we can eat. I'm starving," Fedor said.

The restaurant was advertised as Slinnon cuisine, but Danko thought the claim was dubious.

"My landlady's husband was from Slinnon. Her son lives there."

"And she didn't leave with him?" Calee said.

"Marena has roots in Racellia," Quint said, hoping that would be enough of an explanation for the Dankos. "I've never eaten Slinnon food unless she's cooked it for us and didn't say anything."

"Us?" Calee asked.

"She was the housekeeper for my last flat. I shared with some of my strategic operations colleagues. There were three who tolerated me. Marena was hired as the housekeeper. She offered her son's room. She is my landlady and flatmate."

"Has she behaved herself?"

Quint laughed. "Her son is a year older than I am."

"I'm sure moving to the international quarter has been a good thing."

"It has," Quint said. "Shall we order?"

Fedor laughed. He knew Quint was changing the subject. "Sure. Shall we tell you what we think is good? Narukun food is different from Slinnon since Slinnon is a country filled with polens and polen culture is from a different source than Narukun and Kippun."

After ordering, Quint asked how polen culture was different from hubite culture.

Hubites invaded North Fenola from South Fenola. The polens had developed a different religion and a more bureaucratic culture. Hubites, at the time, were tribal based that promoted individual achievements."

"A warrior mentality?" Quint asked.

"Very much so. The polens learned how to defeat the hubites in battle, but they were only able to claw back the areas now known as Pogokon and Slinnon. Originally, Willots were being pushed out of Baxel by the grans, an offshoot of hubites forcing them to South Fenola, where they eventually pushed the hubites into North Fenola after rebelling against the hubites that had made migrating willots into slaves."

"Has the migrating of races stopped?" Quint asked.

"No. I have no doubt the hubites remaining in Racellia will be pushed out at some point of time. If the Racellians don't do it, the expanding Gussellian empire might cleanse South Fenola of their former slave masters, the hubites."

"And the empires overlay everything?"

"The interactions aren't that simple. The cultures can drive the elements that lead to empire building or it can be the other way around. Although there are similar patterns of empire, the causes that initiate the empires vary. I don't get into that aspect of empire, culture, and migration in my empire book. I didn't want to write more than one volume."

"One thick volume," Quint said.

"You really did read it all?"

"I even wrote a report on what I read."

Fedor leaned forward. "I'd like to read your observations and maybe we can discuss your insights."

"I'm sure they aren't very original," Quint said.

"You might surprise yourself."

The food arrived.

"What are these?" Quint asked.

"Eating sticks, a polen innovation. The cuisine was affected by the polens using these rather than the other way around. We can talk about some of the origins that make up the polen culture later.

Quint wanted to talk about the hubites and Racellia, but it wasn't the time for a serious conversation, and they talked about the food.

"It's close, but not really authentic," Calee said. "I would guess a polen started the restaurant and then it changed hands. The menu didn't change, but the technique and some of the ingredients did.

The meal was over, and Quint paid for it as instructed by the colonel.

"If I can find the right ingredients, Calee and I will make you something more authentic. There are many polen eating establishments in Kippun and Narukun. I suspect you've never eaten traditional hubite food."

"I have. There is a Narukun restaurant, but I thought I would save that for another time," Quint said.

Calee laughed. "Father actually likes polen cuisine more than Narukun."

☙

A message was waiting when Quint showed up requesting his presence upstairs.

"The Danko's aren't coming in today. They'd rather wait for the office to be finished. Fedor has set up an office in the spare bedroom at his flat," Quint said.

"That is fine. Fedor doesn't have meetings scheduled until next week. I want daily reports from you. Henricco would like to know what you talk about with the Dankos and any opinions that might arise from those communications."

"I am to spy?" Quint asked. He was upset enough not to have included an honorific.

"To be honest this time that is exactly what we want you to do, captain," the colonel's tone turned frosty. "If you want to share what you observe with the Dankos feel free. If you are hiding anything from us, your personal situation may be at risk," the colonel said.

"Who is us, ma'am?"

"The foreign ministry, of which you are a part. You are part of us, captain. Did anything happen of note?"

"We ate at a Slinnon restaurant. There are polen restaurants throughout the two hubite countries, Danko said. "He also gave me a history lesson on how one group pushes another off the continent and it becomes a succession of migrations. I never knew that hubites enslaved willots who had immigrated from Baxel."

"I'm sure your knowledge of world history will greatly expand while

Fedor Danko is here. Better you than me," the colonel said.

Quint wanted to follow up, but he had already pushed the colonel too far, something he regretted.

"Is that all? I'm behind in my reading."

"It is. Although you gave me a verbal report, I will still need you to write that up. We will want Doctor Danko's words monitored."

The basket was waiting on his desk. He peeked into the newly painted office and found the bookshelves had arrived, but the desk, table, and chairs were still to come.

On top of the basket were three Gussellian journals. Those had the top priority. The articles were more of the same Gussellian propaganda, but where there were always disparaging remarks about Vinellia, this time there were none. Barellia was attracting the most ire. Since Quint began reading the Gussellian journals, Racellia was always under assault, but the overt insults were growing, especially from one of the authors who hadn't been aggressively anti-Racellian before.

Quint noted domestic references and he detected an increase in the mentions of economic activity. Could it be due to the ramping up of a wartime economy? He posed the question but didn't have any answer. Quint suggested that someone in Vinellia find out if the Gussellian forces were doing any peacekeeping. That was one way for Gussellia to implement a soft invasion.

There was nervousness evident in many articles in the two other South Fenolan countries. Quint looked for evidence of defensive mobilization but didn't find anything.

His analysis took him to the end of his day. He finished his reports and brought the basket up to the diplomatic corps offices. The colonel was still in, so he delivered his notes in person.

"Are we still surly?" Colonel Gerocie asked.

"No, ma'am. I get an impression that the economy of Gussellia is becoming more active. They may be shifting to a wartime footing and that might be driving up Gussellian economic activity. The other note is that I think we should monitor how many Gussellian troops are in Vinellia. Despite their agreement of cooperation, Gussellia could be occupying Vinellia, which would indicate a circling of Gussellian forces around most of Racellia," Quint said.

"That's a lot of 'ellias' for me to keep track of. If I need to get things straightened out, I'll let you know if I need you tomorrow." She gave Quint a smile. "I'm glad you worked out your attitude, captain. Have a good evening."

※

CHAPTER TWENTY-SIX

WHEN QUINT ARRIVED AT THE FLAT, Marena opened the door before Quint could turn the latch.

"We have guests," Marena said.

Quint fully expected to be greeted by Fedor and Calec Danko, but two gentlemen dressed in black sat together on the couch. As Quint stepped in, another leaned against the doorsill of his room.

"You have another copy of the emperor's string journal?" the man standing said in the willot language.

"It's at the corps." Quint said in common. He didn't trust his ability to speak willot.

"I think it is still here," the man said. "Shall we begin to force you to talk?" He nodded to the men in the couch. "Tie her up."

Marena struggled, but not too hard. She was no match for two men.

"Where is it?"

Quint looked at Marena and then at the man who had walked into the room, standing behind the couch.

"I suppose this means that Pacci Colleto has gotten tired of my refusal to join his empire?" Quint asked.

"I wouldn't say that, but he does have second thoughts about you having a copy of his strings."

Quint sighed. "It is in my desk at work. The bottom drawer has a false bottom." He hung his head for effect. "I already know some of the spells. Are you going to kill me?"

The man laughed. "Not at all." He looked at the other two. "Untie her and let's get the book. Tirolo doesn't deserve to have it if he capitulates so easily."

The men walked out with the spokesman strutting, much to Quint's distaste.

"Racellians?" Marena asked.

"I don't know willot well enough to know if they spoke with Racellian or Gussellian accents," Quint said.

"They convinced me," Marena said rubbing reddened wrists.

Quint looked at the front door. "How did they get in?"

Marena shrugged. "Any door lock can be picked," she said. "I came home early since my clients suddenly were asked to dine out."

"Maybe they wanted you here," Quint said. "I didn't dare use strings against them while they were standing next to you."

She managed a smile. "That's comforting to know," she said sarcastically.

"If they ramped up their threats, I would have taken action," Quint said.

"That's a better answer." She shook her head for some reason. "Are you going to retrieve your other copy?"

"What other copy?" Quint said. "What are you talking about?"

That got a nod from Marena. Someone was listening in.

"You said you had made two copies," Marena said.

"No. There were two string books: the original I returned to Colleto and the one I hid in my office." Quint frowned. "And now that is gone. I only remember a handful of strings."

"That's all I needed to have verified," said Amaria Baltacco walking out of Marena's bedroom. "My father will be happy to hear that."

Amaria smirked. "Say bye-bye to your advantage over me," she said as she left.

"And who is she?" Marena said, locking the door behind her as she returned to her living room.

"Amaria Baltacco," Quint said, or as she would say 'Senior Lieutenant Baltacco."

Marena shook her head. "She isn't exactly detached from it all, is she?"

"I think you got a strong enough taste of her." Quint told Marena of Amaria's reporting.

"General Baltacco, whoever he is, needs to put the woman across his knees and give her a good spanking with a studded belt," Marena said.

"I'm sure she desires that the wizard corps will do something more drastic with me."

"What will happen when they retrieve the string book?"

"Probably nothing," Quint said as he tiptoed to the front door. "General Obellia knows I returned the original. No one asked me if I had made a copy. If Colonel Gerocie had asked, I would have been bound to give it to her."

He heard a rustling on the other side of the door and caught the sound of footsteps in the hallway receding and going down the stairs. Quint drew away from the door.

Now everyone would know Quint had a copy, Colleto, Amaria's father, and anyone else who wanted to know. However, whoever eavesdropped, probably Amaria, would leave thinking that she would have the only copy.

The joke would be on them. Quint had memorized all the spells and had practiced quite a few. From what Pozella told him, there weren't many in Colleto's collection that were unique to Pozella's experience.

"We can talk," Quint said. "Whoever was at the door has left."

"The sneaky little witch," Marena said.

Quint winced. It had been a long time since he had heard anyone call a female wizard a witch. It was the worst insult for a woman in the wizard corps.

"No talk about the numbers," Quint said quietly, still afraid that someone would overhear their conversation.

"None at all," Marena said.

Quint had never seen her so angry, but then he was used to Amaria's tricks and had become immune to Amaria's power to aggravate him.

He sat on the couch, recently occupied by Baltacco's thugs. Quint didn't know if they were wizards or not, but he assumed they would have been. Using strings against three wizards, four including Amaria, was something Quint wanted to avoid, and despite what he told Marena, he wasn't sure he would have used his power.

"What do you know about Slinnon cooking? The Dankos took me to the Slinnon restaurant a block away from here."

Marena laughed for too long and took a deep breath. "That was a refreshing question. It isn't bad, but the food there hasn't been authentic for years," she said. "My husband used to know the Slinnon proprietors. There was a death in the family in North Fenola and they sold the restaurant and the recipes."

"And the tastes began to drift from then on?"

Marena chuckled. "That's a good way to think about it. I've eaten at the restaurant and enjoyed the meal, but it is now a Racellian version of Slinnon cuisine."

"If Calee and Fedor offer to cook a Slinnon meal would you agree to come to dinner at their flat?"

"Of course I would. I'm sure the Narukunian version of Slinnon food will be closer," Marena said. "Now, if you don't mind, I'm going to take a bath and go to bed."

⁂

After completing his report about the night's activities and the report about someone breaking down his office door and the destruction of his desk drawer, he dragged himself up to the colonel's office.

"I'm sorry to report an incident last night, ma'am," Quint said, putting his reports on her desk. "I also am reporting that my office was ransacked and a personal copy of Pacci Colleto's string book was stolen. The truth is on your desk. I'm sure you will get a different version later this morning."

Gerocie read through the reports. "Amaria Baltacco again?"

"This time she had more help. My landlady, an innocent, was tied up and threatened."

"So, this says," Gerocie said lifting the night's incident report. "What am I to make of your office break-in?"

Quint shrugged. "They took my copy, ma'am. I told them I only knew a few strings; I didn't tell the truth to them. I memorized the strings weeks ago."

Gerocie's eyebrows rose. "That means you can qualify for Master?"

Quint shrugged again. "I suppose so, but those spells need a lot of practice before I'd be proficient."

"But you could pass a Master test?" she asked.

"I think I could, ma'am."

"I must report this to General Obellia. I don't know what his reaction will be, but I have to see him immediately. Clean up your office and wait there for more orders. Are you calm enough to concentrate on another basket of publications?"

Quint nodded. "I can do that, ma'am." He saluted and left her office.

The office wasn't damaged as much as Quint thought once he picked up the papers and other writing materials that were strewn about. He put the remains of his false bottom in Danko's unfinished office.

The basket hadn't arrived yet, so Quint went over the Colleto spells in his mind and used his hands to make the weaves for the strings, but didn't go farther.

The basket came. There weren't any opinion journals this time, so it didn't take Quint long before he had nothing to do. He heard talking outside his office and observed the rest of the furniture delivered into Danko's office.

The room had been transformed from a dingy storage space to a presentable place to work, if it wasn't in the basement. Quint sat on the desk chair, it was identical to his own, and smiled.

He had been treated well, for a hubite, by Colonel Gerocie. Quint had no complaints.

There were more steps outside Danko's office and the door burst open. Black uniformed soldiers from the wizard corps marched in.

"You are under arrest!" an officer said.

"For what?" Quint asked.

"For withholding valuable information from the wizard corps."

"I'm on assignment to the Military Diplomatic Corps," Quint said.

"Don't say another word or it will go hard against you."

"Does Colonel Gerocie know about my arrest?"

The officer frowned. "This action is outside her jurisdiction. Why would she need to know?"

"I report to her," Quint said.

"Gag him first, then put on the manacles."

Quint rose from Danko's chair but was shoved back down. Two soldiers gagged him while others bound his hands in a framework that didn't allow him to create strings. He was essentially defenseless as they dragged him out of the building through a side door.

The orderly who usually delivered his baskets gave him an evil grin as he opened the door for Quint's abductors. It was useless to resist once he was outside the building and was pushed onto the floor of a waiting carriage and off he went.

Quint recognized the top of the wizard corps headquarters as they passed and turned down an alley. He was pulled out by his feet and had to tuck his chin on his chest, so his head didn't bounce on the pavement.

His captors finally helped him up so he could descend into the wizard corps basement. He was pushed into a cell and a wizard stepped forward and put Quint to sleep.

☙

Quint woke in darkness. He was on a thin mattress on a hard shelf. He couldn't generate a light or a tiny flame, but he could sit up, which he did and waited.

He woke again when someone shook him.

"Time for your trial, traitor," a familiar voice told him.

Quint opened his eyes and pursed his lips. It wasn't a surprise that Amaria Baltacco was glaring at him. She removed his gag.

"What do you have to say for yourself?"

"How am I a traitor? My commanding officer knew all about the copy of Colleto's strings long before you knew."

Amaria slapped Quint's face, something she wouldn't dare to do if Quint was unbound.

"When will I be executed?" Quint asked. "I have no expectation of a fair trial."

"That hasn't been decided yet."

"You mean your father is too busy at present to accommodate your unhinged actions?"

That earned Quint another slap.

"You are slapping a superior officer, lieutenant," Quint said.

Amaria's face twisted with her hatred. "You are no real captain. I've already removed your ill-gotten captain badges."

"Is the prisoner up?" an officer stepped into Quint's cell. He looked closely at Quint's face and then turned to Amaria. "You slapped him?"

"He was being disrespectful."

"Of Racellia? Of the wizard corps?" the officer asked.

"No," Amaria said, lifting her chin. "Of me."

The officer sighed. "If he is acquitted, he can charge you for insubordination, Lieutenant Baltacco."

"Father would never permit it."

The officer put a hand over his face. "We are close enough to the edge by arresting him."

"My father will protect all of us, even after he is executed."

The officer looked at Quint. "Time for a hearing. You are not permitted to cast strings while you are in custody. Remember that."

Quint nodded while a soldier removed the manacles. Quint took a step toward Amaria, who ran to the door.

"I'm ready," he said to the officer.

There were wizards ahead of him and behind him on the steps leading to the main floor where Quint was ushered to a conference room set up for his hearing. Three black-garbed officers, all ranked above Captain, sat at a table. Quint's chair was a respectful distance away and chairs were behind Quint. He had seen two of the three officers before, but he was never introduced to them.

He looked back to see Amaria's angry face, but he also saw Colonel Sarrefo enter the room and take a seat. He gave Quint a nod, but his face remained impassive.

The officer in the middle, a colonel, spoke. "Captain Quinto Tirolo, there are various charges against you which are violations of the rules and regulations of the Racellian Wizard Corps. Do you admit to violating them?"

What a ridiculous question, Quint thought. They weren't going to tell him what he was charged with?

"Yes or no, Captain Tirolo."

"I don't know what the charges are, sir."

The officer looked at someone behind Quint. "He doesn't know what he's been charged with?"

"No, sir," the officer who led Quint from the prison said.

"There are three counts for withholding evidence from your superior officers within the corps. There is a count of seizing Racellian property and using it for your own purposes. The last count is that you have been observed speaking in the willot language."

"There is a formal law against that?" Quint asked.

"You will speak only when spoken to, captain," the colonel said. "Now that you know the charges. Yes or no. Did you violate your oath to the wizard corps.

"No," Quint said. "I did not violate my oath."

"You know the willot language?" the colonel said.

"I know the language, yes. I learned it so I could evaluate opinion journals from other South Fenolan countries. I do not speak the language, although I can understand most of it when spoken."

"Who witnessed the defendant speaking willot?"

Amaria spoke. "How can one not speak willot if they know how to read it? It doesn't need to be observed."

"Lieutenant. You are also advised to speak only when you are spoken to."

Colonel Sarrefo rose. "May I speak, colonel?"

"Go ahead."

"What law prohibits a member of the wizard corps from knowing willot? There are speaking prohibitions, but if no one has heard Quint speak our mother tongue, why charge him for doing so."

The lead officer pursed his lips. "Is there anyone in this hearing who has heard the defendant speak willot?

No one spoke up.

"We will strike that count from the charges. Now, what about the other counts?"

Amaria shot up and left the hearing room.

"I was assigned to work within the military diplomatic corps. I kept my superior, Colonel Julia Gerocie, informed every step of the way or shortly after a significant event, such as the break-in of my flat by members of the wizard corps where my landlady was threatened. She should be asked if she knows of my withholding anything."

"We will save that for your trial, captain. "You said you were forced to reveal where the copy of the Gussellian emperor's string book was hidden?"

"I was. I was threatened by harm to my landlady. The book was hidden to keep it safe. My office doesn't have a lock on the door."

"But you used magical means to seal your office?"

"Whoever burglarized my office defeated the lock with magic. They knew where the copy was kept."

"Would you have surrendered the string book, if asked?"

"Not to a subordinate officer without any orders. I've been working in a different chain of command for nearly a year," Quint said. "I would have complied with any orders from my chain of command. I've not withheld evidence from my chain of command."

"This is irregular," the colonel said.

A tall, thin man barged into the room. "He is guilty and should be executed. End of hearing."

"General Baltacco," the colonel said as everyone in the room stood including Quint. Amaria stepped back into the room.

"I've read the evidence. It is ridiculous to think Tirolo wouldn't speak willot. I reject his reason," Baltacco said.

"You wish to override the matters of this hearing?" the colonel asked.

"I do and who will stop me?"

"I will, General Baltacco," General Obellia said, walking in followed by Henricco Lucheccia, the foreign minister, and Colonel Gerocie. "What is going on here? One of my soldiers has been abducted, and I just heard you condemn him to death."

Baltacco frowned. "It is a matter of speech. Of course I want justice to be served."

"When is the trial scheduled?" Obellia asked.

"After the hearing," the lead interrogator said.

"Without notifying me, without notifying his commanding officer, and without a reasonable consideration of the evidence," General Obellia said.

"I will be putting Captain Tirolo under house arrest in my building until these matters are resolved. What are the charges?" General Obellia asked the lead colonel.

"Three counts of withholding evidence to his superior officer, a count of using Racellian property for his own benefit and a count of a non-willot speaking in the mother tongue."

"Ridiculous. Even I know about the captain's facility for understanding willot. He has never, to my knowledge ever spoken a word, although he uses his knowledge to conduct valuable research on our foreign enemies, some of whom speak willot exclusively. As for withholding evidence, you had better clear those charges through Colonel Gerocie. She tells me that Captain Tirolo has been scrupulous. Scrupulous is the exact word that she said, about keeping her informed. He writes daily reports about his activities. Do any of you?" General Obellia looked around the room. "Even I know about the dictator's string book. I was notified that Captain Tirolo forwarded the original to Colleto soon after he returned to Bocarre. He would have been irresponsible if he hadn't made a copy, and he wasn't commanded to do so. That is not in violation of any order."

Baltacco turned red in the face. "Amaria, I will talk to you later."

Quint thought blaming his daughter on everything was shameless. Her reports required complicity on his part, but Baltacco wasn't going to bring that up to anyone.

"Restriction to your unit is acceptable until charges are formalized, and a thorough investigation is conducted." Baltacco made a military about face and left the room.

Obellia turned to Quint. "Colonel Gerocie will escort you back to the diplomacy corps offices where we will determine where you will be staying for the near future."

Gerocie led Quint out of the room, but not before Quint gave a nod to his old officer in the strategic operations division.

Chapter Twenty-Seven

"I'M SORRY IT'S COME TO THIS, MA'AM," Quint said as they entered Gerocie's office. The colonel had advised silence on their return trip.

"We have a suite for dignitaries on the fourth floor. You may use that for now," she said. "What happened yesterday?"

Quint told her about the wizard corps soldiers barging into Danko's office and didn't forget to mention the orderly who helped them.

"Amaria was there for all of it?"

Quint nodded. "She was directing the activities and remained behind to catch me. She even spoke willot to me, which I didn't reply, since I truly don't know much about the pronunciation."

"Is there anything else that could come up? They will be searching for everything."

Quint shrugged. "That is it. I'm sure Amaria is thinking about what evidence she can fake. Her father…"

'Don't talk about her father, even between the two of us," Gerocie said. "If it wasn't for Colonel Sarrefo, we wouldn't have known. You have at least one willot supporter in the wizard corps." Gerocie went to a window and looked at the council palace. "I'll talk to the general about what to do. There isn't much support for hubites in that building," she pointed a finger at the council headquarters across the grounds.

"Can I get a bag of my things and return, ma'am?" Quint asked.

"You'll be escorted," Gerocie said.

Quint smiled. "I'm amenable, ma'am."

In a few minutes, Quint and three soldiers left the military intelligence building and began the walk to his flat. Quint took them along the alleyway that was a shortcut to his building and as they stepped into the backyard of his building, they were attacked by wizards.

The ambush was so unexpected, Quint was again put to sleep.

He woke bound much the same way he had been on his first abduction, but he was ungagged. The carriage was speeding through the countryside.

"Where are you taking me?" Quint asked, struggling briefly with his bonds, but they were too secure.

"You'll find out soon enough," one of his abductors said. The man held his hands out in front of him and Quint, without any kind of a shield, fell asleep again.

The next time Quint's consciousness surfaced; he recognized his surroundings. They were approaching the city of Nornotta. Quint had been kidnapped by Pacci Colleto, the Emperor of the Gussellian Empire.

Quint's shackles were removed as he exited the carriage. He was escorted through the familiar corridors of the Colleto's palace, allowed to wash up and eat a quick meal in a set of rooms, before he was taken to the door to Colleto's study where his escort knocked on the door and gently pushed Quint inside.

"We meet again," Colleto said with a smile. It was a sinister smile in Quint's eyes.

"I wasn't prepared for such a long trip," Quint said. He thought he'd be afraid, but curiously, he wasn't.

Colleto laughed. "I don't have much time. I've had my people monitoring your activities in Bocarre. It was clear you were headed to the chopping block, so they had standing orders to bring you here. It was only a matter of time before others in the Racellian government ran out of tolerance for a hubite."

"I learned that General Baltacco was the one who spirited you away from the intelligence services. His daughter was involved?"

"She was," Quint said.

"Naughty little girl. Are you still reluctant to serve me?" Colleto asked. "I did just rescue you from certain death."

"I have my supporters," Quint said.

"Let me guess. General Obellia and Colonel," he looked down at some notes, "Gerocie. Baltacco ultimately has more influence, you know." Colleto squinted at Quint. "But you don't know that do you?"

"I only know they are rivals of a sort," Quint said.

"You know more about what I'm doing than what's happening in Racellia, right?"

Quint shrugged. Colleto could be setting him up talking about what Quint knew and what he didn't.

"What are you going to do with me? You could have left me at the capital. They would do the killing for you."

"If that is what I wanted, I'd probably do just that, but your portents remain, shall we say, interesting?"

"I'm not interested in serving you."

"You don't have to work for me to serve my interests, Captain Tirolo. I'm going to take you along on a quick tour of Vinellia and then to your home village."

"Why?"

"I have something to show you. I read your report on my activities in Vinellia. I think your analyses have elements of seeing into the present, which is as important as seeing into the future. But just like portents, the vision of the present is dark and unexpectedly shifts."

"You have access to my work for Colonel Gerocie?"

"I do, but I don't have anyone in her office, but elsewhere."

There had to be a spy in General Obellia's organization, probably the same person who made sure Quint was a member of the border negotiation delegation.

"We will leave tomorrow morning. I will have clothes delivered to your rooms. It wouldn't be advisable to have a Racellian wizard corps officer along for my tour."

༄

Quint was exceptionally uncomfortable riding behind Colleto. He knew where his minders were, and Quint didn't see how he'd be able to break away to escape.

He'd never been to Vinellia, and it wasn't that much different from Gussellia, except for the mountains.

Quint's focus was to verify what he had picked up from the opinion journals he had read. Colleto said he was unconsciously able to see the present with his magic, but without strings, Quint couldn't see how that could happen.

Colleto's entourage took over a large inn at a mountain town in the middle of the country.

"You will begin your Masters trial," Colleto said. "Go to the private room off the dining hall. I won't be involved." The emperor left the inn with a large group of retainers.

Quint found the room that had four wizards sitting at the table, facing the front of the room.

"Shall we get started?" one of the wizards, a woman, said.

Quint went through his string repertoire. A master could cast a minimum of fifty strings, and Quint knew more than that including the ones he picked up from Colleto's journal.

As he demonstrated he could create the appropriate weaves for the strings, one of the evaluators called Quint out. "These aren't in the emperor's journal."

"Is that a requirement?" Quint asked.

"No, but it is unexpected. The emperor said you probably memorized all his strings."

"I have, but I qualified for Level 3 before I ever met Pacci Colleto."

Quint continued and when he was finished, which was past dinner time, the evaluators counted seventy-three strings. The number surprised Quint as he hadn't intended to show so many. He knew more, but those were the marginal strings where he had less control.

"Six psychic and twenty-eight physical strings. You are a true master. How do you remember so many with you being a hubite."

"I can't answer that," Quint said. "Hubites can be smart. Doctor Danko of the University of Narukun is very smart and he's a hubite. It isn't where you are from, but what you can do with what you know."

"Here is your master certification."

Quint pursed his lips. "They will recognize this in Racellia?"

"Who cares about Racellia? They'll be part of the empire before long, and that certificate will be good everywhere in the empire."

Quint took his copy, but it didn't mean anything to him. He didn't intend on joining Colleto's empire, but he was struggling on how he was going to manage his return to Bocarre. With his abduction, Quint might have already had a capital judgement made against him, and he could be returning to a death sentence.

Colleto was right in the sense that Quint didn't know or understand Racellian politics as much as he should. The newssheets didn't address the political undercurrents that pitted General Obellia against General Baltacco, for example.

He was sure there were other influence cliques in Bocarre, but his research had never been directed toward the details of internal politics. Quint would wait for the entourage to make it to southeast Racellia and his home village. From there he would make his move back to Bocarre and face whatever fate had in store for him.

Colleto invited Quint to join his group for dinner. The local authorities were to join their new emperor. It was an opportunity to glean more information on Colleto's newborn empire. Quint had Danko's empire book as a guide.

He put on fresh clothes that didn't quite fit and descended to the main floor. Colleto was already surrounded by sycophants dwelling on his every word. Quint took an open chair at the other end of the table.

Quint decided he wouldn't learn anything from these diners. There wasn't a complaint or an observation or even a good question in the crowd and he found his understanding of willot colloquialisms wasn't very good.

"What does our newest master wizard have to say about the march of my empire?" Colleto asked, putting Quint on the spot.

"Empires need to nurture their citizens at the beginning, so they don't become disenchanted with their new rulers. The march may be violent on the leading edge, but what comes after the conquest will determine if the empire continues or fall due to internal strife."

"Are you claiming the Gussellian Empire has internal strife?" one of the hangers-on asked. Quint was fair game for challenges even if Colleto wasn't.

Quint shrugged. "I'm not an expert in the politics of Pacci Colleto's center of power. The struggle an empire goes through doesn't end with the last war. It is a continual struggle to keep the populace content enough to continue to accept the emperor's rule."

That core principle was right out of Danko's book.

"Acceptance is a continuous state," Quint said. "It ebbs and flows like the tides. Eventually, the balancing act is thrown off balance enough so that the empire disintegrates as they all have."

"But isn't it true that kingdoms and council governments disintegrate, too?" Colleto said from the other end of the table.

"They do. Nothing is forever," Quint said. "A government may take generations to fail, or they might fall apart in months or years. I can't apply any of that to your current situation, sir." Quint couldn't bring himself to call Colleto an emperor. "Frankly, I don't know enough."

"You are perceptive for one of your tender years," Colleto said.

"I recently read a book about empires where I derived most of my perspective. It was clear there is no universal recipe for long-term success."

"And what will you do to keep us happy, Emperor Colleto?" one of the diners asked.

Colleto looked at Quint with an amused look on his face. "You'll find out soon enough. For the present, we will continue to integrate our two great cultures."

To Quint, that meant Colleto would likely apply more administrative pressure through the presence of more troops.

After dinner, the sycophants began to intimate what their prices were for support. He was sure Colleto understood what that meant. He'd have to keep his subjects placated, at least until he had conquered all South Fenola.

Quint excused himself. He wondered if he had exposed his views too blatantly. Quint was sure that he hadn't been subtle enough to slide his anti-imperial views past Colleto. He felt like he was living on the edge of a knife, and Quint didn't expect that to end any time soon.

※

The dinners continued at every stop along the processional. Colleto didn't ask for Quint's views again, and that was a good thing. They reached the southwestern part of Vinellia that bordered Racellia. Quint had expected the border to be filled with Gussellian soldiers, but Colleto still had only his original guard corps with him when the emperor decided to camp rather than commandeer an inn.

They ate a sparse meal that night, and since the emperor was retiring early, the camp was quiet.

Quint couldn't sleep. Racellia was almost a stone's throw from the camp. He thought about sneaking out of camp, but he poked his head out of his tent in the darkness and saw darker shapes close to his tent. It was clear he was being watched.

Would Colleto move into Racellian territory? Quint suspected that was Colleto's plan. Who would fight for the hubite population that lived in the area on the other side of the border?

Quint was tempted to cast a portent spell, but then he remembered Colleto's claim that he employed a wizard who could identify when a person wove a portent string.

He returned to his blankets and went to sleep.

The following morning, Quint rose early with the morning light and spotted a few watchers who had fallen asleep during the night. He folded his blankets and took a walk into the woods. Quint guessed he knew woodcraft better than Colleto's troops and heard movements behind him.

He finished his business and returned to the camp. Colleto sat at a campfire, stirring the kindling into life.

"You aren't using magic?" Quint asked.

"That takes all the fun out of it, don't you think?" Colleto said, as amiable as ever.

"Rules for our incursion. We are not invading Racellia. We are observing, only. I intend to spend two days in Racellia: one day in and one day out. Is your village within that range?"

"I think it is. I never visited Vinellia. It was outside my father's district."

"Ah, yes. The Racellian concept of districts to keep people from mingling has its uses. Did you feel resentful you couldn't spread your wings?"

"My father did. I was too young to care, although I think I was getting restive about the time I was taken into the wizard corps," Quint said truthfully.

"How should an emperor think about districts?" Colleto asked.

"They are useful for controlling populations, but I surmise they end up generating resentment. My father couldn't expand his trading area, and that affected our ability to have enough to cushion the slower times," Quint said. "We almost starved a few times when I was growing up."

"If there was a well-run food distribution system?" Colleto asked.

"The more the government does, the more it costs in taxes. In poor years, tradesmen don't have the resources to buy food but still pay a lot in taxes,"

Quint said. "My father constantly complained about taxes."

"To the government?"

Quint laughed. "No. To his friends in the pub as long as there weren't any willots around."

"He didn't trust willots?" Colleto asked.

"And they didn't trust hubites. It's an ancient rivalry."

"With hubites on the losing end," Colleto said.

"For now, that's the case," Quint said. "People and cultures ebb and flow through the ages. South Fenola was once occupied by hubites. Willots gained enough power to push the hubites out."

"Where did you read that?"

"Doctor Danko, a professor at the Narukun university said history shows that it happens all the time."

"But not at a very quick pace."

"No. It takes centuries, I imagine," Quint said.

"You don't expect your little enclave of hubites will grow and retake South Fenola, do you?"

"Not at all," Quint said. "Hubites have no power base."

"Except for the hubite who became a master wizard."

Quint laughed. "One wizard is not enough to change the world."

Colleto gave Quint a funny look. "I certainly hope not." He rose. "It's time to softly invade Racellia for two days. I'm rewarding you with a visit to your parents. You may be able to do something about your father's situation."

"Within the Gussellian Empire?"

Colleto smiled and shrugged.

They broke camp and entered Racellia through the woods. The main road had a border crossing, but this was to be a clandestine affair.

"I'd ask you to lead, but you don't know the area any better than I do. Let me know if we come to a familiar place." Colleto pulled out a map where he asked Quint where his village was. Colleto's intended path went in a different direction, but the would-be emperor changed his plans.

"That's at the outer limit of our incursion," Colleto said. "We will retreat when we reach that point."

Quint rode in the middle of the entourage. He was hemmed in on all sides in a loose formation that could close at a moment.

The land was familiar in a sense. The layout of the villages they saw in the distance had the same look and the one town they skirted had the same feel as the town in Quint's district, but something was wrong. There weren't any people about.

Quint looked for cooking fires sending curls of smoke from the chimney's but there was nothing. He told his guards he wanted to talk to Colleto, and they moved along with him to the front of the group.

"We should look in a village. I don't see anyone around."

"I suppose that is possible," Colleto said.

In less than an hour they came to the next village and Colleto warned his people to be ready for anything. They drew swords and trotted into the village from the woods.

Quint gasped. There were a few bodies in the main street. Quint dismounted and ignored the shouts behind him as he ran into cottages. People were killed in their sleep. Whoever did the killing, murdered willots as well as hubites. No one was left except for the chickens and goats that roamed the streets.

"Less than a week ago, your excellency," one of the riders reported to Colleto. "That was when we just left Nornotta," Colleto said to Quint.

"Do you still want to see your cottage?"

Quint's stomach was hollow and unsettled. "Yes."

They rode at a faster pace since there was no opposition. Quint's town hadn't escaped the carnage. Pogi the hedge wizard who had sold him into the wizard corps lay dead across his threshold.

There was no sign of wizard castings among the dead. The army had done this without the help of the wizard corps. Did that let General Baltacco off? Quint couldn't see the general restraining the wizard corps.

With a heavy heart, Quint rode into his father's work yard. A horse lay dead in the yard, but Quint found his parents killed in the main room of the cottage. Quint took his father's sheath knife that had laid on the mantle for as long as Quint could remember and sighed as he looked at his parents for the last time.

He staggered out into the yard as Quint tried to make sense of it all.

"Did you do this?" Quint asked. "Did you ask the Vinellians to do this?"

"No. Soldiers shed blood. Commoners are innocent," Colleto said.

"Then, this was likely done to pin this monstrous act on your army," Quint said.

"To energize the Racellians against me?"

Quint nodded. "That's why the willots were slaughtered along with the hubites. You don't care about anyone."

"But that's not correct."

"If anyone hears about this slaughter, what will they assume?"

Colleto stared at Quint. "What they perceive as the worst," Colleto said, visibly disturbed.

"I'd like to bury my parents," Quint said.

"I'm afraid you can't. Whoever did this will come through here again and would know you've returned," Colleto said.

Quint wiped the tears from his eyes. "Then I suggest you turn around and leave through the forest. It may have been a mistake to go into some of the villages leaving possible evidence that you were here, but I'd make sure that there wasn't a rogue Vinellian army at work. Then prepare for the worst," Quint said.

Quint couldn't shake the sickness he felt, but as they rode through the forest that linked village to village and village to town, Quint took off.

"I'll set the record straight!" Quint yelled back to Colleto.

"Let him go," Colleto said. "I know Tirolo well enough to know he had nothing to do with this, and there is no small chance he can establish the fact that we had nothing to do with this."

CHAPTER TWENTY-EIGHT
~

QUINT RODE THROUGH THE FOREST and worked his way toward the west side of Racellia before heading north toward Bocarre. He had his uniform bundled in his bag along with the Gussellian style clothes he currently wore. That had to change.

He stole clothing from drying lines and tossed his Gussellian clothes down outhouse holes. He lived off farmers' personal gardens and drank from streams.

Eventually the forests stopped where the plains that fed Bocarre began.

"Stop right there, hubite," a farmer said, pointing the sharp tines of a pitchfork toward Quint.

The confrontation shocked Quint into realizing that he could be hunted due to his race. Quint took off, again and headed toward the coast where the forest began again.

Quint spent a day searching for food in the woods and found a meadow of peat bogs. He'd seen his mother dye wool brown using peat water. The thought of her made Quint catch his breath as he remembered her sprawled on the floor of their cottage.

The water was dark enough to make a stain for his face and hands. He ended up removing his shirt and darkened everything above his belt. His hair took to the stain and his only problem were his light blue eyes.

The disguise wouldn't stand close inspection, but the first thing in an observer's mind wouldn't be "hubite."

Quint cast a sharpening spell on the knife and was able to put a rabbit to sleep. It didn't seem fair, but he took the rabbit's life. He had skinned plenty of rabbits in his youth and soon he was sitting in front of a campfire watch the rabbit cook.

With a full stomach, Quint kept to the forest and soon came to a small road that led into Bocarre. He joined a line of farmers and when he approached the city gate, he dismounted and walked his horse between a line of wagons, keeping his head down.

Just like that he was inside Bocarre's walls. Now, he had to decide what he would do. Quint realized that he had returned to Bocarre without a plan with perhaps the entire government looking for him.

His flat was sure to be watched. He was tempted to go back to the forest, but that was a very short-term solution. After finding a stable and paying for two weeks board for his horse with the rest of his money, Quint walked to the international quarter and sat in a small park. Perhaps he could pass for a gran who were darker than their cousins the hubites. Possibilities ran through Quint's head, but he couldn't find one that showed promise.

He looked at the buildings around the square and that gave Quint an idea. He patiently waited on a bench on the other side of the street and spotted Calee Danko walking down the steps onto the pavement. Quint followed her and paused when she went in a lady's shop.

Quint couldn't follow her into an establishment like that when he looked a bit rough after his ride from southeast Racellia.

Calee walked out and ducked into a general store. That was a better place. Quint walked across the street and entered the general store. Calee stood looking at spools of string.

"Can I help you?" Quint said.

She looked behind her. Her face filled with alarm at the stranger.

"It's me, Tirolo," Quint said quietly.

"It is you!" she said. "Let me buy this and we can go back to our flat."

"I'll go ahead of you," Quint said.

He approached the building but didn't see any obvious observers before he entered. After walking to the second floor, he stepped into an alcove just past the Danko's door.

Calee stood at her door and paused before retrieving her key. Quint moved out of the alcove. She slipped inside, leaving the door ajar. Quint slipped inside.

Calee turned around. "You stink! Wash up, first," she said.

Quint did as he was told, but he didn't have any clothes to change into. "I need some clothes," he said from behind the bathroom door.

"Step aside. I'll give you something of my father's."

There was a knock on the door. Quint opened it to a crack and Calee stuffed the clothes inside.

Quint came out wearing clothes too short and too wide.

Calee giggled. "That's still better. I don't have to hold my nose while we talk. Where have you been? There was talk about you deserting."

"I was abducted by Pacci Colleto's local spies and taken to Nornotta."

"You have proof of that?"

Quint thought for a moment. "This is all I have," Quint said. He produced his master wizard certificate. "Colleto wanted me tested. I don't know why."

"A master! I hardly believed you were a provost level wizard," Calee said.

"What?"

"We use different names in Narukun. Novice, Acolyte, Deacon, Provost, Prior. Most of our wizards are administered through a cloister. A master is a prior and a Level 3 is a provost, I believe. My father knows more about that kind of thing than I do."

"No wizard corps?"

"No. The cloister manages the wizards. If they are seconded to the army, they work within a company or whatever you call them," Calee said.

"You were kidnapped so he could test you?"

Quint shook his head. "He still wants me to join him," Quint said. "We took a tour of Vinellia."

"Pacci Colleto and you?"

"With twenty other soldiers. I think he wanted to show me how easy it would be to invade Racellia. We crossed into Racellia from southern Vinellia and found that someone had slaughtered all the hubites and willots in the hubite districts."

Calee gasped. "Your parents?"

"Dead," Quint said. "All I have to remember them by is my father's prize possession, this knife. It's an heirloom." Quint put the knife on the table in front of the couch. "I decided I had enough of Pacci Colleto and took off. I tossed my Gusellian clothes and stole what I had on."

"What is on your skin?"

"Peat stain," Quint said. "I can't cover my eyes, but I can darken my skin."

"It didn't come off when you washed," Calee said.

"I suppose that's why they call it a stain," Quint said. He realized he was flirting with her and bit his lip. "They told you I deserted?"

"Father knows more than I do. He has spoken to Colonel Gerocie about it. I haven't heard a word about the slaughter of your family. Why would anyone do that? Hubites are no threat to willots in Racellia," Calee said.

Fedor Danko walked through the door. His eyes grew when he saw Quint.

"I didn't expect to see you in my flat," Danko said. "You didn't really desert, did you?"

"I was abducted." Quint told his story.

Danko gasped when Quint described the hubite carnage, but then he furrowed his brow. "There have been urgent doings at the diplomacy corps. Whisperings and such. It must be that. Colleto is an interesting case. You were with him for almost a week, so he didn't personally supervise the incursion."

"If it was him. I personally think it was Baltacco or one of the other generals as a provocation to get Racellians angered so they will fight Colleto's forces," Quint said. "Willots were slaughtered along with hubites, but I think that was intentional. If only hubites were killed, there are many in Racellia who would rejoice."

"You may be right," Danko said. "But why did you return?"

Quint took a deep breath. "Stupidity. I don't want to join Colleto as the only hubite in his entourage, even if I was so inclined."

"You have no future here," Danko said. "You were tried and found guilty of treason two days after you went missing."

"Why?" Quint said. "Was it Baltacco's doing?"

"Your colonel didn't know. It is all so bizarre."

"Can we ship him to Narukun?" Calee asked. "He's been certified as a Prior."

"A master? You've been tested?" Fedor asked.

Quint handed Danko the certificate.

"I'm sure you can join a Cloister," Danko said. "They would recognize this, especially if you are willing to be tested again."

"Why would I go to Narukun?" Quint asked.

"It is a hubite country. You wouldn't have such a large target on your back. Narukun isn't a perfect place, but better than Racellia," Danko said. "I have a ship in the harbor that is ready to take Calee and me back to Narukun, but I'm not ready to go, yet."

"I'll have to find a place to stay. I can't live here."

"No, you cannot stay here," Danko said. "If you permit, I'll call on your landlady. Perhaps she knows of a safe place."

✧

Quint wrote a note and hoped that Marena was in the flat, a few buildings away. Calee volunteered to deliver Quint's message. In less that half an hour, she returned with a sealed reply from Marena.

"She is glad you are alive," Calee said, "but she wishes you hadn't returned to the capital."

"I understand, but I have nowhere else to go."

Calee nodded. "She realized that when I told her your parents had been murdered. That fact has not reached the city, yet. The good news is she wrote down three places where you can hide out. She doesn't want to know which one you choose and don't try to see her. Marena is being watched, that's why I brought the bag of spices for Slinnon cooking to give her."

Quint looked at Marena's suggestions. One address was on the edge of the international quarter, closer to the council palace. The other two were on the other side of the city.

"I not going to show you the options," Quint said.

"You probably don't have money. Take this purse."

Quint looked inside. "This is too generous."

Fedor smiled. "I have plenty, but I suggest you wait here long enough so I can purchase some better fitting clothes. I presume you don't want to attract attention?"

Quint groaned. "No, I don't."

Fedor and Calee returned from a shopping trip. "Food, a few necessities, and two sets of clothes, one to wear now and another to wear later."

"That's simple enough, Quint said. "I don't know what to say."

"Thank you, will do," Fedor said.

Quint waited for twilight before he went out the back way. As he passed his flat, he saw Marena through the fourth-floor window. Sadness filled him since he couldn't contact those who had helped him in Bocarre.

The address was another flat block. Quint circled the building to the back alley, but the gate was locked. He climbed over the fence and stepped inside. The flat was on the second floor, facing the front. He looked out the window and found the latch. The window opened. Quint could jump to the ground if he had to.

After closing the shutters, he cast a magic light and walked through the flat. It was clean and well-kept. A note was left on the kitchen table.

"Roberto and Anna will return in two months." The dated note was a week old. Quint had a six-week window to figure out what to do. He would have to let Fedor know in case the ship anchored in Bocarre's harbor could be used as a hiding place.

The pantry was restocked recently, and Quint thought he'd have enough food to last until the tenants returned, if he didn't die from his own cooking. He put his head back on the couch and closed his eyes. He felt like he was safe for the moment, but that could change at any time. If his horse was located, those seeking him would know he was in Bocarre and that he had been to the international quarter.

Telling someone else about the hubite massacre took some of the pressure off his return, but he didn't know what to do next. Colleto had spies in Bocarre, General Baltacco was after him, and whoever led the soldiers against the hubites would have people out to kill him as soon as they discovered Quint.

The prospect of casting a portent string came to mind, but Quint's life was in so much peril, he was afraid of what he might see.

CHAPTER TWENTY-NINE

~

QUINT'S FIRST ACT IN THE MORNING WAS TO BUY a wide brimmed hat that was popular among young Bocarren men. The darkness would hide Quint's eye color as well as anything else he could think of. He also noticed that more people had taken to wearing swords recently. Perhaps Colleto's threats were seeping into the consciousness of the general populace. Because of that, Quint purchased a used army sword, a fistful of newssheets, and finished his purchases with a day's supply of market food.

The hat he wore back to the flat, and Quint retired to the kitchen, enjoying his purchases. He cast a string to sharpen the sword and his father's knife.

After Quint had eaten his fill, he returned to the living room to read periodicals. He found paper and pencils in a desk drawer and began to analyze what the people thought of the current situation.

His research wasn't very promising. It was clear that the concern about Colleto's empire-building had picked up during Quint's absence. The swords worn in the open confirmed that.

Comments about the massacre in the southeast hadn't made it into the papers, yet, and that concerned Quint. From his perspective, the repression of the atrocity was being withheld for effect by those in power. Other than Baltacco's feud with General Obellia, Quint learned little about the political landscape in Racellia, but there had to be Council members involved to clamp down on the news so completely.

Master Pozella might have a broader understanding and Quint decided to see if he could track his friend by observing the strategic operations building.

Quint stuffed himself for lunch and walked out through the back of the building and continued for a few blocks out of the international quarter and into the vicinity of strategic operations building.

He found a shady alley across from the strategic operations building and waited. It was mid-afternoon when he spotted Pozella walking down the building steps with Colonel Sarrefo. They walked across the street toward Quint, but then as Quint withdrew a few steps, the pair turned down the street and then walked left toward the international quarter.

Quint followed them, hoping he could catch a few words, but they weren't really talking. He stopped when the pair walked into a pub on the edge of the quarter close to Quint's borrowed flat.

Quint's first thought was perhaps this was a setup to capture him, but if that were the case, how did they know where he lived? Fedor Danko had no idea where Quint had ended up.

He waited a few minutes and then followed a couple into the pub and noticed Sarrefo and Pozella sitting with a non-uniformed person. There was a table close to them next to a window that Quint took.

Others had kept their fashionable wide-brimmed hats on in the pub, so Quint did the same. He could hear snippets of the quiet conversation, but nothing was clear. Quint hadn't learned any strings to enhance his hearing and he couldn't cast a string in a restaurant without someone noticing, he leaned back in his chair and folded his arms, concentrating on the three's conversation.

The server finally arrived, and Quint ordered a plate of fried potatoes and a mug of non-alcoholic beer. It was awful stuff, but Quint didn't want to create a scene. Now he could feel free to concentrate on the conversation behind him. The men switched to the willot language, which Quint found easier to overhear.

"And Pacci is still ambivalent?" Sarrefo asked. "There is too much tension about an invasion."

"Pacci knows that and is still formulating plans. I heard something happened in south Vinellia on his recent tour that made him turn around and head back to the Gussellian capital."

"Do you know what it was?" Pozella asked.

There was a pause. The Gussellian spy was probably shaking his head. "Pacci only tells us what we need to know. That way if we are caught there is less, we can reveal."

"Our participation is even more restricted than yours," Sarrefo said. "My unit isn't on any kind of alert. Everything appears normal, but my people know it isn't. Whatever is happening is building up away from our sight. I'm afraid none of us will be prepared."

"Prepared for what?" Pozella said. "You know how to create a strategy. Have your people come up with ones for every situation."

"And who will convert our strategies into a battle plan?" Sarrefo said.

"I will," Pozella said. "I'm no dummy, you know."

"You are a master," the spy said, "but that is for magic. Are you a general, too?"

"Closer to one than anyone under Sarrefo," Pozella said. "I wish Quint were back. He could see through things better than any of us."

"Why would he return to Bocarre?" Sarrefo said. "He is a wanted man."

"He's still a boy, but a smart, capable one," Pozella said. "He's creative, too, but he lacks experience, something you and I both have in abundance."

Sarrefo laughed. "If he shows up on your doorstep, let me know."

"You are talking about the boy wizard that Pacci is so enamored with?" the spy asked.

"Why is that?" Pozella asked.

"I don't know," the spy said. "We are to report if we see him, but we aren't to capture him."

"Doesn't that sound strange?" Pozella said.

"Pacci considers him more than a master wizard," the spy said.

"He is close to being one now," Sarrefo said. "Isn't that right, Pozella?"

Two new customers walked through the door. One of them was an officer who had shared Quint's flat. Quint turned away from the two newcomers as the pair sat with Colonel Sarrefo and Pozella.

The risk had suddenly risen too high for Quint, so he paid and left the pub, walking in the opposite direction from the window where the others were seated. He thought he had heard enough.

Other than Pozella and Sarrefo working with Pacci Colleto, he hadn't learned a single thing new, but that didn't mean Pozella didn't know more; it just hadn't come up in the conversation. It was nice to hear Sarrefo and Pozella say nice things about him, although Quint didn't believe most of what they said. One of the more important things to remember was that the Gussellian spies weren't actively after him. Even without the Gussellian Empire after him, Quint didn't feel safe in Bocarre, but still, he had no other place to go.

※

Quint practiced magic while he sequestered himself in the flat while he thought of his next step. Early the following morning, he woke up realizing that his first idea, to talk to Pozella was still his best move. He didn't know where Pozella lived other than he and his wife lived close to the strategic operations building to accommodate his limp.

The following afternoon, Quint took up his post in the alley. He almost dozed in the warm darkness, but he caught Pozella walking across the street. He followed his former teacher and stopped when Pozella walked into a modest townhouse on a quiet street.

Quint knocked on the door and a woman answered.

"I'm here to see Master Pozella," Quint said. "I'm a former student."

The woman looked Quint up and down. "I'd say you look young enough to be a current student."

"Show him in Valia," Pozella said from within. "I know the boy."

Quint stepped in.

"You are taking quite a risk coming to my house in broad daylight," Pozella said. The friendliness that Quint had expected was missing from Pozella's voice.

"I don't like disgraced students like you showing up on my doorstep. There is a pub just up the block," Pozella said. "You can say your peace there and then begone." Pozella looked back at his wife. "I doubt if I'll be too long."

"Before dinner?" Valia said.

"I'll be here," Pozella said.

Quint followed a silent Pozella as they walked to a tiny pub converted out of a townhouse no larger than Pozella's.

"In the back where we won't be bothered," Pozella said.

Quint spotted one other customer with a few tankards of something littered around him.

"Maybe they should turn out the drunk," Quint said.

Pozella laughed. "He's the owner." Pozella ordered wine for both. "You are old enough for a sip or two, Quint." He winked at Quint. "I couldn't be friendly to you, or my wife would know who you were."

"I'm the only student you were friendly with?"

"Pretty much. You are the only one with potential."

Quint grinned and pushed his Master certificate toward Pozella.

"What's this?"

"Something that Pacci Colleto had me do after he abducted me to Nornotta."

"A master. I wasn't in favor of testing you before you turned twenty," Pozella said. "No one will take you seriously. It was hard enough for the diplomacy corps to accept a sixteen-year-old Level 3."

"Except for Pacci Colleto. He had one of his wizards cast a portent string on me during the Gussellian border battle and found my future intriguing."

Pozella looked interested. "Did you ask him why?"

"I don't believe in portent strings as much as he does," Quint said. "He thinks I have some grand destiny."

Pozella smiled knowingly. "If you can stay alive, you have the potential and not just as a string caster, Quint. Your commanding officer at the diplomacy corps thought you were special and had you down in the basement so you wouldn't get hurt or discouraged from all the hatred, but she used and forwarded your analysis regularly."

Quint took a deep breath. "I always thought I was in the basement, so I couldn't absorb any sunlight. I have some awful news. I may be the only village-grown hubite in Racellia. Someone in the army massacred the people in the villages and towns in the hubite districts where I grew up. Even the willots living with the hubites weren't spared. It was awful and death on a huge scale."

"Your parents?"

"Friends, family, acquaintances, and enemies. All dead."

Pozella went silent for a moment. "I never went for the hubite hatred. People are people and you can't blame them for something that happened centuries ago. I'm really sorry."

"That's when I escaped from the velvet prison where Pacci Colleto had put me."

"Velvet prison, eh?" Pozella said. "How poetic. He trusts you more than anyone, I'd say."

Quint shrugged. "I don't know about that, but maybe he wants to keep a potential enemy close."

"Perhaps. Pacci Colleto tends to be enigmatic according to my sources."

"Who are his spies?" Quint asked. "Colleto has his tentacles entwined with the strategic operations people. I saw you yesterday with Colonel Sarrefo and one of my former flatmates."

"You were the one in the wide-brimmed hat?" Pozella asked. "I noticed you but didn't recognize you with your stained face and hands." Pozella looked at the dark skin on the back of Quint's hands. "What did you use?"

"I found a brackish pool in a peat bog. My mother used to use that kind of thing to stain wool brown. It did the trick, but it gets lighter with every washing up."

"It looks like dirt at this point," Pozella said. "The hat is good. It's hard to make out your eyes. I knew you when you talked at my front door. You still have a young voice."

Quint smiled. "I'm not going to stay in Bocarre very long," he said. "It's too dangerous, and I don't feel right being at Pacci Colleto's side."

"I wouldn't either," Pozella said, "but Racellian politics are very unstable."

"That's why we had to talk. I have a better feeling for what is happening outside Bocarre, but my publication analysis never dwelled on the capital. I know General Baltacco and General Obellia are rivals, but there must be more undercurrents," Quint said.

"The Racellian Council has three main factions at present. Alliances change from time to time, but for the past few weeks, it has seemed that they change every day or two with the fear of an invasion," Pozella said. "Obellia doesn't have a high-level sponsor, but Baltacco is thick with the Chief Councilmember."

"Is there another army faction?" Quint asked.

"Grand Marshal Guilica is aligned with the former nobility. They have the greatest military power."

"So they were probably the ones who carried out the atrocities in southeast Racellia. Someone with a lot of power is suppressing word of the killing," Quint said.

"They are indeed. Sarrefo and I didn't even know. What is your analysis?" Pozella asked.

"At some point in time, they will either pin the massacre on Pacci Colleto or on Baltacco and the Chief Councilmember. I'm not a willot and can't figure out which would garner the most reaction from the people."

"Most will applaud the elimination of the hubites, Quint, but I'll get the word out. I may even pay your colonel in the diplomacy corps a visit with the rumor. I'd rather she tell Obellia than me."

Quint nodded. "Feel free. The people of Racellia should be told the truth since whatever is going to happen will occur soon. News of hubite destruction can't stay a secret for long, so help it along. What's going to happen to Sarrefo and you?"

"We will ignore the fight between generals as much as we can," Pozella said. "There are others who see the Gussellian Empire succeeding no matter what happens in Bocarre. Racellia has had their day, and it wasn't very successful. You pointed a basic problem that contributed to that early on."

"That there was no creativity at the battlefront?" Quint asked.

Pozella nodded.

"The problem wasn't the motivation of Racellian soldiers." Quint said. "It was the leaders who were and are unwilling to change. The malady isn't restricted to the military."

"I think the Gussellian battle was a turning point for Sarrefo and me. You rubbed our noses in the military's futile strategy. The spy you saw in the pub, has been our go-between with Pacci. We always refer to him by his first name. We don't expect to have to fight against Racellian soldiers, but there must be Racellian officers willing to step up when Bocarre and the rest of Racellia crumbles," Pozella said.

"You know where I live. You can have messages delivered if we need to communicate, again. I won't ask you where you live. I don't want to know."

Quint smiled. "Good! You wouldn't want to know where an antagonistic old student lives, anyway."

"Right! Will I see you again?" Pozella asked.

"I don't know." Quint said.

"I must return to my wife. She is expecting me."

PAGE 234 | The Wizard Corps

CHAPTER THIRTY

~

THE NEW INFORMATION MADE QUINT SAD. He had to talk about his family's demise more than made him comfortable. Life was going to change for Racellians, and it was going to change for him, no matter where he ended up.

Quint needed a safer space in the long term, and he didn't trust being an even rarer hubite in a willot empire. He was continually being pushed by fate or whatever into joining Fedor and Calee Danko on their voyage home. It wasn't a voyage home for him, but a forced emigration from everything that had made up Quint's world.

He walked the streets of the international quarter in a state of depression. Thoughts of his parents and brothers as he grew up kept cropping up in his mind. He was close to his flat when he noticed a person behind him cross from the other side of the street. Quint turned to face him.

The man peered in a shop window, but Quint could see him trying to look sideways. Quint walked up to him.

"You are following me," Quint said.

"I am," the man said, straightening up and facing Quint.

"Who are you with?" Quint walked into the adjacent alley.

"I'm alone, at present," the man said, following.

"No," Quint said. "What faction are you working for?"

"Oh," Quint's follower smiled, "It's permissible to tell you. I am Gussellian and work for the emperor."

"Why are you following me? I'm so insignificant."

The man laughed. "Not so insignificant if Emperor Colleto is keeping an eye on you. Have you told anyone what you saw in the southeast? I was supposed to ask."

"I have," Quint said. "People I trust, but they won't be blurting it everywhere. I don't know if Colleto wants the information spread or controlled."

"The emperor has plans either way. You can do as you wish. What are your plans?"

As if Quint was going to tell this stranger such a thing. "I'm intending to stay alive through this crisis."

"It would be easier to do that in Nornotta," the spy said.

"Until I'm not longer of use to Colleto," Quint said.

"I can see why you might be hesitant."

"Good. That means our little talk is over?"

"It is."

Quint put his hands together and put the spy to sleep. The man fell on Quint, so Quint had to lower the spy gently to the ground. The man had been civilized, at least until the point where Quint put him to sleep. He left the man in the alley and quickly walked to the flat.

It appeared that nothing had been touched as far as Quint could see. The encounter with Pozella and with the spy drained Quint of energy and he laid down for a nap on the couch. He woke and fixed a barely edible dinner from his limited pantry. He continued to work on his list of master strings until it was time to sleep. Quint spent another half-hour perusing a periodical. He searched for evidence of what Pozella had told him, but he couldn't find any confirmation, but Quint also didn't find any contradictions.

He changed clothes but continued to wear the broad brimmed hat. He folded the back of the brim up and the two sides making an echo of a tri-cornered hat. His eyes were still in shadows when he checked in a shop window as he walked to the international quarter market.

Looking for spies all around him, Quint brought himself up to his full height. He was slouching as he looked and realized that he might be drawing too much attention to himself. It wouldn't do to look furtive in the middle of a marketplace.

He bought another change of clothes and a velvet bag to carry them. Quint hoped he looked like a fervent shopper as he handled goods and listened to what people had to say. It was clear that Emperor Colleto was beginning to make a lot of international people uneasy. Quint spotted Calee Danko at a produce stand. He worked his way over to her and held up a melon, looking it over and rapping it with his knuckles. Quint didn't know why people did that, but he tried to make it look authentic. The melon looked ripe enough for him.

He bumped into Calee as he gave the melon to the stall keeper. She glanced at him and then glanced again. Quint noticed her almost silent gasp.

"I didn't expect to see you out and about," Calee said.

"I get anxious not being able to walk outside," Quint said. "Is your father all right?"

"Good enough. Are you coming with us? Father wondered if you have enquired about passage on our ship."

"I've thought about it, and I'm almost committed to leaving Racellia. It is not going to be safe, soon. The government is close to breaking apart."

Calee nodded. "My father agrees. His contract doesn't include working during an insurrection of any kind, and that covers being smothered by an empire."

Quint smiled. "Then consider me a shipmate," he said.

"You have resources?"

"Can I pay my way?" Quint asked. "I'm a Level 3 wizard and some think I'm a Master. I'm sure I can be of use to a smart captain. If I can't use my magic, I possess a youthful body to climb the rigging."

Calee's eyes widened. "You wouldn't do that!"

Quint shrugged. "I would. We must separate. I'll be in contact with the ship on my own."

"Refer to yourself as the local hubite to the purser, then. We will be able to know it's you."

"I'll do that," Quint said as he bowed to her and turned to walk in a different direction.

After another half-hour in the market, Quint returned to his flat. He ate a lonely dinner and at twilight he walked to the docks and after a few questions, he found the purser inspecting boxes delivered to a warehouse space Danko's ship had rented.

"Are you taking on any sailors to Narukun?" Quint asked.

"Are you a sailor looking for a ship or someone looking for passage to Narukun?" the purser asked.

"I'm looking for passage, but I'm short of funds. I'm willing to work my way to Narukun. I'm acquainted with Fedor Danko and his daughter. They know me as a local hubite," Quint said. "I am handy as a wizard, if that would help."

"Are you ranked?"

"I am," Quint said, "but I'm uncomfortable telling you how many strings I can cast. Fedor knows."

"We can always use a wizard. Most of your kind would rather practice your profession on land. You have a name?"

"I'll give it to you when I board. Just put me down as a local hubite and I'll fill any chinks you have on your crew," Quint said.

The purser grunted and wrote a note in notebook that was filling up. "We don't know when we will sail. This warehouse is where we are accumulating our cargo, but we won't load until we are closer to leaving."

"When will that be?"

"At least a week. You can check with me every day until then. I'll be here at midday until we sail."

"Mind if I look around?"

The purser shrugged. "Go ahead. We almost have a full cargo. If you have nothing better to do, you can help me put these crates over there."

"A test?"

The purser laughed. "If you want to call it that, sure. I just want some free help."

Quint spent less than an hour helping the purser and another crew member move crates. Quint looked around the warehouse and found an unlocked door. Inside was an unused office, that wasn't too dirty. Quint found a bedroll in a cupboard and unlocked a window that he could use to get in and out of the room.

"Who uses the office at the back?"

The purser looked up from his desk. "There is an office back there?" The purser shrugged. "I'm already set up in the front. and I can watch our goods better here than inside an office."

Quint nodded and left the warehouse. He turned a corner and ended up at the office window. He slipped inside and looked around. There were solid shutters secured inside the window that would keep the room dark. In a pinch, Quint found a hiding hole.

He climbed out of the window and pushed an empty crate underneath the window before securing the window with a cast string and headed back to his flat.

It was dark when he stood across the street from his building. There were lights inside moving around his flat. Quint sighed. There were possessions in the flat that he wanted, so he counted heads moving through the windows. He sighed again when he caught Amaria Baltacco ordering around three black-clad figures. He wondered if it was the same three who had interrogated Marena.

Quint waited for them to finish and saw all four of them leave his flat. He couldn't see what they had taken. No one carried a sword, so perhaps they left his weapons. Quint jogged across the street and entered an alley a few buildings down and found his way into the building without noticing any watchers. He surveyed his possessions and found everything there except for his master's certificate.

He smiled. If Amaria was the one to find it, she might have even eaten the paper to get over her frustration. He agreed with Pozella's view that Quint was too young to be taken seriously.

It was time to leave. He took what he absolutely needed and finished off what could be easily eaten. Quint headed down to the ground level to go out the back, when he heard a sound in an alcove and then the world went dark.

CHAPTER THIRTY-ONE

~

Quint woke up in a small cabin in the woods. He had no idea where he was in relation to Bocarre, but if he was put to sleep the previous night, he couldn't be too far from Bocarre. His hands were put in fingerless gloves and wrapped together so Quint couldn't cast a string.

He sat up on a dusty cot and looked out a window. No one else occupied the cabin, but Quint heard voices on the other side of the door. Quint rose and walked around; thankful his feet weren't tied together. He fumbled with the cabin's latch, but eventually opened the door that led to a porch the width of the cabin. Two men sat in chairs, facing the woods.

"His highness has woken," one of the men said. "Have a seat and enjoy nature for a bit."

The friendly tone of his captors surprised him.

"You are Baltacco's people?" Quint asked.

"Right, you are, lad," the other, older, man said. "You are complicating what is going on in Bocarre, so the general decided it would be better to remove you. For your information, neither of us are hubite haters, and we are sorry for what happened to your people."

"So Baltacco and the chief council member didn't order the massacre?" Quint asked.

"Not at all, but don't ask us any more questions. We aren't supposed to talk to you," the older man said. "The general will show up by midday."

Quint looked at the sky, determining that it was still morning.

Quint sat down in the third of four chairs on the porch and sighed. "I'm tired of being pushed around. Before it was because I wasn't important enough, and now it's because I'm too important."

"Be patient and your importance will decline," the younger guard said.

"What does Baltacco want with me?" Quint asked.

"Your cooperation with something or he would have had us kill you. That's as specific as we'll get," the older guard said.

"How did you find out about the hubite slaughter?"

The younger guard shook his head. "I lost a few distant relatives, myself. Hubites weren't the only victims. Found out last night, for sure. The general had heard of some action in the southeast and had originally thought it might be an incursion from Vinellia by the pretender's troops."

"Colleto is now called the pretender by Racellians? If he is, Pacci Colleto is doing a good job of pretending."

"You are on his side? After what he's done…"

Quint pursed his lips. "Killing innocent people like that is unforgiveable. Every man, woman, and child were massacred, hubite and willot. I saw them in the streets and in their homes murdered. I parted company with Colletto at that point and headed to Bocarre to figure out what I should do."

"And what you should do is go somewhere else," an older man in a black uniform said, walking around the corner of the cabin and stepping up to the porch. He took the fourth seat. "I'm General Baltacco."

"I know who you are, and you know who I am," Quint said.

"I do indeed. My daughter has kept me informed all along since we last saw each other."

"I'm sure Amaria was very complimentary," Quint said sarcastically.

Baltacco smiled. "In her own way. You found a way to irritate her like no one else. But we aren't here to talk about my daughter. I heard your discussion with my officers."

"Not guards?"

Baltacco shrugged.

"Officers can be guards," the older guard said.

"What are you going to do with me?"

Baltacco turned the chair to face Quint. "Well, that depends on you, Master Quinto Tirolo." Baltacco grinned. "I can say that when Amaria isn't around. Tell me about Pacci Colleto. You probably know him better than all but a few Racellians."

'Know your enemy.' Quint thought. "He isn't a monster, if that is what you are hoping for. He was as surprised by the hubite massacre as I was. It wasn't his men, either. I don't know who did the dirty work, but Coletto doesn't hate hubites. I don't think he even bothers to think about us. He is very smart, and from what I can tell, knows how to use people to his advantage without resorting to strings. He is a master wizard and his interest in me is due to my actions at the Gussellian border battle. I exposed myself using a portent string and he had a wizard cast a string on my future. He thinks I have promise, but I couldn't see myself at his side."

"Your ties to Racellia are too strong?"

"Perhaps 'were' might be a better term. It depends on what happens. If the murdering faction prevails, definitely not."

"And my faction?" Baltacco asked. "I have no love for hubites, although that means much less today than it did a few days ago."

"You didn't kill me out of hand," Quint said. "As your officers said, it's better I'm not around to stir things up in Bocarre, not that I was going to do that anyway."

"You were in contact with a Gussellian spy. We saw you talking."

"He was acting much the same as you are," Quint said. "I wouldn't call him friendly, but he wasn't antagonistic. I was kidnapped by Colleto, by the way. I didn't desert the wizard corps."

"We know that," Baltacco said. "We have our own portent casters and saw something similar to what Colleto's wizard saw."

"What did you see?"

"Quinto Tirolo will rise over time and become a player in the world's affairs," Baltacco said. "Does that sound familiar?"

"It does, but portents are not particularly accurate," Quint said. He was tired of discounting the portents, but they could still be accurate enough to be terrifying.

"Consider this abduction to be like what Colleto tried. I certainly can see his point. I don't want to make an enemy of you, but I remain suspicious of hubites, even now. If the time comes when we face each other in enmity, that you will remember our cordial conversation."

Baltacco nodded to his officers who freed Quint from his bonds. "I'll let you make your way to Bocarre on your own but consider this a truce that can be terminated at any time."

Quint managed a smile. "I'll remember your forbearance, general," he said, resisting the urge to salute the general. Baltacco's relatively civil behavior surprised Quint. Was there another portent cast? Something had to have changed for Amaria's father to change his attitude.

The three willots mounted horses and left Quint to manage his way to Bocarre and then on a ship to Narukun. He still had to see what was left in the flat and then it was spend the rest of his days in Bocarre in a dusty office by the docks.

☙

While Quint rubbed his hands and wrists, he examined the cabin and found nothing to eat and an old broom which he modified into a pointed stick with his magic. Quint was tempted to follow the horse tracks, but he decided to head west and walk through the forest. He'd run into the ocean at some point. Baltacco and his officers hadn't stolen his purse, so Quint could buy whatever he wanted as long as he could convince a willot to sell to a hubite, having lost his wide-brimmed hat in the process of his abduction.

The strategy would work if he could get out of the forest, but Quint had no idea where the forests were within a decent ride of Bocarre. His walk continued, and Quint was getting tired since the forest wasn't level and he was walking up and down hills.

Quint heard a rustle in the bushes not far from him. He faced the sound and backed up. A forest lion emerged and growled. Quint thought they would scream or something, but the low growling was more sinister and set Quint on edge. He hadn't killed an animal so large. Even at home, his father slaughtered the big animals, leaving Quint to help skin their source of meat.

The animal crept closer. Quint couldn't turn and run, or the animal would be on him in a heartbeat. Magic was his only defense. He began to shape tendrils into threads and threads into strings of fire.

When the lion squatted down, gathering itself for a leap, Quint couldn't wait another second. The lion leaped and roared as Quint's fire spear went into its mouth. The roar turned into the gurgle of a scream, and the beast dropped, its head emitting smoke, and fell into Quint's legs, pushing him back and onto his rump.

Quint scrambled backward and then he turned and ran into the forest. He didn't stop until he lurched onto a roadway. A village was less than a hundred yards away from where he emerged. He put his hands on his knees and drew in huge gulps of air until a traveler driving a wagon looked at Quint with a mixture of amazement and revulsion.

"There's a beast in that forest," the man said.

"A forest lion?" Quint asked. "The animal is no longer among the living."

"You killed it?"

Quint waved his sharpened stick at him.

The traveler snickered. "There is no blood on that scrawny pole."

"I used a little magic," Quint said, quickly weaving a magic light string.

"Don't use it on me!" the man said, snapping the reins of the donkey pulling the wagon.

Quint watched the wagon move a little faster than Quint's walking pace. He followed the wagon into the village and saw it travel though the village without stopping.

"I need something to eat and drink," Quint said as he walked into a general store. "I have money."

"Hubite, eh?" the shopkeeper said with suspicion in his voice. "This morning, I heard about a hubite massacre in the south. Did you escape from it?"

Quint shook his head. "I had relatives killed," he said. "Mother, father, brother, old friends, but I've been living in Bocarre for two years. I became lost traveling and decided to head directly west. I have no idea where Bocarre is from here."

"A few hours' walk. Follow the road out of the village and take the south fork." The shopkeeper showed Quint what food he had ready to eat and, in a few minutes, Quint had a new hat, a bag slung over his shoulder with a jug of watered wine, bread and cheese inside.

He ate as he walked and when he heard horses behind him, he left the road to see General Baltacco and the officers ride past. They would arrive in Bocarre before he would, but Quint wouldn't be too far behind.

Quint wasn't shocked that word of the hubite slaughter had arrived at the village he just passed. At least the shopkeeper was able to muster a small measure of pity on him. It was enough for Quint at that point in time.

The forest ended, and in the misty distance, Bocarre stood with the faint outline of the ocean beyond. Quint was coming from the southwest, now that he could get his bearings. He trudged underneath an unmanned gate mid-afternoon, fighting against a stream of citizens leaving the city. The capital was in turmoil. The city guard fought a losing battle against those wishing to flee and as Quint observed the situation, it appeared that the guard was merely providing some order to the evacuation.

Another observer leaned against a building, watching people move past.

"What is going on?" Quint asked.

"The factions finally took arms against each other all the while Emperor Colleto is said to be two days away from the city. Unless they get together to fight off the Gussellians we will be absorbed into Gussellia before the end of the week," the observer said. "You didn't know?"

"I was taking a walking holiday in the forest and have been out of Bocarre for a couple of days. I didn't expect this."

"I heard the fight is for the privilege of handing the keys to the city over to the emperor when he arrives."

"Don't wait too long to leave but be prepared to return in short order. Unless there is resistance, I don't think there will be much bloodshed. Colleto would rather conquer without a loss of life or resources," Quint said.

The observer snorted. "How would you know?"

"I've met him a few times."

"You, a teenager?"

Quint cocked his head. "Amazing how life works."

CHAPTER THIRTY-TWO
~

THE FLAT WAS MOSTLY UNDISTURBED. Amaria hadn't returned to abscond with his sword and knife or any of his notes. Quint gathered what he wanted to take to Narukun and left the flat after writing a note of thanks to Marena.

Quint had never seen the international quarter filled with so many people, but many were willots making their way out of the city through the quarter. Quint walked to the Danko flat, but it looked empty. He had a sudden attack of panic. What if they had left in the ship without him?

He rushed to the docks. There were lines of people trying to get out of the city on ships, but Quint wouldn't get on a ship just to leave the city. It was easier to leave through a gate and find place to hunker down, something much harder to do in the middle of an ocean.

Quint was happy to see men moving crates in the warehouse and the purser at his stand-up desk.

"You are getting ready to leave?" Quint asked.

"Bright boy," the purser said. "We have a problem, however."

Quint raised his eyebrows. "What kind of problem?"

"Fedor Danko and his daughter disappeared from their flat last night. He told us not to worry about him."

"Last night? I was abducted, too," Quint said. "I'm sure we weren't kidnapped by the same people."

"The captain has men looking for them, and as soon as the Dankos show up we will weigh anchor."

"Does anyone have an idea where they are?" Quint asked.

"If they did, our sailors would be following the lead," the purser said.

Quint couldn't hide in a safe place when Calee and Fedor weren't secure at all.

"Can I put my things in your warehouse. They'll be back by the office door."

"Go ahead. We could leave at any time once we have this place cleaned out."

Quint walked past the purser with a wave and opened the door to put his things inside the office after he strapped on his sword and put the knife in his boot. He would start with Pozella.

There wasn't a reply when he pounded on the front door of Pozella's townhouse. He peeked in a window, but nothing looked out of the ordinary. Perhaps Pozella had fled with his wife.

As Quint approached the wizard operations strategic operations building, there were signs of a disturbance in the streets. There were patches of blood and Quint spotted a pile of bodies next to the building.

Quint stopped a female officer walking out of the building.

"Is Colonel Sarrefo in?" Quint asked.

"I think so. You are Tirolo, right?"

Quint nodded. "I didn't desert, but I've been caught up in this mess. When did the fighting occur?"

"Last night. The fighting moved to the council palace and the other buildings. At present, there are two factions."

"Baltacco and Guilica?" Quint said.

The officer nodded. "Now you know as much as I do. I reported and have just been released. There aren't many wizards working right now. If you wish to see the colonel, now would be as good a time as any. Who knows when the fighting will return." The officer looked up and down the street. "If you will excuse me." The woman looked both ways down the street and rushed across, walking quickly.

Quint ran up the steps and disappeared into the building. He went straight to Sarrefo's office. The door was closed, and Quint was hesitant to disturb the colonel, but the door opened, and two senior officers exited. No one was waiting, so Quint walked in after closing the door.

"Tirolo! What are you doing here?"

Quint took a seat that he didn't feel comfortable sitting in.

"Fedor Danko and his daughter have gone missing."

"Guilica has them. The man is crazy and is behind all the infighting when we have a big army heading our way."

"I need to get them free," Quint said.

"You? Why?"

"Because I'm going to leave Racellia and go to Narukun," Quint said. "Baltacco kidnapped me yesterday before Grand Marshal Guilica upset the capital. He wants me out of the city since he sees me as a magical disruptor."

"Just like Colleto?" Sarrefo asked.

Quint nodded. "I don't know how I could fill that role. I'm only seventeen."

"A seventeen-year-old master. Pozella told me. I always thought you were special, but most people had you down as a hubite first, and a wizard second. I'm sorry about your family. It is a bad time to feel sorry for others' misfortunes but accept my sympathy."

"I do," Quint said. Sarrefo had always been a friend from the first time Quint met him. "I'm sure you are biding your time until Colleto arrives."

"Something like that. I cautioned my people from participating in the fighting, but I can only go so far. I wish I could help you, but I can't."

"I don't have any good strategy to suggest," Quint said. "If Colleto invaded today, the military might coalesce against him, but if he waits, there will be more Racellians dead."

"Mostly soldiers," Sarrefo said.

Someone pounded on the door. "Chiglio is sending another wave of soldiers our way. He'll be here in fifteen minutes."

"Then get everyone out of the building," Sarrefo said, stuffing papers in a valise. "I'm going to ask you to leave. If you have a chance, write. I'm hoping I survive this madness."

"You and Pozella," Quint said.

"You might be too late for that," Sarrefo said. "Pozella disappeared about the time Guilica began to fight his own troops."

Quint stood but felt numb. He would have counted Pozella as one of the officers who would be hunkering down far from the fighting. Someone bumped him from behind.

Quint turned around to look into the face of one of his old roommates.

"Sorry about Pozella, but if we don't get out of here, we will feel sorry for ourselves," the officer said.

He found a uniform coat and hat on a hook that someone had left behind and put it on. Quint left with other soldiers and took a side street to avoid the imminent confrontation with Guilica's forces. The streets were almost empty of civilians and uniformed soldiers gathered here and there. Quint did his best to avoid them until he stood in front of the wall that protected the grounds of the council's palace. The military headquarters was on the other side of the palace and Quint needed to be creative to transverse the grounds.

He found a servants' entrance, but it was unmanned and locked. He spotted an overturned cart near to the gate. Quint dragged a pallet off the cart and knelt on it as he cast a teleportation string. He gave the string all the power he could, and it bolted into the air. Quint had never tried such a thing before, so he lowered the height of the pallet and sped across the open field with the pallet a handspan above the grass.

Quint reached the other side without a challenge. He applied more power to his string and moved the pallet over the wall and let the pallet settle, but before it did, Quint sneezed, and the pallet tilted depositing Quint on the dirt below.

After bruising his ego more than anything else, Quint lowered the pallet all the way and quickly looked around to see if anyone saw him. He didn't know the outside of the building on this side, but he crept around the building and entered a door he had used many times while he worked for Colonel Gerocie.

The fighting had reached all the way to the third floor with bodies he recognized and many he didn't still bleeding out. He put his hand over his mouth to reduce the smells and entered the diplomacy corps offices. Colonel Gerocie had died in front of her desk, a sword still in her hand. There wasn't a living soul in the office. General Obellia was a rival of the grand marshal, and it was clear who had prevailed.

The offices had cleared out, but Quint heard voices from below. He took back stairs to the basement and voices were coming from down the hall. There were two soldiers standing guard at the office Quint had made for Fedor Danko. He heard Danko's voice and was about to enter the corridor when he realized that Danko was arguing with someone, which wasn't surprising.

"You promised me safe passage," Fedor said.

"If the coup was bloodless. As you can see that is not the case," a voice said.

"You wouldn't have failed if you could have restrained your soldiers from murdering innocent hubites. That act had two results, the world found out about your hubite hatred and when found out, you moved your timetable up weeks from what we discussed," Fedor said.

Quint realized that Fedor was not an innocent in all of this, and he was in league with Grand Marshal Guilica. How wrong could he have been? Yet, here he was attempting to save the Dankos so he could escape from Racellia aboard Danko's ship.

Quint sat back on the stairs and thought for a moment. He still had nowhere to go in Racellia, especially if Guilica prevailed. Danko's ship still offered him the best way off South Fenola. He could see a way out by helping Danko. His only viable move was forward and that meant taking care of the guards.

Quint slid closer to the edge of the wall hiding him from the guards in the corridor. The shouting continued. Its result didn't matter to Quint other than Fedor had to survive. He created a sleep string and ran into the corridor. When he saw the guards, he didn't have to act to look surprised. They were Gerocie's people and former colleagues. He cast the strings and the men, wearing blood spattered uniforms, dropped.

"Who is out there?" the grand marshal said. "Did you kill my men?"

Quint thought that question had an obvious answer despite the fact the men weren't dead. If Quint replied everyone would know how young he was, so he didn't reply. He cast a magic shield in case there was a wizard in Danko's office.

Prepared with another sleep string, stirring between Quint's palms, he walked closer to the office door. Two more men jumped into the corridor. Both were dressed in black and wore wizard corps insignia. They cast fire spears, but the fire splashed against Quint's shield. He put them to sleep and advanced toward the office.

"Whoever you are, I'll make you a rich man once all this is over," the voice said.

Quint remained silent.

"Tell me who you are!" the voice commanded.

Quint finally stepped to the door and cast another sleep spell at an older man with salt and pepper hair. Danko and his daughter were standing behind Danko's desk. Quint stepped forward to check the general. With all the gold braid, this had to be Guilica.

"Quint. I was hoping it would be you. Is he dead?" Danko asked.

"Sleeping. It's time we got you on the boat."

"How will you ever get past all the soldiers at the front of the building?" Fedor asked.

"The same way I got in," Quint said. "Are you all right?"

Fedor snorted. "We were never in any real danger, until now. You've complicated things."

Quint looked quizzically at Fedor. Why had he hoped Quint was behind the attack when he had made a mess of things? He was about to turn to Calee, when something smashed into his head. As he twisted when he fell, he saw her holding the broken shards of the vase she had just hit him with.

CHAPTER THIRTY-THREE
~

Q UINT'S STOMACH LURCHED AS HE WOKE. He looked up to see sails bowing out with the wind coming at an angle behind them. Someone had put him on a blanket on the deck of a ship. He staggered to his feet and lost whatever had been left in his stomach into the ocean. His eyes, blinking into focus, showed a faint irregular line of a darker blue on the horizon.

His hands and feet were unbound, and he didn't see anything of Fedor Danko or his daughter. Someone had wrapped a bandage around his head.

The purser walked up to him. "Stay on the rail for a bit until your stomach settles, if you're lucky. If you're not, you'll stay on the rail until it does. Some stomachs never do take to the roll of the waves."

"Danko? Did he board the ship? Did Danko bring me on board?"

The purser looked at the quarterdeck nervously and shook his head. "Some of the sailors looking for Danko found you sprawled in the back of the building where Danko had his office yesterday afternoon. They originally thought you were dead, but you twitched or something and brought you on board because I told them about you."

"Does Danko know I'm onboard?" Quint changed his first question a little.

The purser turned to look at the ocean. "Quite honestly, he doesn't. The captain couldn't leave you in a heap after having said you'd be looking for Danko, too. Danko and his daughter made it back just before midnight and are in with the captain now, and we are on the ocean. We won't be turning back to Bocarre for any reason. You said this is what you wanted."

"It is," Quint said. "My possessions?"

"On the ship," the purser said. "I hope you were right about being able to do your sums since you are now my mate. That is the equivalent of an apprentice."

Quint clutched the rail and tried to empty his stomach, but there was nothing left. "I'm willing as long as I can stop the seasickness."

The purser laughed. "Everyone has a remedy. The ship's doctor will give you a choice of them."

Quint took a deep breath and held it for a moment. "It was Calee who knocked me out with a vase. I hope that doesn't make a difference."

The purser looked at the door leading to the cabins. "We thought something odd happened when Fedor Danko and his daughter showed up with an escort of military people wearing black uniforms."

"They might be aligned with the wrong people, but that doesn't make a difference now, as long as he doesn't try to toss me overboard," Quint said.

"Danko can't mess with crewmembers," the purser said, "or he'll find himself in the brig down below for the remainder of the voyage."

The captain emerged from below and walked over to them.

"Evidently, Fedor Danko is disappointed we brought you on board, Tirolo. Is there a reason why?"

"Bocarre was in a bad way when you left, as you probably know. I thought Danko was a friend, but it appears he was aligned with the same ones who massacred most of the hubites in Racellia including my family and friends, but if black uniformed soldiers escorted them onto the ship, he has already changed sides."

"But he's a hubite like the rest of us," the captain said. "He wouldn't support a mass killing."

"Calee was responsible for this," Quint pointed to his bandage. "I'm willing to put all that aside if I can flee from Racellia. It will soon be swallowed by the newly established Gussellian empire, anyway."

"As long as you won't seek revenge on the ship, I will let you work with Horenz, here."

Quint nodded. "I'm not used to the ship," Quint said, "but I appreciate your helping me. I'm a wizard and if you need any magic that I can perform, it will be part of my job."

"That's what Horenz said," the captain looked at the purser, who nodded. "I'll let your superior deal with you and will tell Danko, who is still in my cabin, that you'll be peaceful on board."

"I promise," Quint said.

"Good. I'm sure you have an interesting story, and I'd like to hear it later, especially after Danko tells me his version. I've got to get back to the quarterdeck." The captain nodded, the purser saluted by touching the brim of his cap and Quint turned back toward the sea as his stomach lurched again.

"You'll have to tell me how to act appropriately, sir," Quint said to the purser. "I've been in the military for a few years and know how to act as a soldier, now you'll have to teach me about how to act like a sailor."

The purser took Quint to the ship's doctor who gave some medicine that the doctor claimed never failed. Quint hoped so. His stomach muscles were sore from the constant activity. Then he was shown to a tiny windowless cabin that was smaller than his closet-sized bedroom when he was a servant in strategic operations. He had enough room to turn around and his bunk was on top of a set of built-in drawers. He laid down and felt the swaying of the ship, but it didn't seem to bother him as much.

Someone knocked on the door. Quint slid the door aside and looked into the eyes of Calee Danko.

"Can I come in?" she asked.

Quint gave her half a grin. "You can, but this is a tiny place to talk."

"I'll chance it," Calee said, sitting on the bunk with her legs dangling facing Quint, who had her leave the door open.

"We thought you were dead," she said.

"With all thanks of that to you," Quint said.

"With thanks to my father. He told me to knock out whoever came through the door."

"Did he know it was me?" Quint said.

She shrugged. "He said afterwards that he thought it might be you."

"What did I do to him? All he had to do was say he was safe, and I would have gone away."

"Father didn't know that. You had just killed five men."

"Put them to sleep," Quint said. "I didn't kill anyone. It's easier and less messy to cast a string. As I thought before you hit me, I thought it odd that he would say he expected me and then told me I disrupted things?"

"Anyone else would have killed the guards, wizards and the Grand Marshal if they were anyone but you. The original plan was to blame the Gussellian Empire for the massacre. With your meddling, word spread quickly that it was Giulica's doing. You unwittingly threw everything into an uproar, spoiling my father's plans to save Racellia."

"At the expense of a few thousand hubites?"

Calee bit her lower lip before speaking. "They were Racellian hubites, not hubites from Narukun."

"Even fellow hubites hate us."

"Hate you? There aren't many hubites left on South Fenola," Calee said. "What does that matter in the grand scheme of things?"

Quint shut his eyes. He had promised not to exact revenge, but the anger swelled at Calee's callous indifference at his own tragedy.

"That means that your death and the death of your father mean nothing. You'll both expire at some point and humanity won't know the difference and won't care. Do you see how your father's attitude can justify all kinds of evil acts."

"Evil is in the eye of the beholder," Calee said.

"And that is why wars are fought and people die needless deaths because both sides see their sides as the righteous ones," Quint said. "I promised the captain that I wouldn't exact revenge while on board his ship. I don't know when you'd have me killed before I joined you on this voyage, but I have no illusions and know that you would have tried. You helped me get established when I arrived from the south, and there is still that obligation, however, that ended when you…" he looked coldly into Calee's eyes. "When YOU tried to kill me. I am making my own way to Narukun and will find my way when I arrive. Be civil to me, and I'll be civil to you. I'd rather not talk or even look at you for the rest of this voyage. Please leave."

Calee's eyes widened as she jumped off the bunk and left without saying another word. Quint slid the door closed and climbed into the bunk. He sat, taking deep breaths and trying to put the conversation behind him. He couldn't carry such anger on the voyage.

༄

Quint learned quickly not to call the purser by his first name. That was the captain's privilege. Sir or Mister Pizent was what the purser answered to. Quint was Mister Tirolo if someone was mad at him or Tirolo or boy if they weren't.

The seamen didn't discriminate between Racellian hubites or Narukunian hubites. They were aligned to sailors versus landsmen. Landsmen on board ship were beginning seamen, which was a mild insult to the landsmen.

As a purser's mate, Quint was in between being a seaman and an officer. He had his own tiny cabin and ate in the mates' mess. The food was initially strange to Quint since Narukun cuisine and what he ate in Racellia were quite different.

The purser was patient, but Quint was a quick learner and was soon entering names and numbers into a series of ledgers. In two weeks, the purser had taught Quint the basic duties of a purser. There were secret ledgers that Horenz kept for various officers. Quint was told that there were various petty larcenies that were permitted on board any ship. He had learned in Racellia not to ask too many questions and that helped him as he integrated himself into the day-to-day operations on board the ship.

He rarely ran into the Dankos and gave them curt acknowledgments if he passed them in a corridor.

Quint had rarely exercised his magic on a regular basis, but the captain and his officers, including the doctor, called upon him regularly to complete tasks that were difficult or impossible except by magic. He cleaned the doctor's instruments on a regular basis to keep them from causing infections and officers would ask him to repair lines used in rigging or broken spars.

Some of the tasks required Quint to become creative and Quint surprisingly added more strings that he had to invent to his list.

During the third week, halfway to Narukun, the purser called Quint into his cabin at midday. "You have taken to the sea, young man. I've talked to the captain about the way you've been helping everyone aboard and we've decided to promote you to assistant purser."

"What does that really mean?" Quint asked.

"You are a junior officer, where a purser's mate isn't really anything at all. There is no pay increase because that would go into effect on your next voyage."

Quint shrugged. "I didn't expect anything other than a bed and meals, so I thank you."

"We do have one more question. Danko said to the first officer that you know how to cast portent strings."

Quint nodded. "I can do that, but I'm not a believer in using portents for any kind of decision-making. My original master didn't, either."

"We'd like a little advanced warning on the weather from time to time," the purser said.

"I can do that, as long as you consider it a magic-enhanced guess."

"We can do that. Once a day at sunrise. What will happen at midday, evening and overnight."

Quint sighed. "I am yours to command, I guess. It may take me some time to learn how to control the portent. I've only cast portent threads a few times."

"Can you do it from here?"

Quint shrugged. "I suppose so. If I fail, it won't be so bad if I only disappoint you, sir."

"Don't fail me, Quint. That isn't a threat, but a hope," Horenz said with a smile.

Quint stood, spreading his legs apart as he created the portent string and focused on viewing the deck of the ship.

He saw the wet deck of the ship. There was lightning in the sky. For the sundown portent, the deck was still wet, but the sun was visible slipping beneath the horizon. The last portent was two hours after midnight. The wind filled the reduced sails as the rain continued to pour.

"I've got that written down. Now, tomorrow morning," the purser said.

Quint's last vision wasn't a good one. A burning ship was close to theirs. Fire arrows arced across the gap, striking into the masts. A sail was beginning to burn. There were sailors lying motionless on the deck.

"We are under attack tomorrow morning just after sunrise," Quint said, describing all the details he could.

"Pirates. We will be just past Vicenzi Island in the morning. It is a nest full of them," the purser said. "I'll tell the captain and we will be prepared."

"It might not happen," Quint said.

"But you would agree the probability of an attack has gone up?"

"The probability was always there," Quint said, "but with more certainty you can be more prepared. Do you think they will wait until morning after tonight's rainstorm?"

The purser nodded, getting up from his chair. "It's time to talk to the captain."

Quint followed the purser through the twisting passages that led to the captain's cabin.

The purser knocked on the captain's door.

"Come in," said the captain.

Quint stopped mid-step. Calee and Fedor were sitting at the captain's table eating lunch.

"Our assistant purser has information for you, sir."

Captain Olinko rose from the table and wiped his mouth before stepping away. "It's time I checked the quarterdeck. The sailing master said the weather might be changing." He looked meaningfully at the purser and gave Quint a nod.

Quint was the last to climb to the quarterdeck, a place he had only been twice since he boarded the ship.

"This had better be good, Horenz," the captain said.

The purser took Quint and the Captain to the starboard back corner of the deck. "I asked Tirolo to cast a portent on the weather."

"We already know we'll sail through a wet night," Olinko said.

"What you don't know is that when the rain stops, pirates are going to attack at or before dawn."

The captain turned to Quint and stared. "You saw that?" he said in an urgent, but quiet voice.

"I did. The pirates were about to board the ship. There were flames and fire arrows exchanged on both ships."

"What happened after that?"

The purser broke in. "I brought him to your cabin, captain. Once we've seen that, the future can go anywhere."

Captain Olinko nodded. "I know how portents are supposed to work."

"I don't," Quint said.

Both men looked at the purser's mate. "You know how to cast the string, right?"

Quint nodded. "I know what I see, but I haven't studied portents. I know things change and one shouldn't rely on them."

"That's because whatever you see can be acted on and that affects the future," the captain said. "You didn't learn that?"

"I'm only seventeen, sir," Quint said. "My focus has been to accumulate strings not a lot of magical knowledge. I mean, I'm not totally ignorant, but my knowledge is shallower than perhaps it should be."

"I know you've been liberal with helping the voyage along with your magic." The captain looked at the purser. "You've told him?"

"I have."

"Larger ships often have a Wizard on Board, who has an officer's ranking. We can't afford one, but since you are here, we are happy to use you. What do you suggest?" Olinko asked.

"Me?" Quint asked. "I don't have any idea how to fight a sea battle, sir."

The side of the captain's lip curled. He was teasing Quint. How could the man do such a thing when he was going to battle, and men would be killed. "All right. Tell me exactly what you saw."

Quint was able to recall that portent in detail.

"I'll get together with my officers, and we will have a plan ready for the pirates. Which side will they board?"

Quint pointed to the starboard railing. "There."

"Do you know offensive strings?" the captain asked.

"I do. I can cast fire in a few different ways."

"Anything with some distance?"

"Fifty feet, but it is what I call a fire spear. There isn't much flame."

"That's good enough. Stay in listening distance. Use it on the pirate captain, who will be the best dressed person on board the pirate ship. Wait for three quick toots on my horn."

"Yes, sir," Quint said.

"Issue him armor," the captain said. "He will need protection."

"I'll do that, sir."

The captain brushed off his coat. "If you will excuse me, I will finish my lunch."

The first officer was on the other side of the quarterdeck.

"Rain, as we thought," the captain said. "When the watch changes, come down to my cabin."

The officer touched the brim of his hat in salute and watched the captain leave the deck. "Something big?" the officer asked the purser.

"You'll find out," the purser said, but it was clear that the officer would eagerly await the meeting.

CHAPTER THIRTY-FOUR

~

QUINT FOUND A LEATHER BREASTPLATE and matching backplate that had a thin internal liner of steel between the boiled leather. Finding a helmet to fit was impossible until one of the seamen told him to tie a bandana around his head first. The last bit of armor were bracers made like his breastplate.

"You armor is heavier than what most men wear, but you won't be boarding the pirate ship," the purser said.

Quint headed back to the deck where there was a break in the weather, where he practiced casting fire spears. He used more of his power and the fire spears went out at least thirty yards. If the vessels were as close as Quint had seen in the portent, then if the pirate captain was on the deck, he'd be feeling the heat of the battle.

A seaman woke Quint, who had slept with his armor stacked on the bunk.

"Captain Olinko wants everyone to have an early breakfast. The storm is heading out of our way."

Quint would have admitted to having nerves, but no one asked him. He ate his breakfast next to the doctor, who asked him to help him with casualties when he was finished on the main deck.

The waiting wasn't fun, but Quint was a veteran of two land battles where he had to wait for the action to begin.

As the sky turned pink with dawn, a seaman in the rigging spotted a ship approaching from the direction of the rising sun.

"It's on its way," the captain said, looking down to Quint standing on the main deck. "We have another hour before it catches us, and we are prepared."

The ship finally approached. It sported banners at the top of the two main masts, a red pennant with a black line told the crew it identified the vessel as a pirate ship.

"That's no pirate, sir," the first officer said quietly to the captain, but loud enough for Quint to hear. "It's a military ship."

Olinko grasped the railing. "You are right about portents, lad. We will have to see how this plays out. Since the pirate pennant is showing, we will treat it as such."

The tension began to build. A ballista shot a burning bolt across the gap between the ships. It skidded across the deck, spilling sailors to either side. Sand and water buckets extinguished the fires the bolt had started.

With the pirates making the first move, the captain ordered a hail of arrows shot from the deck and the rigging. Fire arrows followed and the exchange continued as the pirate ship approached.

Quint was surprised when a spear of flame left the pirate ship and hit the rigging. An archer fell to the deck. Quint cast a string bringing a ball of water from the ocean and teleported it to the burning mast. The pirates had a wizard-on-board. Quint immediately cast a shield string.

The pirate ship was drawing closer. Both ships traded fire as crews rushed frantically to quench the flames.

Quint felt a blow to his shoulder, and something skidded ahead. He turned to see Calee frantically winding the wheel of a crossbow. She had just tried to kill him again!

That was too much. He cast wind and blew her into the railing close to where the pirate ship slammed into the side of the ship. His eyes were still on Calee as Fedor, with a large bag, pulled her up and tossed the crossbow overboard. He ran along the railing, dragging his daughter, and jumped aboard the pirate ship.

Quint followed. He was ready with his fire spear, and then he felt the force of a string. Sailors dropped around him. Quint was the only person standing on the ship. Fedor went directly to the captain of the pirate vessel and pointed at Quint. It was a difficult decision to make, but Quint cast his fire spear. An ice spear came from the other side of the pirate ship and slammed into Quint, knocking him against the mast. The blow almost made him faint, but Quint closed his eyes tight and focused on remaining still as his senses returned.

In the meantime, the pirate ship disengaged and headed away from the Narukun vessel, putting Quint's ship in the lee of the pirate's sails. Quint's ship slowed as the pirate ship headed east. Quint looked up and the sails were fluttering in the wrong wind.

Captain Olinko sat against the railing on the quarterdeck. An arrow had pierced his thigh. The wheel was spinning, so Quint ran to the quarterdeck. He worked with the wheel until it slowed. All Quint could do was try to put the ship closer to north. He had no idea how to steer the ship other than to keep it going straight. The sails took on the wind, but Quint was the only one awake. There would be no pursuit.

Quint turned to the deck and saw most of what he had seen in the portent. He hadn't expected the Dankos to escape on the pirate ship. He lashed the wheel so it wouldn't spin and ran from person to person, making sure none were stuck in a position to make their injuries worse before working on the fires. A few sleeping men were entangled with the rigging high above him, but Quint wasn't the person to save them.

Men began to wake within half an hour and continued Quint's work to save their shipmates. Finally, an officer was able to take the wheel. With the situation in other's hands, Quint could help take the captain down to the doctor's cabin.

Quint returned to the deck and used his magic to put out any remaining fires that were difficult for the seamen to reach. Looking east, he could see a column of smoke being spread by the wind, but it was losing its strength. Both ships had survived the fight.

☙

Despite the armor, Quint had sneaked into Captain Olinko's cabin to look in the captain's dressing mirror to see the massive bruise from the ice bolt or whatever it was. Everything had settled down in a remarkably short time. By morning of the next day, the ship was almost normal. Sailors were scrubbing the decks. New sails and line had already been fitted and the ship was headed toward Narukun after checking their heading with compass and sextant.

Quint was summoned to the captain's cabin, where Captain Olinko rested his leg on the seat of another chair. It didn't look comfortable, but the captain was busy with paperwork.

"Yes, sir," Quint said, touching his forehead like he'd seen other sailors do.

Olinko laughed. "Officers salute," he turned to the purser who was at another writing table. "Show him, Horenz."

Quint knew how to perform a nautical salute and did so.

"That's better. Danko left a letter," the captain said tossing an open envelope to the other side of his desk where Quint stood.

Quint didn't want to touch the letter, but he forced himself. The Dankos were not his friends and were plainly enemies. It was all Quint could do not to cast his fire spear at Danko rather than the pirate captain as ordered.

> Captain Olinko,
>
> Thank you for getting me out of Bocarre. As you know by now, I had also planned for another ship to take me on the next stage of my mission. It is a vital assignment for our glorious cause. Our cover will be as victims of a pirate attack. I hope your losses weren't too great.
>
> If Quinto Tirolo survived the fight, something I dearly wish does not happen, arrest him and hand him over to representatives of the green army, who will be waiting at the dock when you arrive. As you know, he is a danger to Narukun and to all North Fenola.
>
> Best wishes from your friend in the cause,
>
> Fedor Danko.

Quint dropped the letter back on the captain's desk. "Am I under arrest?"

Quint asked.

"I'll be honest with you, Tirolo. Fedor Danko and I are not friends. He is aligned with the greens, and all aboard my ship are crimson sympathizers. I pretended to be a green to make the voyage to Racellia and back less contentious. His 'glorious government' is filled with people who want to make the world a darker place. You noticed he didn't care if my crew were killed or not. It might have helped his story if my ship had sunk. Danko is a devil." The captain spat on the floor.

"Narukun isn't united? Danko had told me that Narukun was a land of peace."

The captain laughed. "Not at all. We would be no better off than the Racellians if there was an empire growing on North Fenola ready to swallow us up. If anything, we have more factions ready and willing to fight any time they are provoked. This letter proves that Danko continues to be engaged in making things worse for all Narukuns."

"What will I do?"

Olinko shrugged and grinned at the purser. "You have a berth on any ship I command, but I think, as Danko does, that you are destined for greater things. Danko, however, thinks your actions will disrupt the world, and in my opinion, I think the world needs a bit of disrupting. I think the better course for you to follow will be to spend some time at a Cloister."

"Where wizards live in seclusion all their lives?" Quint asked.

"No! A few do, of course, but there is a Cloister close to our port that is neutral toward the political unrest in our country."

"Is it tinged with crimson?"

The captain pursed his lips. "Perhaps a little. We will sail close to the shore and let you off before reaching our port. I'll get my crew to insist you died in the battle because of that ice spear you described. I had crew enough who didn't make it." The captain sighed.

"Will the Cloister accept me?"

"A young inexperienced Master Wizard?" The captain nodded. "They will if you give them my letter. You have no more than two weeks left as acting Wizard on Board to help repair the ship and help the doctor treat those who will be put ashore at port to recuperate. So, get back to work!"

CHAPTER THIRTY-FIVE
~

Q UINT WAS ANXIOUS. He had another language to learn, he found out. Common was more typically spoken, but the pursuer thought the Cloister insisted on conversing in naru, an old, supposedly unadulterated, language used by the original hubites when they conquered North Fenola.

No one on board could tell him what life was like in a cloister, and not knowing what the future held made Quint uneasy.

He hoped the Cloister didn't accept females. He hadn't had much luck with women. Amaria and Calee had shown him that he couldn't trust women his own age. He had done rather well with older females such as Colonel Gerocie and Marena, his housekeeper.

Quint wished he could send Marena a letter, but that wouldn't be a good idea for someone who was about to be declared dead.

The boat slid up a small beach. Quint looked up at the cliff and the Cloister looming almost overhead. He said his farewell to Horenz Pizent, the purser who had come with the boat to see Quint off.

"You are a man with no name as soon as you jump off this boat," Horenz said. "I wish you could have taken your things, but the more you leave behind, the easier it will be for those at the dock to accept your death."

"I will miss my notebooks."

Horenz laughed. "Your mind is good enough to copy them from memory." He gave Quint a hug. "I wish you the best of luck. I'll always think of you as if you were a son. I have four, you know."

Quint smiled. "You've already told me. I'll regard you and Captain Olinko as good uncles."

Horenz laughed again. "That's appropriate. Remember what your uncles taught you in the last two weeks. Be off with you. The rest of us must get back to the ship."

Quint had a purse the captain had given him, the introductory letter, his father's knife, plus the clothes on his back. He looked back a few times as he climbed the path from the beach to the cloister. When he reached the top, he stopped and backed down out of sight.

A squad of green-uniformed soldiers rounded the edge of the cloister. Could they be after him so soon? He hid behind a scraggly bush and watched them continue their rounds. Quint noticed that none of them bothered to look out to sea where the skiff that brought him to shore was still making its way out to the ship.

Quint followed the soldiers around the walls until he passed a door that was beginning to open.

"In here," a robed man said, holding the door open for Quint. He wore a peculiar beard, but his smile seemed genuine.

Quint decided he didn't have an option as he stepped inside. Even if there were green-uniformed soldiers inside, Quint had nowhere to go, and no support. It had just sailed away.

The monk or whatever he was, cast a string against the door. Quint recognized it. "Wood binder," he said.

The monk turned and grinned. "Very good! Follow me. You are expected, young man."

THE END

STRINGS OF EMPIRE: CHARACTERS & LOCATIONS

CHARACTERS

THE WIZARD CORPS

Quint Tirolo - Fifteen-year-old boy with magic awakening inside him.
Zeppo Tirolo - Quint's father
Master Geno Pozella - magic trainer
Amaria Baltacco – junior officer in the wizard corps
Colonel Sarrefo - commander of Strategic Operations
Field Marshal Chiglio – Army commander
Specialist Gaglio - old friend of Pozella
Pacci Colleto. Master Wizard in the Gussellian army.
General Emilio Baltacco - of the Wizard Corps. Amaria's father.
Zoria Gauto - assistant to Colonel Sarrefo
Marena Categoro - housekeeper of Quint's shared flat
Colonel Julia Gerocie - head of the Military Diplomatic Corps.
General Obellia - Head of Military Foreign Affairs
Henricco Lucheccia - Racellian Foreign Secretary reporting to the council.
Calee Danko - daughter to the Narukun professor.
Fedor Danko - Narukun professor teaching at Racellian University.
Grand Marshal Tracco Guilica - War Minister and Head of Racellian Forces
Horenz Pizent – Purser of Narukun ship
Captain Goresk Olinko – captain of Narukun ship

LOCATIONS

CONTINENTS – COUNTRIES - RACES

AMEA – last expanded into by gran race - offshoot of hubites
Honnen
Progen
Chullen
Lekken

North Fenola - Oldest settled - by hubites and polens
Pogokon - polens
Slinnon - polens
Kippun - hubite
Narukun - hubite

South Fenola – Willots pushed most hubites out of continent
Barellia - willots
Gussellia - willots
    Nornotta - capital of Gussellia
Vinellia - willots
Racellia - Till's home country willots, hubites
    Bocarre - Capital of Racellia
    Fort Draco - wizard training

Resoda - Most recently settled - first by grans, but other two races followed
Volcann - all four
Akinnonn - gran/hubite
Logedonn - gran - hubite
Wippadann - gran - polens
Loppodunn - willots - polens

Baxel – most recently settled by grans Willots coalescing in New Baxel
Boxxo - grans
Loppo - grans
New Baxel - Willots

A Bit About Guy

With a lifelong passion for speculative fiction, Guy Antibes found that he enjoyed writing fantasy, as well as reading it. So, a career was born, and more than fifty books later, Guy continues to add his own flavor of writing to the world. Guy lives in the western part of the United States and is happily married with enough children and grandchildren to meet or exceed the human replacement rate.

You can contact Guy at his website: www.guyantibes.com.

†

Books by Guy Antibes

Justin Spede
An Unexpected Magician
An Unexpected Spell
An Unexpected Alliance
An Unexpected Betrayal
An Unexpected Villian

~

Gags & Pepper
Plight of the Phoenix
The Wizard's Chalice
A Tinker's Dame
A Spell Misplaced
Comrades in Magic

~

The Augur's Eye
The Rise of Whit
The King's Spy
The Queen's Pet
The Knave's Serpent

~

The Adventures of Desolation Boxster
Prince on the Run
Theft of an Ancient Dog
The Blue Tower
The Swordmaster's Secret
A Clash of Magics

~

Wizard's Helper
The Serpent's Orb
The Warded Box

Grishel's Feather
The Battlebone
The Polished Penny
The Hidden Mask
The Buckle's Curse
The Purloined Soul

~

MAGIC MISSING
Book One: A Boy Without Magic
Book Two: An Apprentice Without Magic
Book Three: A Voyager Without Magic
Book Four: A Scholar Without Magic
Book Five: A Snoop Without Magic

~

SONG OF SORCERY
Book One: A Sorcerer Rises
Book Two: A Sorcerer Imprisoned
Book Three: A Sorcerer's Diplomacy
Book Four: A Sorcerer's Rings
Book Five: A Sorcerer's Fist

~

THE DISINHERITED PRINCE
Book One: The Disinherited Prince
Book Two: The Monk's Habit
Book Three: A Sip of Magic
Book Four: The Sleeping God
Demeron: A Horse's Tale - A Disinherited Prince Novella
Book Five: The Emperor's Pet
Book Six: The Misplaced Prince
Book Seven: The Fractured Empire

~

POWER OF POSES
Book One: Magician in Training
Book Two: Magician in Exile
Book Three: Magician in Captivity
Book Four: Magician in Battle

~

THE WARSTONE QUARTET
Book One: Moonstone | Magic That Binds
Book Two: Sunstone | Dishonor's Bane
Book Three: Bloodstone | Power of Youth
Book Four: Darkstone | An Evil Reborn

~

THE WORLD OF THE SWORD OF SPELLS
Warrior Mage
Sword of Spells

~

THE SARA FEATHERWOOD ADVENTURES
Knife & Flame
Sword & Flame
Guns & Flame

~

OTHER NOVELS
Quest of the Wizardess
The Power Bearer
Panix: Magician Spy
Hand of Grethia

~

THE GUY ANTIBES ANTHOLOGIES
The Alien Hand
SCIENCE FICTION
The Purple Flames
STEAMPUNK & PARANORMAL FANTASY with a tinge of HORROR
Angel in Bronze
FANTASY

~

Printed in Great Britain
by Amazon